A RIVER OF LIES

John Crossan

Printed in the United States of America
Print ISBN: 978-1-956019-14-8
eBook ISBN: 978-1-956019-15-5

Library of Congress Control Number: 2021919609

Published by DartFrog Plus, the hybrid publishing imprint of DartFrog Books.

Publisher Information:
DartFrog Books
4697 Main Street
Manchester, VT 05255
www.DartFrogBooks.com

Join the discussion of this book on Bookclubz. Bookclubz is an online management
tool for book clubs, available now for Android and iOS and via Bookclubz.com.

To my wife, son and daughter—thank you so much for your support and encouragement. Timothy and Adrian would not have come to life had you not pushed me to pursue a dream.

CONTENTS

PROLOGUE

SUNDAY, MARCH 3

The Merrimack River rarely gives up its secrets.

The river is over one hundred miles long and flows through two states. Its name is believed to have originated with the Penacook or Agawam Tribe and loosely translates into "the place of the strong current." On its surface, the river typically appears calm, inviting, and peaceful. However, the United States Coast Guard has classified the Merrimack as one of the most dangerous waterways along the Eastern Seaboard. A few feet below the surface is a treacherous current that can drag an object for miles underwater and through a phalanx of jagged rocks, sunken tree trunks, and rusted remnants from an industrial age long gone by.

East of the Massachusetts community of Haverhill, the river is flanked along the north bank by an old roadway aptly named River Road. It matches every turn and curvature of the Merrimack from a little hamlet called Rocks Village through the town of Merrimac and into the city of Amesbury. In some spots, the road overlooks the waterway from high cliffs, while in other locations, it is low enough to flood during spring storms. Because of its scenic beauty, River Road often attracts joggers, hikers, birdwatchers, and lazy Sunday drivers.

Of course, every now and then, the Merrimack River gives up a secret. And on this Sunday afternoon in early March, it did just that.

Michael and Nina O'Rourke, a local middle-aged couple, were out for their weekly afternoon power walk along River Road. Antique houses built in the eighteenth and nineteenth centuries dotted the roadway and reminded the walkers of the small village that once occupied this section of the town of Merrimac. With the temperatures rising, the snowpack was quickly melting, spilling water onto the street, and causing the pavement to become caked with wet sand and road salt. Nevertheless, the pair sloshed through the dirty road and pressed forward.

The couple started to ascend a hill that rose slowly toward an old Methodist church that was perched on the crest and overlooked the river. As they did, Michael would occasionally look to his right and study the opposite shoreline. Afterward, he would turn his attention back to Nina to acknowledge he was half-heartedly listening to her tale about her wine and drawing night the previous evening in Amesbury. Once at the top of the hill, Michael gazed back out toward the waterway and eyed the chunks of broken ice that were bobbing up and down in the waterway as they floated downstream toward Newburyport. He studied the blocks carefully, noting the brown dirt stains and the random piece of plastic trash that was intermingled with the frozen debris.

As the pair started to descend the opposite side of the hill, Nina pointed out the remnants of an early-nineteenth-century riverside dock that once catered to fishing sloops and dories. All that remained now was a crumbling stone foundation, a mound of overgrown grass, rotting pilings, and several yards of rusted anchor chains. However, the couples' attention was quickly drawn beyond the deteriorating pier to a large block of ice that was approximately ten feet from shore. After it gently bounced off the abandoned dock, the block of ice started to coast closer to the shore. A moment later, it slowly scraped the sandy floor of the Merrimack and came to rest.

The couple instinctively stepped off the road and walked toward the old dock. Nina gasped and brought her hand up to her mouth. Her husband stood motionless for a moment, struggling to speak.

As river water lapped around the beached ice chunk with soft splashes, the couple continued to gaze in horror at the large object wrapped in a gray tarp resting on top of it. It was over five feet in length and was heavy enough to push the back end of the ice block slightly under the waterline. There was no doubt that the object was a body. As she visibly shook, Nina raised her hand and silently pointed to Michael that it was bound with duct tape in three locations—the top, middle, and bottom.

After a moment of fearful silence, the pair started walking toward the object. Neither uttered a word as they advanced. The only sound was river water rhythmically splashing against the shoreline. As they closed in, Michael held his arm out in front of his wife, signally that they should stop. He fought back the sour taste of bile that climbed up his throat, loudly gulped, and then nodded toward the black and blue swollen foot that protruded from underneath the tarp.

"Dear God!" Nina cried loudly as she turned away and retched. Moments later, her husband observed a long, waterlogged strand of mahogany-colored hair float out from the other end of the tarp and gently twist with the river current. After his wife regained her composure and straightened herself up, the two looked at each other for several tense seconds. Finally, Nina tugged at her husband's arm and exclaimed, "Michael, call 911!"

He stammered for a second and repeated her instructions as he pulled out his iPhone. "Yes. . . yes, call 911."

Moments later, the rippling sounds of the Merrimack River were drowned out by the emergency sirens of an approaching police cruiser.

ONE

Spectators stood outside the perimeter of yellow and black "Police Line: Do Not Cross" and "Caution" tape lines that bordered the roadway above the crime scene. Massachusetts State Police detectives worked feverishly, photographing and collecting potential evidence around the wrapped body that had been dragged ashore an hour earlier. A Merrimac Police Department detective interviewed the couple that found the body, while an attending Essex County assistant district attorney argued with the town's chief of police over the necessity of following crime scene protocol. A pair of uniformed officers cautiously eyed a local newspaper reporter and warned her several times about the consequences of entering the restricted area.

About ten yards behind the barricade tape, Merrimac resident Adrian Watson took a sip of his coffee and leaned up against a nearby tree. Surveying the scene, the six-foot-tall black man with broad shoulders, a cropped haircut, and goatee shook his head and silently chuckled to himself. He had repeatedly told his neighbors that it would only be a matter of time before the river would cough up a body. Naturally, they scoffed and said he was crazy. Waterlogged bodies washing up on the shoreline were typically Lawrence and Lowell's problem, not Merrimac's. How wrong they were.

At forty-two years old, the private investigator had pretty much seen it all. Growing up in the Arlington District of Lawrence, Adrian had been exposed to both the good and ugly in humanity. He had watched with amazement as his parents worked two, sometimes three, jobs each to raise enough money to send him, as well as his two brothers and sister, to an elite private high school located in one of the city's toughest neighborhoods. He understood the sacrifices his family made to ensure he and his younger siblings all received a quality education to get out of the City of Immigrants once they graduated from college. At the same time, he routinely stared in awe as a select few of his neighbors rolled the dice and started small but successful restaurants, auto parts stores, and tire shops throughout the city.

Of course, Adrian was also aware of the darker side of Lawrence. In the nineteenth and twentieth centuries, the city was considered the capital of America's Industrial Revolution. Sadly, following World War II, the economy had shifted to other demands, and by the 1980s, Lawrence was an empty shell. Worse, within two decades, the city was known to law enforcement as the heroin capital of New England. Adrian watched with sadness as illicit drugs infested his community and drove young men toward gangs, theft, and violence. He struggled to understand why cops and prosecutors made deals with drug dealers in exchange for questionable and often unreliable intelligence, and he bristled at the constant pandering by politicians who made generalized and halfhearted promises to cure the problem in exchange for political power.

As the epidemic worsened, thousands of heroin junkies, most local but some as far away as Maine, Connecticut, and New York, arrived in the city simply to score a gram or two of the brown substance that was known to be remarkably cheap but gave one hell of a high. Adrian's younger brother, George, eventually became one of those addicts. The summer after his high school graduation, the young man was introduced to cocaine at a party in Andover, Massachusetts. By August of that same year, he had graduated to heroin. Adrian recalled how George initially tried to hide the addiction from his family but eventually ceased to care. At first, he stole small things from the house to support his habit. As the months passed, George grew more desperate and started to pawn family jewelry, electronics, and cherished personal belongings. The teen even stole kitchen utensils and supplies such as spoons, tin foil, and bottle caps so he could liquefy the heroin before injecting it into his veins.

By the time George had turned nineteen, he had dropped out of college and started to simply waste away. The addiction consumed his life. He lost all his money and physically began to waste away. Adrian watched helplessly as his brother deteriorated before him. George lost a significant amount of weight, was always sweating heavily, and suffered from erratic mood swings. He would also disappear from days and sometimes weeks on end. Adrian's father would beg officers of the Lawrence Police Department for help, but they were so overwhelmed and unprepared for the crisis that they lacked the resources to help a black family locate their addicted son. As a result, Adrian and his father would often drive for endless hours throughout the city trying to locate his brother. On the occasions they were successful, the pair would often find George underneath a city bridge or in an alleyway incoherent, limp, and lying in a pool of his own vomit.

It took almost two years to get George the help he needed. However, not all Lawrence families were so lucky. The heroin blight eventually led to the breakdown of many families as they were overwhelmed by the crushing weight of addiction and hopelessness.

But even worse, there were the homicides, many of which were tied directly to the city's narcotic epidemic. Adrian saw more than his share of death growing up, and by the time he started working as an investigator for the Massachusetts public defender's office, known as the Committee for Public Counsel Services or CPCS, one would assume Watson was immune to the bloodshed. However, despite the constant exposure to the raw violence of this dead mill town, he could not find the strength to desensitize himself from the horror of the sudden and often tragic ending of one's life.

After some time of studying the crime scene, Watson pushed himself off the tree, took another gulp of his coffee, steeled himself, and walked forward toward the police tape line. As he casually strode past several teenage spectators who leaned forward on their mountain bikes and gawked at the crime scene, a Massachusetts State Police detective in plain clothes discreetly waved at him and gestured toward an unoccupied section of the security line. The trooper chuckled slightly and then extended his hand toward Watson.

"Nice to see you, Adrian. It's a little soon for a CPCS investigator to be sneaking around the crime scene, don't you think?" the trooper asked.

Watson laughed, turned to his left, and pointed to a nearby street. "I live about a block away, Bobby. I did not want to miss the neighborhood show. This is the most entertainment this town has had in over fifty years."

"Well, when the cultural epicenter of your town is the Richdale's, I can understand why people are drawn to something like this."

The private investigator looked down toward the river. From his vantage point, he could see the body had been placed on a patch of nearby grass. The gray tarp had been cut open and peeled back, exposing the discolored body of what appeared to be a young female. A detective armed with a high-powered digital camera approached, knelt next to the body and began to take pictures of the woman's face, neck, and hands.

After several moments of awkward silence, Adrian exhaled softly and turned his attention back to the trooper. He motioned toward the body. "What happened?"

The trooper looked over at the body and then back at Watson. "I can't tell you much other than this one's a bit of a shitshow. The victim is a young woman, maybe about nineteen or twenty. She was bound up with duct tape at the wrists, ankles, and around the mouth. Her face looks like it was beaten for hours with a hammer. The guys from crime scene services are still processing the area, and the coroner is on his way to take the body."

"Do we know who she is?" Watson asked with a tone of curiosity.

"No, it's too soon," Bobby quickly retorted.

Adrian nodded and gestured toward the couple being interviewed. "They know something. What are the witnesses saying?"

Before Bobby could answer, a stocky woman confidently strode over toward the pair, stopped about five feet away, and then stared intensely toward the river. She did not acknowledge either of them, but it was clear to both Adrian and Bobby that she was trying to eavesdrop on their conversation.

Watson looked over at the woman and immediately recognized her as a reporter for *The Lawrence Star*. He rolled his eyes and snorted softly with contempt.

Adrian despised the *Star* and considered it a sensational rag that was long overdue to go out of business. The newspaper, if one could call it that, generated sales by typically stoking up the racial fears and hostilities of the local white residents. It was not uncommon for its reporters to portray all Dominicans and other Hispanic groups as corrupt drug dealers hell-bent on raping women. Rarely did the *Star* write a positive news article about the city's minority population. In 2004, when a Hispanic candidate defeated the incumbent white mayor in a hotly contested election, the paper retaliated by publishing countless inflammatory stories focusing on his ethnicity and familial ties to the Dominican Republic.

Watson's dislike of the *Star* paled in comparison to his hatred of Harriet Jenson, the crime reporter who had just slithered up next to him. From Harriet's own warped perspective, she played a critical role in the criminal justice system and was long overdue for several Pulitzer Prizes. She rarely hesitated to remind prosecutors, probation officers, and police officers that she was part of their law enforcement "team" and openly bragged of her contempt for public defenders and minority defendants, especially Dominicans and Haitians.

In reality, Harriet was a lazy reporter who lacked even the basic journalistic skills to write a newspaper article. She routinely lifted stories, word for word, from local police reports and submitted the material as her own work. Worse, her follow-up stories usually consisted of cutting and pasting her original story and combining it with one to two new sentences. Her reports were frequently slanted in favor of white police officers and typically turned a blind eye toward police corruption and accusations of brutality. Many attorneys, defendants, and cops simply steered clear of her and refused to give her any tips or story leads because of her reputation of destroying or exposing confidential sources once they were no longer of use to her.

Adrian became slightly annoyed that Harriet chose to stand next to him and bristled at the thought that she was trying to grab what little scraps of information she could from his conversation with the trooper. Bobby recognized the situation as well, nodded at Adrian, and quickly walked away. The investigator took another sip of his coffee and looked over at her. "I guess you decided that you were going to park your ass next to us in the hopes we're going to give you a tip?"

"I can stand wherever the fuck I want; it's a free country, Watson. I don't appreciate your efforts to prevent me from getting a story." She hissed loudly, hoping to attract the attention of nearby spectators. "Then again, it is a typical tactic of the public defender's office to try and drive the press away."

Adrian laughed. He knew that last dig was about the public defender's office routinely filing motions in court to have Harriet and the *Star* excluded from accessing court records, including impounded police reports and affidavits. He gestured toward a group of state troopers standing about five yards away along the tape line. "Should we see if we can get one of them to write your next story? I am sure they have a report or two they could loan you. Tell you what, when you and your lumpy ass graduate from a high school newspaper and develop some basic ethics, then I'll give you a tip."

Harriet stiffened, glared at Adrian, spun around, and walked farther down the security line. Watson grinned from ear to ear and turned his attention back to the crime scene. As he did, he heard a car door slamming and a woman shouting. Adrian turned around and observed a senior prosecutor, armed with a tablet and a cell phone, walking hurriedly over to the investigators. She gestured at the spectators and ordered a pair of troopers to move the tape line back another one hundred yards. Harriet immediately objected to the order but was met with a curt "fuck you" from the prosecutor.

Adrian immediately recognized the prosecutor as the number-three-ranking person in the entire Essex County District Attorney's Office. She typically oversaw sexual assault, child abuse, and domestic violence cases. As far as the investigator could recall, she had not touched a homicide case, let alone supervise crime scene processing, for over a decade. Likewise, many of the attorneys he worked with repeatedly told him that the last time she saw the inside of a courtroom was in the mid to late 1990s. Adrian found her arrival at the scene highly unusual. He watched with curiosity as she crossed the grassy field toward the body.

As the troopers ushered the crowd back almost half a block, Adrian started to move back with the spectators but then peeled off and walked up the street toward the crest of the hill that overlooked the park. Along the river side of the road, there was an old antique brick house that dated back to the War of 1812. It was owned by a local attorney and close friend of Adrian, David Salamone. He was away on vacation in Florida and had asked the private investigator to check on the property from time to time. Adrian noted to himself that he was long overdue to check the backyard—especially since it just happened to overlook the crime scene.

Upon reaching the top of the hill, Adrian looked back over his shoulder. Seeing everyone was still transfixed on the arrival of the prosecutor, he turned immediately to his left and stepped onto the property. He passed along the right side of the home, curled leftward into the backyard, and walked directly toward a wood storage shed that sat on the precipice of a thirty-foot-high cliff above the river. The investigator pressed himself against the right-hand side of the shed and slowly stepped forward. Once at the back of the structure, he peered down at the scene below him.

A pair of state police detectives and the female prosecutor were standing around the body, now covered with a blanket, and staring down at it. After a brief discussion, the woman crouched down, studied the body for several seconds, and then pulled the blanket back. She lifted her cell phone and appeared to take several images of the dead woman. Afterward, the prosecutor stood back up, walked away from the detectives, and began to tap on her phone as if sending a text message. Once done, she tucked her phone into the back pocket of her jeans, spun around, and gestured for one of the detectives to join her.

Adrian watched as the senior detective walked over and spoke with the prosecutor. She gestured angrily toward the body several times. In response, the trooper raised his voice and stepped closer toward the prosecutor. Unfortunately, Watson could only hear the two speaking to each other with raised voices but not the substance of their conversation.

The private investigator stepped back and leaned against the woodshed. He really needed to find new ways to keep himself busy, as eavesdropping on the early stages of a homicide investigation was not the best way to spend a Sunday afternoon. Then again, he also knew that most criminal defendants accused of murder were routinely represented by the senior trial attorneys of CPCS. So, the odds were in Adrian's favor that he would be working on this matter eventually.

His musings were interrupted when a uniformed state trooper emerged and stepped into the backyard.

"Hey!" the trooper barked. "You can't be back here. You need to be behind the rope line about a block from here."

Adrian raised his hands and apologized as he walked toward the officer. "Sorry, sorry. I live around the corner from here. I'm watching my neighbor's property, and curiosity got the better of me. My bad."

"You got an ID?" the cop demanded, as he eyed Adrian somewhat suspiciously.

"Really?" he replied, somewhat taken aback. "I just told you I live a block away from here. I know you live in Merrimac too. I've probably bumped into you every other week getting breakfast down the street at Andyman Cafe."

"Your license or another form of identification, now," the trooper repeated, ignoring the investigator's last comment.

Adrian felt his chest tighten and his breath shorten. He could feel himself quickly becoming aggravated by this trooper. However, he checked himself, took a deep breath, pulled his driver's license out of his front pocket, and handed it over to the trooper.

The trooper studied it for a second and then returned it back to Adrian. "You're free to go, Mr. Watson."

Watson muttered silently to himself, brushed past the trooper, stepped back onto River Road, and started to slowly walk back to his own home. In the distance, a hearse had parked next to the crime scene, and a pair of medical examiners exited the vehicle to collect the body.

TWO

The professor quickly parked his dilapidated Toyota Prius and hopped out of the vehicle. He was already ten minutes late for his Monday morning class. He slung the strap of his briefcase over his shoulder and started to hoof it across the small parking lot toward a two-story brick building. Once he reached the main entrance, he swung open the glass double doors and burst into the main lobby. He brushed past a campus coffee shop occupied by several students, turned right, and quickly strode down a narrow, poorly lit hallway toward his classroom. Once at the door, he briefly paused to collect his thoughts and adjust his blazer. Afterward, he entered the room. Almost instinctively, the students shot up in their seats. Some quickly pulled out their laptops while others put their cell phones away.

"Good morning," professor Timothy Pickering announced as he walked to the podium. "I apologize for being a bit late. Traffic on Storrow absolutely sucked."

A few students nodded in sympathy. Storrow Drive was the only major Boston thoroughfare that led students and faculty traveling from northern Massachusetts through the city to Brighton College. To complicate matters, it was always clogged during the morning rush hour because of heavy traffic, accidents, and road construction.

Pickering dropped his briefcase onto the table adjacent to the podium, reached into it, and withdrew a laptop. After a few seconds of fumbling with the device, he successfully connected it to the classroom smartboard. As the laptop warmed up, he looked up at the class and warmly smiled.

At first blush, Timothy Pickering was somewhat physically intimidating to his students. Standing at six feet two inches in height, the forty-five-year-old professor was well built, clean-shaven, and wore his dark brown hair short and tight. His cold green eyes seemed to easily pierce his students' innermost thoughts while his booming voice created an air of authority as it echoed throughout the classrooms and hallways of Brighton College. Many of his students initially mistook him for a hardened federal law enforcement officer or a military veteran. However, his broad smile, sense of humor, and genuine sincerity both inside and outside of the classroom quickly removed any fear and easily fostered an atmosphere of mutual respect with his students.

Before Timothy Pickering was a college professor, he had been a prosecutor in Essex County, the northeastern territorial district of Massachusetts, for almost ten years. He handled a variety of criminal offenses, including gang-related offenses, narcotics crimes, firearm-related activities, sexual assaults, and homicides. Afterward, he worked for almost eleven years at a prestigious Boston law firm as a criminal defense attorney. He represented clients charged with a variety of offenses, including drunk driving, arson, murder, rape, drug trafficking, and domestic violence. To his colleagues, he was known as a "trial horse" because, throughout his entire legal career, he had taken to trial over one thousand felony and misdemeanor cases.

However, there was also a downside to life as a criminal litigator. Unlike real estate or tort law, criminal law was a blood sport that gambled with people's lives. It was a high-pressure occupation where one misstep could result in ruined reputations, scathing newspaper articles, death threats, malpractice lawsuits, or the loss of professional licenses. On more than one occasion, Pickering felt helpless and sickened as criminal defendants, desperate for freedom, would blame him for their misfortune and accuse him of not acting in their best interest. Fellow attorneys, jealous of his success and eager to steal clients from him, would often whisper behind his back or actively dissuade defendants from hiring him.

Eventually, the stress and pressure caught up to him. At first, Pickering experienced chest pain and shortness of breath. This was followed by a morning ritual of vomiting and diarrhea. These symptoms eventually graduated into full-blown panic attacks accompanied by an unusual fear that his world was collapsing around him. When sleeping and anxiety pills prescribed by his physician did not curb the anxiety, he turned to alcohol. By his sixth year as a criminal defense attorney, his wife watched in horror as Timothy's evening routine shifted from reading his history books to consuming several glasses of rum to combat the stress of the occupation.

Pickering finally threw in the towel and gave up practicing law following the representation of a defendant accused of drugging and raping a teenage girl. The client was a twenty-one-year-old man from Quincy, Massachusetts, named Gideon Broadbent. He had been asked by a family friend to "house sit" a home located along the waterfront in the seaside community of Beverly, Massachusetts. In the days after Gideon moved in, he ingratiated himself with a pair of local teenage girls who were no more than fifteen years old.

At first, Gideon merely flirted with the pair and bought them small presents such as fast food, cigarettes, and vape cartridges. However, a week later, he was providing the two with an endless supply of Klonopin, whiskey, and cheap beer. One Saturday, the three spent the morning downing shots of vodka and snorting crushed pain killers. After one of the girls passed out, Gideon led the second out of the house and down the street to a waterfront park. Once there, he let the semi-conscious girl collapse onto the sand before he removed her shorts and underwear and proceeded to rape her in broad daylight.

Unfortunately for Mr. Broadbent, there were at least a dozen people who were present in the park at the time of the assault. The Beverly Police's 911 system lit up like a Christmas tree as multiple people called to report the ongoing rape. A pair of young fathers quickly rushed Gideon, pulled him off the victim, and pinned him to the ground. When the police and EMTs arrived, they found the young man laughing at the entire spectacle.

The girl was rushed to the Beverly Hospital, where her stomach was pumped, and a nurse performed a highly invasive sexual assault physical examination. Between the eyewitness statements, the forensic evidence recovered off the victim's body and Gideon's own confession to investigators, he was quickly charged with a variety of offenses, including child endangerment and rape of a child. An indictment quickly followed.

Gideon's mother, one of the wealthiest socialites in the expensive Cape Ann community of Rockport, decided to hire Timothy Pickering to represent her son. When she produced a certified check for $35,000, he reluctantly accepted the case.

Pickering recognized immediately that the government had Gideon dead to rights and that a negotiated settlement was his client's only option. However, despite Timothy's repeated pleas to his client to admit responsibility and receive a light prison sentence, Gideon insisted on going to trial. As the case played out in a courtroom inside the Salem Superior Court, Pickering's client sat at the defense table and repeatedly became sexually aroused as his victim recounted how she was drugged and raped. When the jury came back in record time with a guilty verdict, Gideon turned to his attorney, leaned in, and stated with a soft voice that dripped with ooze, "She enjoyed it."

As his client left the courtroom in shackles, Pickering felt the bile rise in his throat and his chest tighten. He quickly exited the courtroom, stumbled into a nearby men's room, and proceeded to vomit all over himself. Horrified at defending a child rapist who displayed absolutely no remorse, Pickering collapsed to the floor in grief and began sobbing. About thirty minutes later, a court officer found him visibly shaking in the corner of the bathroom. Pickering's wife arrived sometime afterward and brought her emotionally exhausted husband home.

One month later, and to the shock of no one in his law firm, Pickering left the practice of law for good. At his wife's insistence, he significantly cut back on his drinking, developed a passion for mountain biking, and took up teaching history and criminal justice on the college level. After spending two years bouncing around several New England area colleges and universities, Pickering finally landed a full-time teaching post at Brighton College. Now he spent his days lecturing students on the intricacies of constitutional law, criminal law, search and seizure, and crime scene forensics.

The class this morning was about three-quarters full and made up of sophomores and juniors. The students who attended Brighton College were not the best or brightest of the Massachusetts educational system. In fact, most had barely graduated from high school, and a select few could barely string together three sentences on paper. Pickering was fairly certain several of his students were typically high on locally sourced cannabis, and it was not uncommon for his classroom to smell like a skunk sprayed the walls.

Not surprisingly, most of his students had expressed an interest in working in the criminal justice field after graduation. Over half wanted to become cops. A few wanted to become probation or parole officers. More than one expressed a desire to become a criminal attorney. When Pickering would ask them why they wanted to get into this line of work, the standard responses typically were, "I want to help my community" or, "I want to catch bad guys." Somewhat unimpressed at such vague answers, he knew that only a few students in his classroom had the intelligence and perseverance to succeed in law enforcement.

Nevertheless, his classes were entertaining, relaxed, and, most importantly, filled with examples of real-world crimes. However, Pickering did not want his students to simply listen to his war stories from the courtroom. He wanted them to learn from his examples and be able to utilize them in future scenarios. More importantly, he wanted to make sure each of them walked out of his classroom with a firm understanding of what their constitutional rights were. It was not uncommon for the professor to constantly pepper his students with news reports of recent arrests, criminal investigations, and trials. Afterward, he would relentlessly quiz them on whether the conduct of law enforcement, the prosecution, or the court was proper. He knew that if a citizenry were unaware of their civil rights, the government would simply roll over them. Hell, he saw it daily as both a prosecutor and defense attorney. As a result, Pickering took to heart President Lincoln's constitutional lesson: "Don't interfere with anything in the Constitution. That must be maintained, for it is the only safeguard of our liberties."

The students leaned forward in anticipation of Pickering's talk and prepared to take notes. They loved his lectures, not only because they were informative and entertaining but because Pickering knew his shit.

"We had left off last week discussing what could be considered specific and articulable factors that could justify a *Terry* stop by a police officer." The professor reminded them. "Today, we're going to look at when a police officer would be justified to performing a frisk of a suspect during a *Terry* stop."

Pickering spent most of his class trying to walk his students through the various factors necessary before a police officer could order a suspect out of a car and frisk him for safety. For some reason, the students seemed to be stuck on the concept that a *Terry* frisk was only limited to a "pat down" to detect the presence of weapons and that a search for evidence of criminal activity was not acceptable. It only got worse when the professor started to grill his students about searches of pocketbooks, backpacks, and nearby cars. In response, the class kept trying to use episodes of *Law and Order* and *Blue Bloods* to justify what they believed should be considered unconstitutional behavior. When he demanded to know whether they had read the search and seizure review documents he uploaded the previous Friday to the course's online learning platform, his students met him with blank stares.

Pickering smirked slightly and recognized his students had hit a wall, and any further attempt to jam constitutional principles down their throats would be futile. He looked at his cell phone and noted it was 9:53 a.m.—there were still seven minutes left of his class.

"All right, it's probably 10:00 in the morning somewhere, so we're going to call it a day now," he announced loudly.

Students shot out of their chairs and started to walk toward the classroom exit. More than one pulled out their cell phones and started to check their Instagram and Snapchat accounts. Pickering sighed in disappointment before speaking loudly again.

"Just a reminder that there is a quiz this Friday. I expect you to study for this one! Your last test results were atrocious," he proclaimed as his students exited the room. He watched in silence as they slowly filed out and then called to one of the remaining students as she neared the door.

"Ms. Vincente, a word, please."

Yulissa Vincente stopped, turned around, and bounced over to Pickering's podium. Generally, she was a polite, good kid who worked extremely hard to get Bs in his class.

"Yes, professor?" she asked.

"Mr. Vaughn has been among the missing for the past week. Since you are his partner in crime, I figured I would ask if everything is all right?" Pickering inquired.

Yulissa and Carmen Vaughn were best friends and were inseparable during their time at Brighton College. Initially, Pickering thought the two were dating until Yulissa explained that Carmen was in an on-again, off-again relationship with a girl who attended a college somewhere north of Boston. The professor also discovered in his conversations with the young woman that she was more interested in the nitwit lacrosse player who sat four seats over from her and was actively failing his class.

After Pickering's question, Yulissa's usual cheerful demeanor disappeared, and a look of dread spread across her face. She looked around to see who remained in the class, waited until the students left, and then leaned toward the professor.

"I guess no one told you," she whispered. "Carmen and his girl went out a week ago last Saturday. I know they hit a couple of clubs up in Lawrence to go dancing. A few drinks later, they got into a pretty ugly fight. She stormed out of the club, he followed. They argued some more in the parking lot, and then she took an Uber home. That was the last he saw of her."

"Yulissa, are you telling me Carmen is skipping my classes because he got into a fight with his girlfriend?" Pickering struggled desperately not to make a face of disgust upon hearing this alleged excuse. He also resisted the urge to immediately open his grade book and start taking Vaughn several points off his participation grade for skipping his class.

"No, professor. But I didn't finish," Yulissa replied with some hesitation. "No one knows where she is. He called her Monday after he cooled off, and she never returned his calls or answered his texts."

"Did he call her dorm or check in with her parents? I am sure there must be some logical explanation for all this. Maybe she's still pissed at him and decided to dump him," Pickering mused.

"Carmen's girl never returned to her dorm room, and her parents haven't seen or heard from her since that weekend," Yulissa announced as she struggled not to sound emotional.

Pickering felt his stomach tighten up. This was not a good sign. He quietly swore under his breath.

"What about the police?" he demanded. "Has Carmen or this girl's parents contacted the police?"

"Carmen started with the Lawrence Police last Tuesday because that's where the club is. They did not do shit and basically chased him out of their nasty-ass station. He then went to the North Andover Police because the college she attends is in that town. They simply shrugged their shoulders and said they could not do anything yet. He finally reached out to the Salem Police because that is the city she lives in when she's not at school. I guess a captain over there felt bad for Carmen, made a few calls, and was able to convince a few cops to start looking around Salem for her."

"Salem, New Hampshire, or Salem, Massachusetts?" Pickering asked. It was quite common for New Englanders to confuse the two towns that were less than fifty miles apart from each other.

"Salem, Massachusetts," Yulissa quickly answered.

"And what about her parents—did Carmen ever reach out to them?" Pickering questioned.

"Carmen contacted them the day after he spoke with the police. He's not on the best terms with them."

"Why?" Timothy pressed.

"They're not thrilled she was dating a Hispanic kid," she announced with a tone of disgust.

"She's white, I take it?" Pickering asked matter-of-factly.

"Hell yeah. She's a Becky," Yulissa exclaimed with a slight smile.

"A what? No, never mind. I don't want to know," he replied as he brushed off the comment with a wave of his hand. "So, where is Carmen now?"

"When he is not in his dorm room bed in a funk, he's bouncing around Salem and Lawrence trying to find her. He's absolutely scared the worst has happened to her."

Pickering remained silent for a few moments. This was a conversation he was not sure he wanted to continue participating in. Nevertheless, he felt compelled to ask.

"Yulissa. What do you think happened?"

"Me?" she exclaimed with surprise as she straightened her body up. "I think she's bat shit crazy, off her meds, and is probably riding around with some rich white dude and spending his money. She was always playing fucking mind games with Carmen and letting him twist in the wind. The sad thing is that fool is madly in love with her."

Pickering nodded in understanding and then politely led Yulissa to the classroom exit. "Thanks, Yulissa. I appreciate you clarifying a few things for me regarding Carmen. Tell him I'm pulling for him, and we can chat about making up his assignments when he gets his head together."

After the conversation ended and both had left the classroom, Pickering exited the building and walked back across the small parking lot to a late-nineteenth-century Victorian house that contained the school's faculty offices. He walked up to the back porch, passed through a doorway, and ascended a flight of stairs to the second floor. After navigating past several empty desks in the main hallway, he unlocked his office door and stepped inside. Immediately, he was met with a wave of heat and realized the thermostat must be broken again. Pickering cursed and spent the next ten minutes struggling to open a pair of heavy office windows to let some cool air into the office.

Once successful, he collapsed in his office chair, exhaled loudly, and cracked open his laptop. He had at least an hour to prepare for his next class. Rather than reviewing his next lecture, Pickering visited a local news website. As he scanned the headlines, his attention was directed to the flashing yellow and red banner that scrolled across the top of the page:

Breaking News: Body of Missing Salem Girl Found in Merrimac.

THREE

TUESDAY, MARCH 5

The trooper reached across the conference room table and grabbed his third donut. His coworkers watched in horror as he gobbled the blueberry-filled pastry with a pair of large bites and then slurped white powdered sugar off his fingers. He concluded his feast by sliding his index finger out of his mouth with a loud pop.

His immediate supervisor, Sergeant Dennis McCam, quickly chided him. "You have to be one of the most disgusting people I know. Did your mother ever teach you any manners?"

"The donuts are from Ziggy's!" Trooper Brian Bancroft retorted. "Who the fuck doesn't like Ziggy's?"

"Do you think for once you can act like a human being and not a fucking goat when Geoff gets here?" Lieutenant Jacqueline Lammoth loudly snapped.

Lammoth commanded the Massachusetts State Police detective unit assigned to the Essex County District Attorney's office. According to Massachusetts law, the district attorney's office oversaw the investigation of all suspicious deaths that occurred within its jurisdiction. In turn, the office was supported by investigators from the state police detective unit. Typically, these investigators were experienced and well-trained professionals who were tasked with the gruesome responsibility of examining difficult cases that involved suspicious or questionable deaths.

This Tuesday morning, Lieutenant Lammoth impatiently waited in the District Attorney's personal conference room with five of her troopers for the arrival of Geoffrey Walker, the number-two prosecutor in the office. According to protocol, Walker was responsible for the oversight of all suspicious deaths and missing person investigations within Essex County. It was his meeting; where was he?

Sergeant McCam stood up from the conference room table and casually strolled over to a large window that overlooked Salem Harbor. The trooper plunged his hands into his pants pockets, stared out the window, and silently wished to himself that he had a cigarette. McCam started his career at age twenty-five, patrolling the highways and secondary roadways of Central Massachusetts. After his fifth year of service, he was assigned to a narcotics investigative unit and participated in over one hundred operations in an undercover capacity. By the time he was thirty-five, he was tackling arson investigations and working closely with federal investigators from the Bureau of Alcohol, Tobacco, Firearms, and Explosives. At forty, he was recruited to join the detective unit attached to the Middlesex County District Attorney's Office in Cambridge, Massachusetts. Three years later, he was promoted to the rank of sergeant and transferred to the Essex County District Attorney's office. For the past fifteen years, he helped solve some of the most difficult and high-profile homicides in the county.

As he looked out the window, he bristled at the bullshit requirement that members of his detective unit routinely meet with prosecutors to discuss the progress of their investigations. From his point of view, his men should be out on the street solving cases, not appearing in front of armchair warriors who were incapable of understanding the difference between a theoretical scenario hashed out in a law school classroom and the real world. If anything, these protocol meetings were a colossal waste of his time.

His thoughts were interrupted when First Assistant District Attorney Walker finally entered the room. In tow, directly behind him was Assistant District Attorney Victoria Donovan.

McCam snorted silently to himself. He had been told Donovan had shown up to the crime scene but assumed it was only because she was the "duty prosecutor," an assistant district attorney responsible for fielding legal questions from law enforcement on any given day. However, her presence at the meeting meant that she was now involved in the Russo matter.

The sergeant passionately believed Donovan was an inept prosecutor. She rarely handled her own caseload, was oblivious to updates in the law, routinely disregarded input from her staff, openly mocked the constitutional safeguards afforded to the accused, and treated the criminal defense bar with utter contempt. She should have been fired years ago. However, it was widely believed among various circles both inside and outside of the Essex District Attorney's Office that her father's post as a powerful state senator all but guaranteed her role as the number-three prosecutor in the office. Some even whispered that Victoria Donovan was the "power behind the throne" and dictated office policy on public safety matters and internal procedures to the district attorney himself. It was an openly known secret that her long game was a judicial appointment to the highest court in the Commonwealth—the Massachusetts Supreme Judicial Court.

Donovan's presence at this meeting did not bode well for the McCam. He noted one of the newer troopers assigned to his unit, Brian Eriksen, shifted uncomfortably in his chair when she entered the room. The sergeant stepped away from the window, walked over to his chair, and sat down. He nodded at Geoff and looked over at Lieutenant Lammoth, who was struggling to connect her laptop to the conference room smartboard. After a moment of awkward silence, a projector cast the computer's screen onto the interactive whiteboard.

Walker cleared his throat and smiled at everyone. Unlike Donovan, he was generally an affable person who was typically calm, approachable, and generally admired by both his coworkers and law enforcement. Defense attorneys respected him because he treated their clients with respect and almost always tried to ensure their constitutional rights were well protected both inside and outside of the courtroom. Of course, First Assistant Geoffrey Walker was also a morbidly obese man who moved in a manner that more closely resembled a bear on the verge of hibernation than a seasoned criminal litigator.

Before speaking, the prosecutor looked to the center of the table and noticed the box of donuts. Instinctively, he leaned forward, seized a glazed donut with his right hand and a jelly donut with his left, and sunk back into his chair. Afterward, he glanced at Lieutenant Lammoth.

"Jackie, let's talk about the recent developments in the Jillian Russo case," Walker announced as he stuffed the jelly donut into his mouth and continued to speak. "From what I understand, this girl was a Salem resident who attended Merrimack College in North Andover. She disappeared approximately a week ago after last being seen outside of a Lawrence nightclub. This past Sunday, a body of a dead female washed up on the shore of the Merrimack River in ... Haverhill?"

"Merrimac," McCam quickly corrected.

"Right, Merrimac. It's a small town, isn't it?" Walker inquired, changing the subject slightly.

"It is," McCam affirmed. "You blink; you miss it."

The first assistant nodded in understanding and then gestured for the lieutenant to continue. "Let's back up for a moment. The deceased girl that was pulled from the river—Jillian Russo?"

"It was," Lammoth replied almost automatically. "Her father identified the body early yesterday morning."

"Must have been extremely difficult," Assistant District Attorney Donovan noted without any emotion.

"It was," the lieutenant replied matter-of-factly. "Of course, it didn't help that her father saw her face all smashed up."

"Oh?" Walker quickly asked as he scribbled notes onto a yellow legal notepad. "What did your team observe in regard to facial injuries?"

Lammoth stepped toward the conference table, picked up her copy of the case file, opened it, and began to read aloud from her notes. "Three of my detectives on the scene are of the opinion that her facial injuries are consistent with repeated blows to the face. I wouldn't be surprised if the autopsy report came back indicating multiple facial fractures."

"With all due respect to the lieutenant, I think it's important to highlight that her face was beaten to a pulp," McCam interrupted with a tone of annoyance in his voice. "If I had to make a prediction, I would say autopsy report will come back highlighting severe injuries to her nose, jaw, orbital bones, and back of the head."

The first assistant nodded silently and reflected for a moment before turning his attention back to his lieutenant. "Jackie, what other injuries were observed?"

Lammoth shot a sideways glance at her sergeant. It was obvious she was annoyed at McCam's editorial comments regarding Jillian's injuries. She cleared her throat and then resumed her presentation. "There were several dark-brown ligature marks on her neck consistent with strangulation and were similar in shape to fingers. There were also several contusions and gashes along her back and legs, but we suspect those injuries were the result of the body striking either rocks or debris in the Merrimack River and not from her assailant."

"Do we have any idea how long Jillian had been in the Merrimack River for?" Walker inquired as he tried to calculate in his mind a date range for Jillian's death.

"Well, we have an idea," Sergeant McCam chimed in. He had been working with two of his troopers on the timeline of events leading up to and immediately after Jillian's disappearance.

Walker gestured to one of the attending troopers to help himself to the donut he was eying before motioning to the sergeant to continue with his response. After the trooper took two bites of the glazed cruller, McCam spoke.

"Ms. Russo was a nineteen-year-old freshman at Merrimack College. She lived on campus with three roommates, of which two were apparently her sorority sisters. When not at school, she lived on Federal Street in Salem with her parents and brother. She has a previous criminal record—"

"That's all well and good, sergeant," Walker interjected, "but can you speed it up a little bit, please? How long do you think the body was in the river?"

"Yes, sir," McCam replied with a hint of frustration as the donut-munching trooper choked nervously nearby on the crumbs of his donut. "According to her college roommates, last Saturday they went to the Centro Lounge in Lawrence to go dancing and drinking. They arrived after 9:00 p.m. There were three males that accompanied them to the club, including Jillian's on-again, off-again boyfriend, Carmen Vaughn. According to one of the roommates, they specifically picked that club because the bartenders do not ask college students for IDs to prove they are over the age of twenty-one. The roommates believe everyone was drinking that night, and two confirm that Jillian consumed at least four rum and cokes over a two-hour period. Security footage retrieved from an ATM directly across the street from the club captured four images of Ms. Russo leaving the club at approximately 11:45 p.m."

McCam nodded at Lieutenant Lammoth, who silently pulled up the first of a series of images on her laptop and then projected it to the attendees on the whiteboard. The black and white image depicted a young woman exiting the club's front entrance with a purse in one hand, a cell phone in the other. She was wearing a low-cut blouse, short skirt, and knee-high boots. Approximately five feet behind her was a Hispanic male. After about a minute of silence, two more pictures were displayed on the smartboard by Lammoth. Both suggested Jillian and the young man were engaged in a heated argument. The male's arms were raised, and it appeared he was shouting at the victim. Jillian, in turn, was pointing a finger toward the male and had taken a somewhat defensive stance. The final image showed Jillian entering a dark-colored SUV without the male.

Everyone stared at the pictures in silence. McCam continued, "These pictures were taken over a ten-minute timeframe. All of Jillian's roommates have positively identified the man in the pictures as Jillian Russo's on-again, off-again boyfriend, Carmen Vaughn."

"Those pictures suggest the pair were in a pretty heated argument. Did anyone tell you whether they were?" Walker asked as he started to focus on Carmen Vaughn as his prime suspect.

Lammoth nodded and joined in the conversation. "According to the victim's roommate, Abigail Roberts, the pair spent most of the night arguing over Carmen's belief that Jillian was cheating on him with an unknown man. At the height of the fight, Jillian decided she was going to leave the club. We believe she called for an Uber and left to wait outside. Vaughn followed her, and the argument continued until her ride pulled up."

"Are these images the last of her alive?" Walker asked.

"Yes," McCam quickly answered, "although we expect cell tower ping data, app usage, and her phone records might give us a better picture of how long she was alive after leaving the club."

"When do you expect that information to come in?" Walker asked softly as he continued to stare at the final image on the smartboard.

"We're drafting a warrant as we speak," Lammoth reported. "Assuming it gets approved, we could have the information before the end of the week."

"Have you been able to find her cell phone?" Victoria Donovan inquired.

"If we had the damn cell phone, there wouldn't be a need for a warrant to secure cell phone data, would there, Vicky?" McCam snapped as he grew impatient with the woman's irrelevant question.

An awkward and uncomfortable silence hung about the room for several seconds. Finally, Lieutenant Lammoth cleared her throat and directed the meeting back on track. "If we had to estimate a time of death at this time, we think Ms. Russo was killed early Sunday morning, and the body was dumped into the Merrimack the same day."

"Jackie, any thoughts on how the body ended on top of a chunk of ice?" McCam inquired with a hint of curiosity.

Lammoth paused for a moment to reflect on the question before answering. "Once the body was dumped into the Merrimack, the current of the river immediately pulled the body downstream.

However, as the days passed, the body slowly started to rise toward the surface. How she ended up on top of a chunk of ice is anyone's guess, but if I had to speculate, I would say at some point, the force of the river current probably pushed the body up onto the ice."

Walker thanked Lammoth for her speculation and then looked over at McCam. "Any deterioration of the skin as a result of being in the water for so long?"

"Nothing really beyond the skin being white and wrinkled. We think maceration was delayed because she was still clothed and wrapped in the tarp," McCam reported.

"Any possibility of forensics being recovered?" Donovan asked quietly.

"There is," Lammoth replied. "The coroner has collected fingernail scrapings and mouth and vaginal swabs for evidence. We're waiting to see what if any material has been recovered and if any is suitable for testing."

"Any fingerprints recovered?" Walker inquired of Trooper Brian Eriksen, who in turn shifted uncomfortably in his chair. The first assistant eyed the investigator for a moment, unsure why he seemed so anxious, before turning his attention back toward Lammoth in disbelief.

Trooper Brian Eriksen had been a member of the State Police Detectives Unit for a little under a year. His father was the head of the Massachusetts Environmental Police and had to call in many favors just to get his son accepted into the Massachusetts State Police Academy. Upon graduation, he spent four years on road patrol. During that time, Eriksen did extraordinarily little to impress his superiors or to stand out. Nevertheless, with the assistance of his father, he was able to secure a coveted post within the state police detective unit at the Essex County District Attorney's office. Within a short period of time, he quickly demonstrated that his investigative work was sloppy, his reports were poorly written, he was a terrible witness in court proceedings, and he was in a position that far exceeded his intellectual capabilities.

However, what worked for the trooper were his good looks and charm. Standing at six-foot-one in height, Eriksen typically sported a military-style haircut, a healthy tan, and the latest fashion trend in business casual. His bright green eyes, hard body, and broad grin easily captured the hearts of many members of the opposite sex, especially prosecutors, defense attorneys, and defendants. It was repeatedly whispered that he had several girlfriends throughout Essex County and southern New Hampshire.

"Were any fingerprints recovered, Trooper Eriksen?" the lieutenant softly hissed as she glared at the trooper. While many women were enamored with the trooper, Lammoth was not one of them.

Eriksen stopped fidgeting in his chair and looked over at Walker sheepishly. "Two latent prints were recovered. Both were found on the adhesive side of the duct tape wrapped around Jillian's wrists."

"Their condition?" McCam interjected, somewhat annoyed with Eriksen's lack of preparation.

"In good enough condition for us to visualize the prints, photograph them, and then preserve them through transparent fingerprint-lifting tape." Eriksen nervously answered.

"The fact prints were still recoverable suggests she was in the water for no more than a week," Lammoth noted.

Walked nodded in silence and then lightly tossed his pen onto the notepad that rested on the conference table. He wiped his eyes, blinked a few times, and then redirected his attention back to the meeting at hand. "How long before we'll have a preliminary autopsy report and death certificate?"

"Within the next twenty-four to forty-eight hours. A full detailed autopsy report is likely going to take upward of several weeks," Lammoth declared with a tone of frustration.

"All right. Lieutenant, do we have any suspects?" Walker knowingly asked as he let out a loud yawn. The meeting was quickly sucking the energy out of him.

"Yes," Lammoth quickly answered. "At the suggestion of Jillian's parents, we're looking at her boyfriend, Carmen Vaughn. He is a nineteen-year-old Salem resident and has been in an on-and-off-again relationship with her since their junior year of high school. Her parents described the interaction between the two as 'toxic', and on at least two occasions, she took out restraining orders against him."

"Oh?" Victoria Donovan blurted out as her interest piqued. "When was the most recent one?"

"Nine months ago," McCam announced. "She let both of the restraining orders lapse after ten days."

Sergeant McCam leaned forward in his chair to continue the discussion. "We're already in the process of getting copies of her restraining order applications and affidavits. We also think there may have been a domestic violence incident that may have been dropped. We're hoping to have a clearer picture by this afternoon."

"Where is this young man now?" Walker inquired.

McCam paused for a moment as he reviewed his handwritten notes. "We think he's either at home with his mother in Salem or in his dorm room at Brighton College."

"Has he been laying low?" Donovan queried.

"Surprisingly, he was very active in trying to locate Ms. Russo," Lammoth declared. "He was checking in with the police and going to areas she was known to hang out at to see if anyone saw her."

"And what do you think of that, sergeant?" Walker asked, convinced he already knew the answer.

"Not much. Could be evidence the kid is innocent or simply he is trying to create an impression of innocence to cover his tracks. It's too soon to tell," McCam mused.

"Very well," Walker blurted as he stood up and stretched. He pushed his chair in, picked up his notepad and pen, and started to walk out of the conference room. Donovan and the troopers started to follow him out. Once at the doorway, Walker stopped and looked back at Lammoth. "Lieutenant, find Vaughn immediately and start questioning him."

"Yes, sir," the lieutenant replied as everyone emptied out of the room.

Trooper Eriksen left for his cubicle. He heard the clicking of heeled shoes coming up quickly behind him. He looked over his shoulder just in time to see ADA Donovan seize him by the left arm, spin him into a vacant office, and then follow him inside. The office door slammed with a loud bang. He stood silently as she neared within inches of his face.

"You have a lot of fucking balls working on this case," she declared with nothing but contempt in her voice.

"Why? I am more than qualified, and I've earned the right to work on this case," Eriksen replied, somewhat taken aback.

"You, of all people, have no business on this case, let alone coming even remotely near fingerprints, forensics, or any other physical evidence which could lead to you fucking up this case. You are going to tell Sergeant McCam to reassign you."

"Fuck you. I'm not going anywhere." Eriksen retorted.

Donovan seethed at Eriksen. This trooper was a risk that could not only hurt the progress of this case but her chances for career advancement. She struggled to contain her rage and deeply exhaled through her nostrils twice before continuing. "Let me be fucking clear," she coldly whispered as her eyes narrowed and her face hardened. "If you in any way fuck up my case, I will bury you and make sure you never, ever, see sunlight again."

Before Eriksen could respond, she stepped back, spun around, and stormed out of the office, slamming the door once again. The trooper muttered "bitch" to himself once confident that she was no longer within earshot. Afterward, he continued toward his cubicle but made it a point to wink and smile at the attractive twenty-something administrative assistant as he passed her desk.

He was Trooper Brian Eriksen, and there was no way some bitch like Victoria Donovan was going to keep him off a case that he was determined to see to its conclusion.

FOUR

THURSDAY, MARCH 7

The hot shower water cascaded water around his head and down Carmen Vaughn's body toward the drain. He leaned forward and pressed his hands against the bathtub wall, letting his mind revisit the final moments he spent with Jillian outside of that Lawrence nightclub. After playing out in his mind several scenarios about how the evening could have ended better, he pushed himself backward, shut off the water, and stepped out of the tub.

Carmen grabbed the towel that sat on top of the toilet water tank, wrapped it around his waist, and stepped to the sink that was across from the shower. He wiped the condensation off the mirror and stared long and hard back at the reflection of himself. He sighed twice as he felt a wave of sadness overcome him. His stomach tightened, his eyes welled up with tears, and his breath shortened. After a few more moments of shaking in silence, Carmen managed to somehow regain his composure. He exhaled loudly, stood up straight, and started to dry himself off.

At nineteen years of age, he had already experienced more than his fair share of sadness, disappointment, and heartache. As a young child, he was constantly exposed to the violent outbursts of his father against his mother. On one occasion, when he was merely eight years old, he was awoken out of a sound sleep to the sounds of his mother shrieking in pain as his father drove her head repeatedly against a kitchen cabinet until it splintered into several pieces. She probably would have died that night if not for a neighbor who lived above them called the police. Yet, despite her injuries, Maria Vaughn refused to testify against her husband and asserted her marital privilege in court. After a few months of relative tranquility, the beatings resumed once again.

Shortly after his tenth birthday, his father grew tired of his wife and son, and one morning, simply abandoned them. Carmen never saw or heard from the man again. Although his mother occasionally hinted that he returned to his native city of Montreal, the boy always suspected he was either dead or incarcerated somewhere.

With the pressures of being a single Dominican mother with no emotional, financial, or spiritual support from her own family bearing down on her, Maria often turned to alcohol and weed to help her get through each day. By age twelve, while other boys were spending their time after school flirting with girls or playing pickup games of football or baseball, Carmen was always waiting outside of a Salem bar to walk his mother home. It was only when a neighborhood Congregationalist minister discovered what was going on and personally intervened that Carmen's circumstances changed.

The Reverend Martin Thoreau was an imposing six-foot-five black man who hailed from the projects of Philadelphia and had clawed his way to success. He outright refused to listen to excuses, believed that failure was never an option, and the path to one's redemption depended solely on hard work and perseverance. He took Maria and her son under his wing. Over the next year, he helped her sober up, find a better apartment, and secure stable employment. In exchange, he demanded that Carmen report to him daily after school so that he and his wife could personally oversee his educational progress and social development. By the time he was sixteen, Carmen's performance at Salem High School was somewhat above average, and he was active in school sports.

It was around that time he started dating Jillian. Neither the Reverend Thoreau nor his wife approved of her. Both felt she was hot-headed and a bad influence on Carmen. On more than one occasion, the minister warned him that he was going to go down a dark path if he continued to see this girl. Naturally, Carmen didn't care because he was a fool in love.

But now Jillian was gone. Carmen reflected one more time on the final moments he was with her before he resumed getting dressed. He dropped the towel onto the floor, stepped into his boxers, pulled a t-shirt over his head, pushed open the bathroom door, and was met by his mother coldly staring back at him.

"Jesus, Mom. You could have told me you were standing there," Carmen snapped as he stepped back in surprise.

His mother remained silent as she continued to glare up at him. Although he stood at five-foot-ten in height, he feared his barely five-foot-tall mother. He shifted nervously in place until she finally broke the silence and whispered, "Carmen, there are two Massachusetts troopers downstairs that want to speak with you."

Carmen's stomach turned once again, and he gulped hard as he fought back the urge to vomit. He felt his mind race as he desperately tried to convince himself that the investigators were there to seek his help. He brought his hands up to his face, paused for a moment, and then dropped his arms to his side. "I've been trying to talk with them since the day after Jillian left that club. They want to talk with me now?"

"Yes. Please, don't talk to them," his mother pleaded in a hushed tone.

"I want to talk to them," her son replied somewhat unconvincingly.

"Carmen, listen to me!" she growled as she stepped into the bathroom and closed the distance between her and her son. "If they were here to get your help, they would have called before coming over to see you. These two assholes showed up unannounced at seven o'clock in the fucking morning. They're only want to talk to you because they think you did something to that girl."

"I didn't do anything to Jillian!" Carmen protested as he looked around nervously.

"Shut up, Carmen!" she hissed as she grabbed his left arm and held onto it with a vice grip. "I'm telling you, you don't say a word. They will twist whatever you say to them and use it against you."

He stewed over her advice for a moment before breaking free of her iron grasp and walked past his mother and to his bedroom that was adjacent to the bathroom. Maria instantly followed, growing even angrier that her idiot son was not listening to her warnings.

"Are you listening to me? You are not talking to them!" she murmured as her son spun around to face her, raised his hand, and gestured for her to be silent.

"Mom, they're downstairs waiting. I need to get dressed. Please tell them I'll be down in a moment," he calmly answered.

"You promise me you're not going to say anything stupid to them," his mother demanded.

"I'm not promising anything. I've got nothing to hide." Carmen retorted.

"You stupid, stupid boy." His mother sighed in disappointment as she started to back out of his room. Suddenly, she stopped retreating and pointed her finger at him. "They will blame the Hispanic kid for killing the white girl. You better keep your fucking mouth shut, or I'll personally shut it for you."

Carmen nodded in silence. His mother glared at him for a prolonged moment, convinced that her son was about to dig an excessively big hole for himself. She struggled for a moment over whether to call the Reverend Thoreau to her home before deciding to hold off. She turned around and went downstairs to wait with the troopers.

Carmen quickly finished getting dressed and cautiously walked down to the first floor of the condo he and his mother shared. As he stepped into the kitchen, he saw his mother leaning up against a counter and eyeing a pair of white men dressed in suits seated at their table. One looked to be in his mid-fifties, while the other was likely in his early thirties. Both studied Carmen as he entered the room.

"Carmen Vaughn?" the older trooper inquired with a slight smile.

"Yes," he answered somewhat hesitantly, unsure how to respond.

"Good. Son, have a seat," the trooper announced as he pushed a table chair back and gestured for Carmen to sit down. "My name is Sergeant Dennis McCam, and this is Trooper Brian Eriksen. We're with the Massachusetts State Police, and we'd like to chat with you about Jillian Russo."

Carmen hesitated as he lowered himself into a chair across from the two troopers. He looked over at his mother, who had cocked her head and appeared to be chewing on something sour. He looked back at the officers.

"You obviously knew her, right?" the younger trooper asked as he studied Carmen closely.

"Yes ... yes, I know Jillian," Carmen replied but corrected himself. "I knew her. She's dead now."

"Unfortunately, yes," Sergeant McCam noted softly in response. "Tell us, what was your relationship with her? You were her boy-friend, correct?"

"Yes," Carmen replied as his mother muttered under her breath. Sergeant McCam straightened up in his chair, turned to the mother, and stared in disbelief at her for several seconds. In turn, Maria icily glared at the sergeant. Finally, the sergeant cleared his throat, narrowed his eyes, and growled at her.

"Ma'am, you're allowed in this room as a courtesy. Carmen is over eighteen, and there is no requirement that you be present during this meeting. Do you understand?"

Maria said nothing as she tapped her foot, clenched her jaw, and continued to eyeball the troopers. McCam continued.

"If you would prefer, I could easily toss your son into the back of my cruiser and drag him down to the Salem Police Department for questioning. I have not done that because I do not want to jam this kid up if I don't have to. Right now, you are starting to jam this kid up. So, I suggest you drop the confrontational attitude, shut the fuck up, and allow us to speak with your boy."

His mother cursed under her breath again, shook her head, folded her arms, and then waved in exasperation at the officers. Carmen, who had been watching the exchange in horror, looked away from his mother and nervously toward the troopers. McCam turned his attention back to the young man.

"Carmen," the sergeant stated in a tone that suggested the argument with his mother never happened, "we're trying to get a sense of what happened to Jillian. We think you're one of the last people to see her alive, so we need to ask you some questions."

The young man nodded silently as he listened to the trooper. His mind started to race once again as he failed to recall the minuscule details of his time with Jillian that evening.

McCam continued, "It's always standard for us when we speak to witnesses and suspects—and we're not saying you're a suspect—to advise them of their Miranda rights. We are going to do that here with you as well. Do you understand that?"

Carmen felt his heart start to beat rapidly and his mouth dry up. He looked over at his mother, who was silently shaking her head side to side in disgust. His attention shifted to Trooper Eriksen, who unexpectedly leaned back in his chair, rested his right arm on an adjacent chair, and exposed a Smith & Wesson M&P pistol that was secured in a shoulder holster underneath his suit jacket. Carmen felt as if electricity was running up his legs, and he became lightheaded.

Suddenly, his focus shifted, and he struggled to remember what his professor had always warned him if the police ever came knocking on his door.

"Carmen!" McCam snapped angrily to regain the young man's attention. "Are you listening to me?"

The young man sat forward, propped his elbows on the table, and rested his head in his hands. He sniffed loudly and looked up at the sergeant. Beyond the trooper, he saw his mother starting to slowly pace like a trapped animal.

"I'm sorry, sergeant, I got a bit distracted. I'm just overwhelmed right now."

"That's okay. I understand," McCam said reassuringly. "This is not a position I would want to be in. What I said was I am going to read you your Miranda rights from a sheet I have. After I read you each right, I am going to ask you if you understand that right. If you do, I am going to ask you to place your initials next to the right I read to you. Do you understand what I just said?"

Carmen nodded in silence. He kept asking himself, what was it that Professor Pickering had told him to do if the police wanted to speak with him? Didn't he say if the police start any conversation with Miranda rights, it is never a good sign? His thoughts were interrupted as the sergeant loudly slapped a piece of paper onto the kitchen table, passed it to Carmen, and then handed him a pen. On the top of the sheet, it read "Miranda Rights." McCam got out of his chair, stepped behind Carmen, and leaned down toward the table. His left hand rested on the back of Carmen's chair while his right hand pointed to the sheet. Carmen could smell Dunkin Donuts coffee and cigarettes on the trooper's breath.

"Do you need to hover that close to him?" his mother interjected.

"Stop talking, please," Trooper Eriksen barked as he stood up, sidestepped a few paces toward Maria, and stood between her and her son.

"Carmen, I am now going to read your Miranda rights one at a time," McCam informed Carmen in a very calming tone. "Carmen, you have a right to remain silent. Do you understand that right I just advised you?"

He nodded in the affirmative as his mind continue to race back to his criminal justice classes. What the fuck did Pickering tell him? Why the hell did he skip so many of the professor's classes?

"Excellent, Carmen. Since you understand that right, I am going to ask you to write your initials next to that right I just read to you. By initialing, you are telling me that understand that right." The sergeant picked up the pen and offered it to Carmen. "Go ahead and initial the sheet, please."

Carmen sheepishly took the pen held the pen above the Miranda sheet for a moment. Suddenly, his eyes grew wide, and he dropped the pen onto the table. He remembered what his professor said. He turned slightly around and looked up at Sergeant McCam.

"Is there a problem?" McCam inquired, somewhat confused at the sudden hesitation. "Do you want me to read the right to you again?"

Carmen smirked slightly. "Sergeant, as my professor told me,

'When the po-po rolls up, your first call should be to your lawyer, not your mom.'"

"What the fuck does that even mean?" Eriksen blurted out as he turned away from Maria and looked back at his boss. McCam instantly recognized that the situation was deteriorating very quickly.

"It means he doesn't want to talk to you, and he wants a lawyer!" Carmen's mother announced as she sprang forward from the kitchen counter and pushed past Eriksen.

"Is that what you want? A lawyer?" McCam demanded, now clearly annoyed.

"It's exactly what I want," Carmen retorted as he stood up from his chair, forcing the sergeant to back away. The young man quickly walked over and stood next to his mother. "If you're coming into my house and advising me of Miranda rights, then I'm a suspect. And I'm not saying shit without a lawyer."

The two troopers and Carmen watched each other for a moment before Eriksen decided to take a different approach and break the silence. "It sounds like you have one hell of a professor, Carmen. You want to roll the dice with us, as well as your future based upon the advice of a college professor?"

"I'm not talking to you without a lawyer," Carmen repeated.

Eriksen scowled at Carmen and his mother before McCam interjected. It was clear the sergeant was very pissed off at Carmen for asserting his Miranda rights so early in the interview. "Very well, Carmen, but I want to be perfectly clear. It does not and will not get any easier from this point forward. If you had anything to do with Jillian's death, I will make your life exceptionally difficult. That is a promise to you. Are you sure this is what you want to do?"

"If you're finished, you can leave now," Maria replied as she stepped between Carmen and the troopers gestured for the two investigators to leave.

"We're not done with Carmen," Eriksen responded with a sly grin as he rested his hand on the grip of his pistol and stepped toward Maria. Sergeant McCam pulled a folded paper out from his suit pocket and handed it to Carmen. "We've got a warrant for your cell phone, son. Hand it the fuck over, now."

"What?" Carmen replied in shock as he glossed over the paper. In the upper left-hand corner, in large bold letters, the caption read, "SEARCH WARRANT G. L. C. 276, §§ 1-7."

"That's not a birthday invitation, son. I can see the outline of your phone in your front jeans pocket. Take it out, and hand it the fuck over," the sergeant snapped as Trooper Eriksen stepped away from Maria and withdrew a clear evidence bag from the knapsack he brought with him into Carmen's home.

"Fine." Carmen sighed as he pulled the Galaxy S7 phone out of his pocket and dropped it into the bag. Eriksen sealed the bag with adhesive tape and made a series of shorthand notations on the front of the bag. Afterward, he nodded at McCam.

"Should have talked to us, Carmen," the sergeant warned as the two started to leave the house through the kitchen doorway. When Trooper Eriksen reached the threshold, he stopped and looked back at Carmen and his mother.

"Tell me, Carmen. You're Dominican, right?"

"Half."

"Where's the name Vaughn come from? That's an unusual last name for a Hispanic kid."

"My father's white asshole. He's from the Quebec Province of Canada."

Eriksen grunted softly, looked around the kitchen one last time, and then eyed Carmen. "Interesting. I wonder if ICE knows about you."

"You mother—" Maria blurted out as Eriksen gave a quick wink, blew a kiss at Carmen, and stepped outside.

After a moment of cursing in Spanish and knocking random items off a kitchen counter, she looked back at her son. His hands were up to his mouth, and he had a wild look of terror in his eyes. There was a soft, high-pitched whine as he started to sob. She quickly rushed over to her and hugged him. He was physically shaking.

"Momma, they think I killed her. What are we going to do?"

Sergeant McCam stood on the street that ran past Carmen's residence for a moment, listening to the frightened wails of the boy and his mother that could be heard outside. He smiled slightly, knowing that his point had been made. He continued to listen to the disturbance for a moment before turning his attention back to his partner.

The sergeant spun around and walked briskly back to his unmarked Ford Explorer. He quickly hopped into the driver's seat and eyed Eriksen as he climbed into the passenger side. He started the engine of the unmarked cruiser, took one last look at the Vaughn household, and pulled away.

"You really can't be that dumb," he snarled as a confused look spread across Eriksen's face.

"What, what did I do?" the trooper replied.

"You threatened our primary suspect with a visit from ICE? Why didn't you simply tell him to make a run for it? We don't have probable cause to arrest him yet, and you just gave him an incentive to flee. Walker is going to be all over our shit because of your stupid cowboy statement," McCam barked at the trooper.

"I doubt it," Eriksen responded with a sense of confidence as he regained his composure. "The kid knew he was a suspect once you advised him of his Miranda rights. Why did you even do that? I mean, he wasn't in custody."

McCam chose to ignore the foolish, condescending statement and instead reflected upon just how stupid his partner truly was. He always believed Eriksen was nothing more than a hack who relied upon his father's political connections to secure undeserved advancement after undeserved advancement. Vaughn jeopardized the investigation today. He was cocky, self-assured, and convinced he knew better than the other members of McCam's team. In short, he was a liability, and it was time for McCam to snap him into line. He pulled the cruiser over to the side of the road, slapped the gear shift into park, and turned in his seat to address the idiot that occupied the seat next to him.

"Have you even bothered to read our policies and procedures while you were in the academy, you dumb fuck?" McCam demanded angrily. "You always advise a suspect of his Miranda rights so we can avoid a fucking motion to suppress a suspect's confession when the case is in the courts."

Eriksen stared blankly as his commanding officer continued.

"Don't you ever—and I truly mean forever—pull a stupid stunt like you did back there. You better get your shit in line, or I will find a way to have you transferred to a road barrack in western Massachusetts. Am I fucking clear?"

"Yes, sergeant," Eriksen stammered, somewhat surprised at his superior's reaction.

"We better hope this phone yields something; otherwise, we're going to hit a friggin' dead end, no thanks to you," McCam announced with exasperation as he slipped the vehicle back into drive and pulled away from the side of the road.

"It will," Eriksen instantly replied with a hint of confidence.

"It better," McCam snarled as he pulled a cigarette out of his shirt pocket. "And remind me someday to find this kid's professor and put my boot up his ass."

FIVE

The Everett Mill Building has dominated the Lawrence skyline for the last century. Construction of the brick complex commenced in 1909 and finished the following year. At the time of its completion, it was the largest cotton mill in the world. The site employed well above two thousand people and produced 1.2 million yards of cotton cloth every week. By 1912, the mill was known nationally for its high-quality ginghams, denims, and shirtings, which were affectionately referred to as "Everett Classics."

Following a combination of federal regulations and shifts in the American economy, demand for Everett Classics dropped off significantly, forcing the mill owners to sell the property to a real estate management company in 1929. By the late 1970s, the textile industry had all but died in Lawrence, and the Everett Mills fell silent. Nevertheless, in 1981, a developer purchased the property and announced his commitment to revitalizing Lawrence through the redevelopment of the Everett Mills. Although the effort has been largely unsuccessful, the mill complex currently houses social advocacy groups, health care organizations, light manufacturing, warehousing, high-tech firms, and a cafe.

Approximately fifty yards to the left of the Everett Mill's brightly painted wood and granite main entrance was a smaller glass door. Above the doorway hung a white sign with black and gold letters that read "Committee for Public Counsel Services." Also known as the public defenders or "CPCS," this government organization was charged with the difficult task of providing criminal defense services to poor persons who could not otherwise afford an attorney. Despite being underpaid and overworked, most, if not all, of the members of this organization felt a compelling sense of devotion to the concept of justice and due process for the accused.

CPCS was routinely portrayed by the *Lawrence Star* as the bad guy. Countless editorials slammed the organization as a waste of taxpayer dollars and a collection of political "hacks" and misguided social justice warriors. *Star* reporter Harriet Jenson typically fanned the flames of racism with one-sided tales of Hispanic defendants who were represented by court-appointed attorneys on the public's dime. Even high-profile criminal defense attorneys slammed the organization and warned potential clients they ran the grave risk of losing their freedom if they went with a public defender rather than hire one of them.

Yet, despite all the negative attention, Maria Vaughn chose to come to the public defender's office for help. She paced outside the front door of the Lawrence division of CPCS, attempting to work up the courage to go inside. Just a few hours earlier, two Massachusetts state troopers were sitting inside her home trying to question her son about a dead girl. Now she had to be proactive and find a lawyer for him before the police returned to arrest Carmen.

She glanced across the street toward the old brick and wood Roman Catholic church that had been built a century before by Italian immigrants. She crossed herself, took a deep breath, swung back the heavy glass door back, and entered the office. A handicap ramp led up to a thick glass plate window behind which a pair of administrative assistants sat. She felt her chest tighten up and her breath shorten as her mind raced through the various scenarios of her son's fate. She stopped halfway up the ramp and leaned against a railing. She fought back the tears as they welled up in her eyes and started to pray out loud.

One of the administrative assistants, an extremely attractive redhead in her mid-forties, looked up and saw Maria gasping for air.

She instinctively sprung up out of her chair, walked to her left, and entered the reception area via a side door. She rushed over to Maria as she crumbled to the floor. She caught the woman by the left arm and, with some effort, managed to help her stand back up. The assistant made a few assuring comments, tightly grasped Maria's arm, and led her over to a row of chairs located at the top of the ramp near a brick wall. End tables flanked both ends while a series of pictures of the Everett Mill from the early twentieth Century hung on the wall above the seats. After Maria sat down, the blond woman left and returned several moments later with a bottle of water and tissues. She handed both items to Carmen's mother and began to ask some basic questions as to why she was visiting the public defender's office.

"I—I need a lawyer for my son," Maria blurted out with embarrassment. Hours earlier, she was arguing toe-to-toe with police officers who were clearly after her only son. Now, she was sobbing helplessly in front of a stranger. "I need help!"

"Okay," the redhead responded sympathetically and with a heavy Boston accent. "Has he been charged with a crime? Is one of our lawyers currently representing him?"

"No." Maria gasped as she struggled not to physically shake in front of the woman. "I think he's a suspect in a murder. The dead girl who washed ashore earlier this week in Merrimac. My son is her boyfriend, and the police tried to question him today."

"Oh my God," the woman replied with shock as she sat down next to Maria and leaned in toward her. "I want you to listen to me very carefully, all right? What is your name?"

"Maria Vaughn."

"Okay, Miss Vaughn. I'm not sure what we can do for you just yet," the woman softly explained. "CPCS usually doesn't get involved with a criminal case until after someone is charged with a crime."

Maria nodded in silence and wiped the tears from her eyes. She wondered if this trip was a waste of time. She started to review in her mind how she could possibly come up with the money to hire a criminal defense attorney.

The receptionist stood up and studied Maria for a moment. Afterward, she smiled reassuringly at her. "From one mother to another mother, let me see if there's someone who can speak with you and explain what you and your son need to do right now." The receptionist paused for a moment. "Where is your son right now?"

"With his professor," Maria replied with a slight tone of aggravation.

"I'm sorry, did you say his professor?" the receptionist responded with a confused look on her face.

"Yes. His professor teaches criminal justice at Brighton College. I told my son he needed to come with me to meet with someone from your organization, but he insisted he wanted to talk with his professor instead."

The receptionist cocked her head slightly back in surprise before regaining her composure. "All right, Ms. Vaughn. I'll be right back."

Maria felt another wave of emotion starting to overwhelm her, and she choked back tears. "I begged him to come with me here, but he insisted he wanted to talk with Professor Pickering."

The assistant nodded silently, spun around, and walked back through a side door and into her office area. She immediately turned left and walked down a hallway to a cluster of offices located near the agency's rear entrance. She stopped at the last one on the left, knocked on the door, and stepped inside. She found Adrian Watson leaning against a ledge and peering out his window at a vehicle parked in a nearby lot.

"Anne, see that blue Honda over there?" He chuckled as he pointed to the dilapidated vehicle. "Whoever owns that car left a pistol on the front seat. I mean, it's just sitting out in the open for everyone to see."

"Oh?" Anne responded, somewhat curious and horrified at the same time. "Did anyone call the cops?"

"That's the thing," Adrian replied with a large grin. "The building manager approached me about an hour ago. He thought the car and the gun belonged to one of our clients. Of course, I told him that was

not possible because none of our clients are here right now. So, he immediately called the Lawrence Police. I bet him ten dollars they would be a no show."

"How long did you give him before you win the bet?"

"Three phone calls to the station or two hours. Whichever happened first."

"And where are you right now?"

"It's been ninety minute,s and the manager has already made two calls." Adrian proudly announced before pushing himself away from the window and turning his undivided attention to his favorite receptionist. "So, what's up?"

"None of the lawyers are in right now so you would be doing me a huge favor if you could speak to a woman who's in the reception area. She's looking for a lawyer for her son because she thinks he might be a suspect in the murder of his girlfriend."

Adrian perked up slightly. "Not the Jillian Russo case? The girl who washed up from the river near my house in Merrimac?"

"The exact one," Anne replied, her eyes growing wide. "She said the police paid her son a visit a few hours ago."

"Where's the kid now?" Watson inquired.

"With his professor."

"His what?" he replied with disbelief. "C'mon, Anne, you're not serious."

"I wish I was full of crap, but that's what she told me," the receptionist replied.

"Has he been charged?" Adrian asked, his interest in the matter quickly growing.

"Nope. Not yet," she declared, seeming somewhat unsurprised. Murder investigations were often methodical and slow-paced. The Jillian Russo case appeared to be no different.

The private investigator reflected in silence for a few moments and then spoke. "I'm not sure how much we can do since the kid hasn't been charged yet."

"That's what I told her," Anne quickly reported. "But it wouldn't hurt to get some basic information. We can pass it onto one of our attorneys, so it stays on the radar."

Adrian nodded in agreement. He walked with Anne down to the reception area. Once there, he stopped and looked over at the Hispanic woman who was hunched over in a chair, rocking back and forth. He could tell she was emotionally exhausted.

"What's her name?" he softly asked Anne.

"Maria Vaughn."

Adrian walked over to the woman, extended his hand, and introduced himself.

"Ms. Vaughn, my name is Adrian Watson. I am a private investigator with CPCS. Unfortunately, none of the lawyers are available to speak with you right now. If it is okay, I'd like to take a few minutes of your time to get some basic information from you about your son and his situation so I can forward it to our supervising attorney. Can you do that for me?"

Maria never made eye contact with Adrian. She sniffled softly and then shook her head in the affirmative. The private investigator gestured for her to follow him to a conference room. Once there, he pointed to a chair for her to sit down in and then dropped a notepad and pen onto the table. Anne wished the woman good luck and left the room.

"First off, tell me a little about yourself," he asked.

"My name is Maria Vaughn. I live in Salem, Massachusetts, with my son, Carmen."

"Is it just the two of you who live together, or does anyone else live with you?" Adrian inquired.

"No, just the two of us," Maria replied in a soft, monotone voice.

"Is dad in the picture at all?" the investigator pressed.

"Dad is nowhere in the fucking picture," Maria sneered as she looked up and shot an icy stare at Adrian. "He hasn't had any contact with his son since he was a young boy."

"I see," Watson replied, attempting to appear sympathetic. "All right. Tell me a little bit about your son."

"What do you want to know? He is twenty years old and attends Brighton College. He's a hard worker and decent student."

"I'm happy to hear that," Adrian noted. Tell me, what's he's majoring in at Brighton?"

"Criminal justice," she replied.

"Does he work?"

"Yes. On weekends and during the summer, he works at an auto body shop in Lynn. He also volunteers at our neighborhood church."

"Is your minister aware of what is going on?" the investigator calmly asked.

"He is and he isn't. He's aware that Carmen has been looking for his missing girlfriend, but he doesn't know yet that the police visited him this morning."

Adrian paused for a moment before asking a follow-up question designed to address his own curiosity about Mr. Vaughn. "Has your son ever been in trouble with the law before?"

"Yes," Maria replied with some hesitation.

"It's all right. There's no judgment here," Adrian stated reassuringly.

Maria sighed. "He stayed out of trouble most of his life. It wasn't until he started dating Jillian."

"The dead girl?" Adrian asked instinctively.

Maria studied him momentarily before answering softly, "Yes, the dead girl."

"What happened with Jillian?" he asked.

Maria paused for a moment before continuing. "The relationship between those two was like a roller coaster. If they were not fighting, I swear to God, they were all over each other."

"Go on," Adrian replied.

"I know she took out a restraining order against him on one occasion and accused him of punching her another time," she stated as she wiped a tear from her eye.

"What happened with those matters?" the investigator questioned.

"Dismissed. Both were dismissed."

Adrian paused for a moment and made several notations before dropping his pen and looking back up at Maria. "You said you live in Salem?"

"Yes."

"All right. Have you spoken with any other criminal defense attorneys?" the investigator pressed.

"No, I haven't," she stated with some hesitation.

Adrian nodded in the affirmative as he studied Maria. After a moment of awkward silence, he finally spoke. "Why us? Why not speak to our sister office in Salem? I mean, they have an office right on Congress Street. It shouldn't be too hard to find them."

Maria flushed with embarrassment. "Mr. Watson, I came here because I can barely rub two nickels together, and I sure as hell can't afford an expensive Boston or Andover lawyer. I work upstairs in the light manufacturing company. I see you guys every day, and you always look as if you care about the work you do. Are you telling me I'm wrong about the people in this office?"

"No, no. I'm just trying to get a sense of why you decided to knock on our particular door," Adrian responded with a grim look. "Ms. Vaughn, I'm not sure if our administrative assistant said anything to you or not, but I'm not sure if there's anything we can do about your son's situation—"

"You're not sure if there's anything you can do about my son's situation because he hasn't been charged with a damn crime yet," Maria interrupted. "I heard that the first time from your receptionist. You mean to tell me my son will be out there twisting in the wind with no help because a police officer hasn't slapped handcuffs on him yet?"

Adrian stared at Maria in surprise and then reluctantly nodded in agreement. The woman cursed silently under her breath before wiping fresh tears from her eyes. Watson looked down and started to quickly write a series of brief notes about Maria on his notepad. Afterward, he looked back up at the woman.

"I can't ask you too many questions about the case itself because I don't want to make myself a possible witness against your son. That said, you mentioned that a pair of police officers paid your son a visit this morning. I assume they started asking him questions, so tell me, did he say anything to them?"

"Thank God, no," Maria stated as she sat back in her chair and folded her arms. "They started to advise him of his Miranda rights, and he said he wanted a lawyer almost immediately."

The investigator nodded with approval. "Good, that's good. Did they take anything from him, or did they try to take evidence from him? For example, did they take a hair sample, scrape underneath his fingernails, or seize any of his clothing?"

"They took his phone."

Adrian stopped and put his pen down. He folded his hands on the table and looked directly at Maria. "Well, if they took his phone, then he's definitely on their radar screen."

Maria's eyes welled up with tears again. "That's what I was afraid of."

The private investigator continued, "I'll be honest, from what little you've told me so far, I'd say the police are looking very closely at him. He is the boyfriend, so it's a routine procedure to look at him. He may end up lucky and their attention shifts to someone else. On the other hand, they could come at him hard and try to pin this girl's death on your son."

"What do I do now? What does Carmen do?" Maria asked as she lowered her head onto the conference room table.

"If that kid were my son, I'd be telling him the best thing he can do right now is to keep his damn mouth shut," Watson whispered as he leaned toward Maria and pounded his index finger on the conference room table for emphasis. "He needs to keep his fucking mouth shut and not do anything stupid. You need to tell him that he cannot talk about this on Facebook or post anything on Twitter or Instagram about this matter. He absolutely talks to nobody about this case."

Carmen's mother looked up and nodded in understanding. Adrian eyed her intensely before continuing. "If he is charged, someone from our office will represent him, and believe me—they'll do one hell of a job. But the best thing he can do right now is just to lay low, shut up, and not bring attention to himself."

"I understand," Maria replied, her voice trembling with fear.

"Where is he now? You need to speak with him about how important it is for him to not talk to anyone."

"He went to his school to see his professor to talk about his case."

Adrian exhaled loudly. "Okay, that is a perfect example of what not to do. You need to get in touch with him and make him understand that there is no such thing as professor-student confidentiality. Am I making myself clear?"

"I pleaded with him to come here with me, but he insisted he wanted to talk to Professor Pickering."

The investigator instinctively sat up straight in his chair, cocked his head slightly, and eyed Maria carefully. "Did you say, Professor Pickering?

"Yes, his professor's name is Pickering."

"Are we talking about Timothy Pickering?"

SIX

THURSDAY, MARCH 7

Timothy Pickering sat at his desk, rubbed his hands together, and eagerly leaned toward the screen of his laptop. For several moments, he carefully studied the digital images of an early-nineteenth-century Boston newspaper, quietly hoping he would come across any minute reference of Essex County ship carpenters being hired to repair the USS *Constitution*.

Many of his coworkers and his family found the professor's obsession with early nineteenth-century American naval history to be painfully tedious and quite boring. However, for Pickering, the untold adventures of historical nautical research served as an avenue of escape from the daily toils of difficult students, nagging administrators, and incompetent research assistants.

However, the brief respite came to a sudden end with a loud knock on his office door. At first, Pickering ignored the unannounced caller and continued to study a broadsheet containing a variety of advertisements, but when a series of quick, repetitive knocks followed, he was forced to end his diversion and address the intruder.

"You can come in," he exclaimed with a tone of slight annoyance as he slapped his laptop shut and looked at his office door. "Enter!"

The door slowly opened with a long-prolonged squeak to reveal Carmen Vaughn standing in the entrance. He looked gray and very anxious. The young man was physically shaking, sweating heavily, and quickly looking both ways over his shoulders. He leaned onto the door frame to support himself, and after a series of loud, shallow breaths, he stepped forward and staggered into his professor's office.

Pickering shot up out of his chair, walked around his desk, and guided Carmen to a seat located in the corner of his office. He then retrieved a bottle of water from his mini-refrigerator and handed it to the student. Afterward, he sat down in a chair adjacent to Carmen and visually examined his student for several moments. His thoughts drifted back to his conversation with Yulissa earlier in the week. Carmen had been missing classes because he had been searching for a missing girlfriend—the young woman who washed up on the shores of the Merrimack River a few days ago.

"Mr. Vaughn, you don't look too good," Pickering declared in a calm voice. "I know from speaking with Yulissa that you've been going through an exceedingly difficult time these past few days. Perhaps it would be in your best interest to speak with a school counselor or go to the infirmary?"

Carmen remained silent as he visibly shook in his seat and looked around the office in terror. After a moment of awkward silence, Pickering leaned forward and spoke once again to his student.

"Carmen, listen to me," he stated softly but in a firm tone. "I know you're going through a difficult time right now. Hell, I cannot think of an uglier position to be in. If you are here to discuss the assignments and tests you've missed, rest assured, I am more than happy to work with you."

"They think I killed my girlfriend, professor!" Carmen abruptly announced as he snapped out of his trance and stared intensely at his teacher. "They think I killed my girlfriend."

Pickering leaned back into his chair, held up his hands in protest, and growled at his student. "You don't want to be having this conversation with me, son. If you are in trouble, you need to talk to a lawyer."

"You're a lawyer, aren't you, professor?"

Pickering felt his stomach turn and his chest tighten. He knew where Carmen was going with the conversation and why he visited him instead of the school counselor. The last thing he wanted was to return to the profession that almost destroyed him emotionally and physically. Nevertheless, he chose to respond to the question.

"Yes, I am."

"Well, I want to talk to you," Carmen announced as he took a gulp of water from the bottle his teacher had given him.

Pickering laughed nervously. "Mr. Vaughn, I don't think you want me as a lawyer. I haven't seen the inside of a courtroom in over three years, and I'm not sure I feel comfortable representing one of my students in a murder investigation."

"Why?" Carmen demanded, his voice briefly raising.

"Carmen," Pickering continued, "the potential conflict of interest issues with the school alone may prevent me from providing you with a zealous defense. On top of that, I think there's a good chance this institution would prohibit me from coming within ten feet of your matter just to avoid any hint of bad press."

Carmen gawked in horror before speaking in a low, cold voice. He stared icily at his professor. "I want to speak with you, Professor Pickering. I do not trust anyone else, and I don't give a fuck about any conflict issues or school rules. I will gladly sign paperwork waiving any conflicts. All I want to do is talk and get an idea of what I am looking at. At the end of the day, if you don't want to help me, fine. This poor Hispanic boy is probably going to end up with a court-appointed attorney anyway, so it shouldn't be any skin off your fucking shoulder to give me the big picture as to what I'm looking at."

The professor reflected cautiously on his student's remarks. Admittedly, Pickering was unsure whether any conflicts truly existed that would have precluded him from giving advice to his student. On the one hand, since Vaughn was seeking guidance from an experienced attorney and not his professor, it was likely any statements Vaughn made were shielded by an attorney-client privilege. However, on the other hand, the last thing Pickering wanted to do was return to the criminal litigation stage. After some time of internal debate and conflict, Pickering relented and decided the meeting was a mere conversation that likely could go nowhere.

"All right, Mr. Vaughn," he announced. "We'll talk hypotheticals and what you could potentially be looking at. But let us be perfectly clear. You need to tell me the absolute truth. I do not want any sugar-coating or bullshit. You also must answer all my questions honestly. If I feel you are full of shit, I will shut down this conversation immediately. I just hope to God our conversation falls under attorney-client privilege, and the police cannot use it against you down the road. You understand what I'm saying?"

"Yes, professor," Carmen replied with a curt nod.

"You do understand that if you're charged with a crime, the school is going to move to either suspend or expel you. Of course, that's going to be the least of your worries," Pickering mused.

"Yes."

"Very well. I am not going to take any notes or record this conversation. We are just going to have a chat. At the end of it, I will give you some suggestions on what you need to do next. Are we clear?" the professor cautiously stated.

"Yes, Professor Pickering," Carmen replied, his voice shaking.

"Yulissa told me you were having a girlfriend problem. Is that correct?"

"Yes."

"What is your girlfriend's name?" Pickering inquired cautiously, unsure if he wanted to hear the answer.

"Jillian Russo."

The professor's stomach turned slightly. He senses warned that he was going down a road he did not want to. Nevertheless, he pushed forward and continued to ask his student questions.

"How long were you dating her for?" He demanded.

"For over two years," Carmen replied.

"You two meet at school, at work, or where?"

"Salem High School. We started dating our junior year when we were both sixteen," Carmen replied.

"All right. How would you describe your relationship with Jillian?" Pickering asked, unsure if he wanted to hear the response.

"Difficult," the student replied with some hesitation.

Pickering cocked his head slightly in confusion. "What do you mean by 'difficult'?"

"I think my mother described it best. The bitch was always getting me in trouble, leading me around, cheating on me, and talking smack about me."

The professor cleared his throat and stared intently at Carmen. "Really? That is how you want to describe your relationship with Jillian to me? My early advice to you would be do not talk like that, especially around the police. Otherwise, you'll be handing them a potential motive for murdering this girl."

"Yes, professor," Carmen responded, almost sheepishly.

"So, the two of you graduated from high school together?"

"Yes."

"What did Jillian do after graduation? Did she go to work or school?"

"She was a student at Merrimack College and lived on campus in North Andover," Carmen replied.

"Well, you're attending a Boston area school; she's attending a college up on the New Hampshire border. How often would you guys get together?" Pickering inquired with a slight tome of disbelief.

"I would try. I'd try to get up to see her every other weekend at best or once a month, worst-case scenario."

Pickering reflected on that comment for a moment. "How often would she come down to visit you?"

"Not often. She didn't have a car and couldn't afford the train."

The professor did not believe it. It was clear Jillian was slowly trying to distance herself from her high school sweetheart.

"How did you get along with her roommates?"

"No problems. When I would visit Jillian, they would often ask if I could bring some of my friends with me for them. They liked to party with them."

"Did you bring any of your friends with you?" Pickering asked.

"Yes. Sometimes Jake and Tyler would come with me."

"Were they friends from home or from school?" Pickering pressed.

"School," Carmen nervously answered.

"When was the last time you saw Jillian?" Pickering asked as he studied Carmen's body language.

Carmen visibly fought back tears. "It was about a week before she was found in the river."

"All right. Where were you when you saw her last?" the professor demanded as he struggled to fight back the idea of becoming emotionally attached to his student.

"Two of my friends from school and some of Jillian's friends all got together at Merrimack College before we decided to hit some of the nightclubs in Lawrence. We all met about nine o'clock at night and took a pair of Ubers over to Lawrence. Ultimately we ended up at the Centro Nightclub on Common Street."

"Would these two friends be Jake and Tyler?" the professor inquired.

"Yes, professor," Carmen curtly answered with a nod.

"How did the evening go, Carmen?" the professor inquired as he carefully studied his student's demeanor and expressions.

Carmen sighed for a moment as tears rolled down his cheeks. "We got into a fight. She told me she was dating an older guy she met at another club in Lawrence."

"Obviously, that news upset you," Pickering replied as he struggled to sound sympathetic.

"It pissed me off," Carmen announced as his body stiffened and his eyes started to well up with tears. Pickering reached over to a nearby table, retrieved a box of tissues, and handed it to him.

"What time did this happen?"

"She had been drinking and I really didn't have anything. We chose that club because they do not ask for IDs and will serve just about anyone. She was pretty buzzed and—"

"Carmen, what time did the argument start?" the professor interrupted as he became annoyed with Carmen's beating around the bush.

Carmen shifted uncomfortably in his chair. "I don't know; definitely before midnight. We got into it good."

"Did you hit or grab her?" Pickering demanded with a stern tone.

"No, no," Carmen replied as he tried to remain calm. "But she shoved me a few times. She was so mad that she left all our friends behind, walked out of the club, got into an Uber, and took off. I never heard from her for the rest of the night or on Sunday."

"Were you concerned that you never heard from her?" the professor asked as he carefully studied his student.

"By Monday, I started to panic and was going all over the place trying to find her."

Pickering held up his right hand, gesturing for Carmen to stop talking. "You said you never saw her the rest of Saturday night. Did you try to call her or text her?"

"Of course," Carmen exclaimed. "But she never responded."

"Did you threaten her in any of your calls or texts? Did you leave voicemail messages you are going to regret down the road?" Pickering demanded.

"Absolutely not," Carmen retorted as he waved his hands in protest.

"And your friends would be able to testify that you remained with them in the club until you went back to Brighton College?" Pickering sharply retorted with a hint of suspicion.

"No." Carmen sniffed and sunk his head down into his head.

Pickering moaned slightly and slumped back into his chair. After a moment of reflection, he sat up straight in his chair and looked directly at his student. "Where did you go?"

"I left about an hour after Jillian and took an Uber ride by myself back to my dorm room here on campus," Carmen replied, matter-of-factly.

"Oh!" Pickering blurted out, somewhat relieved with his student's answer. "That is very good. If you can identify who the Uber driver was, you've got an alibi witness."

Carmen smiled slightly. "It sounds like I might have some good news."

"It is," Pickering replied with slight enthusiasm. "Ultimately, you're going to need to produce witnesses or information that shows when you arrived at the dorm. If you do that, there's a good chance the police might back off looking at you as a suspect."

It was not a rock-solid alibi, but it was a pretty close second place. *If Carmen's story checked out,* the professor thought to himself, *the police would have to back off and focus on other leads.* He quickly shifted focus and turned his attention to his student's actions in the days after Jillian's disappearance.

"Did you ever report her missing to the police?"

"Yes, on Tuesday."

"Which department?" the professor inquired.

"Three."

"Three?" Pickering interrupted. "Which ones?"

"Lawrence, North Andover, and Salem Police," Carmen answered.

"Did any of them ever ask you to give a statement to them?" Pickering asked.

"Yes."

"Who?" the professor pressed.

"Salem," Carmen replied in a tone that was much calmer than before.

That surprised the professor. He would have expected the Lawrence Police Department to ask for information surrounding Jillian's disappearance. "Did you say anything to them?"

"Of course," Carmen replied with a hint of confidence.

"What the hell did you say?" Pickering demanded, growing annoyed that his student clearly ignored his lessons and spoke with the police.

"All they did was ask me to write out a statement as to what happened at the nightclub and what I did to try and locate her before reporting her missing."

Pickering silently cursed to himself. If this kid was even remotely a target, the district attorney's office was going to twist that statement into evidence of Carmen's guilt.

"Carmen, listen to me very carefully." Pickering growled as he pointed a finger directly at Carmen. "From this point forward, you keep your fucking mouth shut. You do not give any additional statements to the police. Any statement you give them is going to be used against you. Do you understand me?"

"Yes, professor, I know that," Carmen stammered. "When the state police visited me this morning, I told them I wanted to stay silent and talk to a lawyer."

Pickering replied with a wave of his right hand. "Did you just say the police visited you this morning? Where?"

"At my mom's house," Carmen announced.

"What did they ask you?" the professor demanded.

Carmen recounted how the two troopers arrived at his mother's house, presented a warrant, and then seized his cell phone. He then described the threats Trooper Eriksen made to have ICE check on his immigration status.

His instructor stared at Carmen with his mouth open. However, after he regained his composure, Pickering leaned back in his chair and contemplated his student's situation. Assuming the young man's statement to the Salem Police did include references to a fight with his girlfriend, it was that likely that the Essex District Attorney's office would start building a case around a domestic violence homicide theory. It was an argument Pickering would have made as a prosecutor. Carmen, the ever-jealous boyfriend, attacked and killed his helpless girlfriend after an embarrassing verbal argument at the nightclub.

Even worse, since the police had his phone, they would be looking for threatening text messages, a pattern of harassing phone calls, or cell tower pings that placed Carmen near Jillian after she left the club. Pickering knew the writing was on the wall—his student was more than a casual suspect; he was the primary target.

He cleared his throat, eyed Carmen for a moment, and then resumed his conversation with the student.

"Carmen, I've got some serious concerns that a prosecutor may claim that you killed Jillian because you were an abusive and jealous boyfriend."

"A domestic violence killing," Carmen sadly stated as his head sunk back into his hands.

"Exactly," the professor responded, a little surprised at the young man's response. "I need to ask you some questions about your past relationship with Jillian that may be relevant in this case. All right?"

"Of course," Carmen replied with some hesitation.

"Jillian ever accuse you of hitting her?" Pickering inquired as he carefully studied his student and his response.

"Yes, twice," Carmen replied softly, as he avoided making eye contact with his teacher.

The instructor ground his teeth. This revelation was not good under any circumstances.

"Did she ever take out a restraining order against you?"

"Twice. About nine months ago," Carmen responded, sounding somewhat reluctant to reveal the information.

"Do you know if it's still active?" Pickering asked.

"No. She went into court shortly after each one was taken out and dropped them."

"I assume you got back together after that?" the professor asked, already knowing what the answer would be.

"Yes."

"Were you ever arrested because you were accused of hitting or her?" the professor continued.

"Yes. It was last year in the Salem District Court, but she admitted to making up the allegations, and the charges were dropped."

"Are you sure?" the professor demanded dubiously.

"That's what my court-appointed lawyer told me," Carmen retorted, slightly annoyed that his professor would doubt him.

"Is there any record of her telling the court, under oath, that she made up the charges?"

"I don't remember," Carmen hesitated.

An uncomfortable silence fell on the room. Pickering folded his hands, leaned back in his chair, and looked out a nearby window. He sighed in disgust. Carmen glanced about the office nervously, and after a moment of reflection upon the conversation he just had with his instructor, he spoke.

"Am I in trouble, Professor Pickering?"

Pickering stared at his student and studied his facial expressions. Carmen looked terrified. His eyes were wide, his breathing shallow, and he looked as if he were about to vomit. There was no way Pickering could minimize or sugar-coat the bad news.

"Carmen, based upon what you have told me, there is no doubt in my mind the police are trying to build a case against you. You, sir, to put it bluntly, are in deep shit."

The young man slumped back in his chair and started to cry. "I'm going to jail for something I didn't do!"

The professor stood up and stared down at Carmen. He gestured for the young man to stand up. Once he did, Pickering placed his hand on the young man's shoulder and shook him gently.

"What you need to do now is keep your mouth shut and lay low. If I were you, I'd get my ass home now and stay there until either this blows over or they arrest you."

Carmen nodded, his face lacking any signs of emotion. He looked up at his professor. "I'm going to need a lawyer?"

"Absolutely," Pickering replied as he struggled to sound optimistic. "If you and your family cannot afford one, then CPCS will appoint one to you after you're arrested. Trust me; they are not your typical court-appointed attorneys. Murder list attorneys are usually the best of the best."

Carmen slowly nodded in understanding and then stared at Pickering in desperation. His lips quivered as he struggled to speak. His professor looked at him and smiled in sympathy. He hugged his student, slapped him loudly on the back, and then stepped back to address him.

"Carmen, you're going to get through this, but you need to go home now and get an attorney immediately."

"Professor Pickering?" Carmen replied as his voice quivered.

"Yes, Carmen?"

"I want you to be my lawyer," the young man pleaded.

Pickering froze momentarily before his heart started to beat so rapidly it felt as if it was going to burst out of his chest. He felt his blood pressure drop, his head spin, and the room close in. The professor started to review in his mind the various scenarios he could face if he returned to the courtroom, including contempt, ridicule, scorn, and embarrassment. Pickering gasped for air, stepped back from Carmen, and turned away momentarily to fight back the urge to start gagging. After he regained his composure, he took several deep breaths, turned to face Carmen again, and spoke.

"I'm sorry, Carmen, but I won't represent you."

SEVEN

MONDAY, MARCH 11

The water from the Merrimack River quietly lapped up against the gray mud shoreline. Nearby, a thin cluster of trees screened the waterway from a small grassy field located between an eighteenth-century saltbox and a nineteenth-century Victorian home. Typically, this waterfront park rarely attracted visitors. However, a little under ten days ago, the field was the sight of a homicide investigation. Today, two police cruisers and an unmarked SUV were parked on a roadway adjacent to the park.

The Merrimac police chief leaned against his cruiser and watched from a distance as First Assistant Geoff Walker strolled about the park with one of his patrolmen. As the two moved across the lawn, the prosecutor occasionally asked questions of the officer about what he saw when he first arrived on the scene following the initial 911 call. From time to time, Walker would stop and take pictures of the field with his cell phone.

After about a half-hour of the pair walking around the park, the prosecutor motioned the officer to follow him down to the river. After they passed through the tree line and stepped down onto the mud-covered beach, Walker asked the officer to describe his initial observations when he discovered Jillian Russo's body. Again, as the patrolman recounted what he saw, Walker took pictures of the waterline from different angles.

"Once again revisiting a crime scene, Geoff?" a voice boomed at the pair from the field above the river. Walker turned around to see Sergeant McCam looking down at him, his arms crossed and shaking his head in disappointment. The first assistant chuckled slightly to himself.

"You know why I do this, Dennis," Walker replied as he returned to taking pictures of the beach. "I want to have a firm understanding of the crime scene because, at some point, a defense attorney who knows what he's doing is going to argue that your team tainted or damaged the forensic evidence recovered here. You don't want a repeat of the Jiminez case, do you?"

McCam stewed silently for a moment. The Jiminez case was McCam's first homicide investigation as the lead detective. The Methuen Police, as well as members of his investigative team, allowed *Star* reporter Harriet Jenson and her photographer to trudge through the crime scene before any evidence was properly secured. Mr. Jimiez's defense attorney discovered the mistake and argued to the jury that any evidence recovered was tainted by the misstep. The prosecutor handling the trial was completely unprepared for the issue and, as a result, chose to ignore it. However, the jury latched onto the error, and Mr. Jiminez was quickly acquitted of the crime.

"Tell me, sergeant, why are you here in the lovely town of Merrimac?" Walker asked as he looked across the river to the opposite shoreline.

McCam's thoughts shifted back to the present as he responded to the first assistant. "We have an update on the Russo case, and I wanted to discuss it immediately with you."

"And you couldn't have called me?" the prosecutor retorted as he gestured for the Merrimac patrolman to follow him back up onto the field. As the two stepped onto the grass, Walker thanked the officer for his time and motioned for him to rejoin his chief. Once the officer left, Walker turned his attention back to McCam. "Tell me, Dennis, what have you got?"

"A few things, but I wanted to review it with you immediately so we could make a call whether or not to move on this Vaughn kid," the sergeant replied as he watched the patrolman cross the grassy field.

Walker looked around and then gestured for McCam to continue.

"First, there are the cell tower records," the sergeant stated as he opened the binder he was carrying and began to review his notes.

"We have a series of pings off a Lawrence cell tower put that Jillian near the Centro nightclub. We were then able to triangulate her route of travel from the club due to the multiple cell towers between Lawrence and Haverhill. You'd be amazed how many of those things litter the hillside of the Merrimack Valley."

"How sure are you of where she went?" the first assistant interrupted, growing annoyed that the sergeant could be wasting his valuable time.

"We're comfortable we've got her location down to within three-quarters of a mile," McCam announced.

"That pretty confident, but not impressive," Walker replied as he studied his counterpart. "Go on."

McCam ignored the critical remark and continued with his report. "It appears she traveled north on Route 495 until she crossed into the city of Haverhill. She then got off the highway and traveled to the downtown area. The cell phone tower records suggest she remained in the general vicinity of the downtown for about twenty minutes. Unfortunately, we have no further ping data from her phone after that."

"She shut her phone off?" the first assistant pondered.

"Possibly, or the battery died," McCam replied before continuing. "Once a cell phone powers off, it will stop communicating with nearby cell towers."

"What did the Uber driver say?" Walker inquired.

"He was completely cooperative," the trooper replied matter-of-factly. "I think the poor bastard was afraid we'd pin the crime on him. He corroborated the cell phone data."

"Dennis, what did he say?" the first assistant repeated.

"He says he dropped her off near the railroad station, which is about a block from the Peddler's Daughter Pub."

The prosecutor nodded in understanding. "Anything else?"

"Of course. We also have the cell phone tower records for Mr. Vaughn's phone."

Walker perked up and leaned slightly toward the sergeant. "Oh? Do not leave me twisting in the wind, McCam. Spill it."

McCam cleared his throat and continued, "The boyfriend lied to the Salem Police when he said he stayed at the club and eventually took an Uber home. Video surveillance from the club has him leaving the establishment no more than twenty minutes after Jillian did."

"Where did he go?" Walker asked as he cocked his head to the side and looked over at McCam's notes.

"The cell phone tower triangulation from Carmen's phone also has him traveling to Haverhill and getting off the same highway exit as Jillian did," the sergeant reported. "We have him entering the downtown area approximately thirty minutes after the victim."

"Is there any evidence that Carmen was in communication with Jillian during this time?" the first assistant inquired.

"There is," McCam replied without hesitation. "Carmen was texting and calling her for at least an hour after she left the club."

Walker's eyes widened. "Then I take it the seizure of Carmen's phone yielded a jackpot?"

McCam's stern face broke out into a wide grin. "He called her no less than a dozen times within the first half-hour after she left Centro. Better yet, he texted her sixty-two times for over an hour."

Walker gaped in disbelief at the sergeant. After regaining his composure, he eyed his investigator inquisitively. "Is it possible to get his exact location through the phone's GPS? That could help us identify where exactly he encountered Jillian."

"We're looking into whether we can recover the GPS tracking history. Trooper O'Reilly thinks there is a strong possibility we can pull it from Carmen's phone," McCam affirmed.

"What does Jillian's Uber driver say about the phone calls?" the prosecutor pressed. "Did he hear any conversation between the two?"

"No." The sergeant sighed in disappointment. "However, he did say her phone was constantly going off while she was in his car. She just never answered."

"Tell me about the text messages," Walker asked bluntly.

McCam smirked again. "Carmen did most of the texting. He

threatened to kill or beat her 'ho ass' more than a dozen times. An additional fourteen times, he said he was going to torch her car, vandalize her parent's house and kill her pets. She'd occasionally respond with comments such as 'fuck off, 'you suck,' and 'leave me alone.'"

"Holy shit," Walker exclaimed in disgust. The sergeant watched as the first assistant took a step back, turned around, and studied the movement of the river.

"Where's the Merrimack River located in relation to where Jillian was last seen?" Walker asked.

"The Peddler's Daughter is less than three blocks away from the river. But there's no way he'd dump her there," McCam replied confidently.

"Where do you think he dumped her?" the prosecutor replied as he turned back around to listen to the sergeant's response.

McCam looked at the ground, kicked the dirt once, and looked back up at Geoff. "There would be too many witnesses in the down-town area. We are operating under the theory Carmen would have dumped the body in a less-populated area with tree or brush covering. The Bradford, Ward Hill, and Riverside Park sections of Haverhill are all ideal locations to put a body in the river."

"Where would you dump the body, Dennis?" Walker asked calmly and coldly.

The sergeant reflected in silence before speaking. "If I were to do it, I'd go to the private boat ramp about half a mile down the road from the Crescent Yacht Club in Bradford. It's located behind a few abandoned industrial buildings."

"Why?"

"It's really simple, Geoff," Walker mused. "It's easily accessible but off the beaten path. Nobody would be watching because there is nothing in the immediate area of that ramp. It is just an open field with a dirt ramp down to the river. There are no street or floodlights, and the nearest house is about half a mile away, so dumping the body at night would be a cakewalk."

The prosecutor carefully contemplated McCam's comments before continuing. "You looking to charge him?"

"Absolutely," McCam stated as he closed his binder and tucked it under his right arm. "It's circumstantial, but I think after we tie up a few loose ends, it's an open-and-shut case."

"I think you need more," Walker countered.

"What? Cut the bullshit, Geoff; we've got more than enough to charge and convict him," the sergeant snapped. He was starting to feel hamstrung by the attorney.

"No. We've got enough to charge him," Walker disagreed. "You still need more so I can get a jury to convict him. Can you give me an exact location in Haverhill where he may have killed her?"

"There's plenty of locations, Geoff—multiple alleys, a couple of abandoned buildings, and a parking garage," McCam responded in exasperation.

"Plenty of locations isn't good enough," the prosecutor retorted. "Have you recovered building surveillance footage or ATM security images in this general vicinity that shows where Jillian was, that Mr. Vaughn was also present, and the two interacted with each other?"

McCam saw where the prosecutor was going. He exhaled loudly and then nodded silently in agreement. "I'll get Eriksen to look into that right away."

"Thank you," Walker replied with a smile. "Has the coroner's office disclosed the cause of death?"

"Yes. The medical examiner released her findings this morning. She believes Jillian was killed by blunt force trauma and strangulation. She also said the victim's damn windpipe was crushed."

Walker felt his jaw clench. Strangulation was a slow, painful, and terrible way to die. However, it was also a method that occasionally yielded forensic evidence. "Dennis, hit his house, dorm room, and car with a search warrant. I would like to try to see if we can locate bloodstains, broken fingernails, strands of Jillian's hair, remnants of duct tape or tarps. Find me something that can put a final nail in Vaughn's coffin."

"I'll see to it personally," the sergeant replied instinctively.

McCam glanced back across the field toward the Merrimac police officers and noted they were in a deep but friendly conversation with each other. From the sergeant's perspective, they were completely oblivious of their conversation. He looked back over at the prosecutor.

"Geoff, there's one more thing you need to be aware of," he said in a low whisper. "Crime scene services was able to compare the latent fingerprints recovered on the interior layer of duct tape used to bind Jillian's wrists."

"What the fuck, Dennis? You wait until the last minute to tell me this?" Walker roared, once again becoming annoyed with his investigator. The Merrimac officers stopped their conversation and looked over toward the pair. There was an awkward momentary silence before Walker regained his composure and continued the conversation. "What was the result? Is it a match? Jesus Christ, tell me it's a match. I'll authorize you to arrest his ass right now."

The sergeant averted his eyes away from Walker. "You know Vaughn has a prior arrest for assaulting Jillian, and we were able to get his prints from the Salem Police."

"And?" Walker growled softly.

"It's not a match," McCam replied softly.

Walker stood in silence with his mouth hanging open. He stepped away from the investigator and stared once again at the river. After listening to the water brush up against the shore for several seconds, he clasped his hands behind his back and glanced over at McCam. "Was it even close to a match?"

"Not by a mile," McCam replied, somewhat frustrated by Geoff's flair for the overdramatic. "The report being prepared is going to say the two prints don't even remotely match Vaughn's prints."

Walker reflected on the news and mentally reviewed the potential scenarios. "Is it possible that there was an accomplice?"

"That's a theory my team is exploring," the investigator replied. "We're already trying to identify potential suspects, namely friends or relatives, but—"

"Building a stronger case against Vaughn is your priority, Dennis," Walker interrupted. "We'll eventually weed out any accomplices. Do you need help with drafting a search warrant application or affidavit?"

"No. Eriksen and Davies can do that," McCam replied.

Walker took one last look around the field before he started to walk back to his vehicle. McCam followed. As the two neared the roadway, the prosecutor quickly thanked the chief and his officers for their time. He then waited for the local cops to enter their respective cruisers and drive away. Afterward, he turned to the trooper, raised his finger, and pointed it directly at him.

"Not a single word to anyone outside of our team about the print results. Nothing. Last thing I need is the press or some defense attorney sticking their nose in our investigation before we are done. Not a fucking word, Dennis; to anyone."

McCam started to protest. He wanted to discuss the print results further with Walker, but the prosecutor raised his hand and gestured to him to stop talking.

"This conversation is over, Dennis," Walker barked. "Do what I told you to do and bring me Vaughn. The remaining chips, including any fucking accomplices, will fall into place. But I mean it, no one is to talk about these fingerprints until I say so."

EIGHT

The hallway echoed with booted footsteps as a pair of uniformed Massachusetts state troopers, a Brighton College security guard, a crime scene services technician, and Sergeant McCam all advanced toward the classroom located at the end of the corridor. The detective was in a pleasant, if not cocky, mood and was eagerly looking forward to meeting with Carmen Vaughn once again. He knew that young son of a bitch killed Jillian, and he was determined to nail his punk ass to the wall.

Over the past week, McCam had a pair of his best detectives conducting visual surveillance on Carmen while two more investigators traveled back and forth between Brighton and Salem to question his classmates as well as his friends back home. The effort paid off as the sergeant was able to quickly ascertain that during the previous week, Vaughn had met for over an hour with one of his professors. Afterward, he immediately left campus and drove to Salem to be with his mother. He stayed with her for a little over a day before returning to school. Since then, he had been going to classes and hanging out in his dorm room as if nothing happened.

Unfortunately for Carmen, things were about to change. Thirty minutes earlier, over a dozen state police detectives, uniformed troopers, and forensic evidence collectors from crime scene services descended upon Brighton College armed with search warrants for Carmen's car, dorm room, and personal belongings. Trooper Eriksen had already located his vehicle and was preparing to search it. Meanwhile, Lieutenant Lammoth and her team had met with the school's resident life department and were en route to his dorm room.

The arrival of McCam and his team had completely rattled Brighton College's campus police department. Most of the security officers were either retired mall cops or young men barely out of high school with no law enforcement training. When McCam entered the department office, he found one man dozing off in the corner while another was engrossed in her Instagram posts. The sergeant slammed his fist onto a countertop to get the pair's attention. After the two jumped at the loud noise, he immediately demanded to speak with their superior. Fifteen minutes later, the department's director arrived and was given a brief overview of why law enforcement officers were visiting his campus. The poor man desperately tried to keep up as McCam explained what was going to happen, but all he could do was nervously stammer and mumble softly. After he had finished, McCam demanded to know where Carmen Vaughn was located. The director quickly turned to his laptop and pulled the school's online student record database. He then wrote down the classroom number on a piece of paper, handed it to McCam, and then nervously instructed a young guard to lead the sergeant and his team to Carmen's classroom.

As the officers approached the classroom door, the security officer motioned for the sergeant and his team to stop.

"Sir," the young guard anxiously stuttered, "our school's policy is that I ask the student to step out of class so we minimize any disruptions to the lesson."

"That's fine, but I'm coming into the classroom with you," McCam hissed. He knew the guard was intimidated by his presence, and the sergeant was determined to keep it that way. "The last thing I want to see is that shit diving out a classroom window trying to escape because you didn't want to disrupt a classroom environment."

"Yes—yes, sir," the guard replied as he stumbled over his words. He stood there, eyeing McCam in abject fear.

McCam pointed at the classroom door and then glared at the guard. "Well, what are you waiting for?"

The security guard gulped, nodded, and then knocked on the windowless door to the classroom. He pulled the door back and stepped inside the classroom. The sergeant followed. As he entered, he saw a room filled with about twenty young college-aged students, all staring at him and the security guard with curiosity. He scanned the classroom until his eyes met Carmen's. He then smiled thinly as he watched the man's color drain from his face. He then continued to survey the room until his gaze rested upon the professor standing at the head of the class. The two eyed each other for several seconds.

"Son of a bitch," the trooper muttered underneath his breath. The security guard glanced nervously at Timothy Pickering and then back at McCam.

"Sergeant McCam," the professor asked in a low, cold tone as he slowly leaned against his podium. "Is there any reason why you're interrupting my class?"

"My apologies, counselor. This will only take a moment," Dennis replied with equal contempt as he turned and gestured for Carmen to stand up. "Mr. Vaughn, could you please come with me? Please bring your backpack with you."

Yulissa gasped in horror and brought her hands up to her mouth. Her eyes started to well up with tears. Other students in the class murmured audibly, looked around the room at each other, and then shifted uncomfortably in their chairs. Pickering silently seethed, knowing this was a typical tactic of McCam—embarrass and shame a suspect who refused to cooperate with his investigation.

Carmen looked over at Pickering, back at McCam, sadly nodded his head in agreement, and then slowly stood up. He collected his belongings and walked toward the officer without his backpack. McCam stepped forward between the row of desks and quietly picked up the bag. Afterward, he gestured for one of the uniformed troopers standing at the doorway to escort Carmen out of the classroom. As the group started to file out of the classroom, McCam looked around the classroom one last time. He studied Pickering, snorted in contempt, and shook his head in disgust. Afterward, he exited the classroom. The security guard who was with the sergeant walked over to Pickering and softly apologized for the intrusion that had just occurred. He started to explain, but before he could continue, Pickering waved him off.

The professor tapped his finger against his podium as he watched the collection of law enforcement and Carmen departed from the room. He knew that with such a show of force, his student might not last long and would likely start making incriminating statements against himself. Pickering turned back to his class and surveyed the room. Almost every student stared back at him in stunned silence. A few whispered to each other in disbelief and occasionally uttered words such as "suspect," "he's fucked," and "he did it."

Timothy internally struggled with himself. He felt his chest tighten and his breath start to shorten. A sharp pain started to erupt in his right shoulder and shoot down his right arm. Bile crept up his throat, forcing the professor to cough twice to suppress the sour taste. Pickering's internal voice screamed in his head, reminding him to look the other way and let someone else deal with the matter. His hands started to shake. He quickly shoved them into his pockets so as to conceal from his students his growing distress.

He knew if he became involved in Carmen's matter, he would be returning to a world he had hoped to leave behind him years earlier. On the other hand, if someone did not intervene on Carmen's behalf immediately, McCam and his troopers would steamroll over the student and likely coerce an incriminating statement from him.

Yulissa gazed desperately at Pickering as if to will him to do something on behalf of her best friend. Twice she mouthed the word "please" and then glanced nervously at the classroom door. Timothy knew he was the only person who could assist Carmen at this critical moment. He cursed silently for the foolish decision he was about to make, cleared his throat, and addressed his students.

"Ladies and gentlemen, I am not going to discuss what just transpired here with any of you. However, I am going to step outside for a moment to check on Mr. Vaughn. In the meantime, please go to the course page on Blackboard and review the online lesson I uploaded for you yesterday evening."

Pickering quickly exited the classroom, shut the door behind him, and loudly exhaled. He took two deep breaths and steeled himself for what he was about to do. He stood up straight, adjusted his suit jacket, and strode down the hallway. As he rounded a corner, he observed Carmen seated on a bench with his mouth wide open. A crime scene technician was rubbing a cotton swab along the inside of his cheeks and under his tongue. Two uniformed troopers stood over him while McCam rummaged through Carmen's backpack. Less than fifteen feet away, several students and a dean watched the show with morbid curiosity.

Pickering felt his courage and his litigation instincts quickly return as he quickened his pace. As he neared the group, he called out to Carmen.

"Carmen! Carmen! You better not have consented to that swab!"

The larger of the two troopers spun around to face the professor, his right hand moving quickly to the grip of his firearm. "Step back, sir!" he growled. "Do not approach the suspect!"

McCam gestured with his hand for the trooper to stand down and walked over to Pickering. The two knew each other well. McCam and Pickering had worked together years ago at the Essex District Attorney's office and had successfully dispatched multiple gang members, rapists, and killers to the Massachusetts Correctional Institution for lengthy stays. However, the sergeant lost most of his respect for the man once he became a criminal defense attorney and chose to represent scumbags who were clearly guilty. Three times Pickering handed McCam his ass in court, resulting in criminals walking free while innocent victims were left with their lives in shambles. What galled McCam even more was he knew Pickering only did what he did for money.

Of course, McCam laughed out loud when his coworkers reported to him that Pickering suffered a complete breakdown in an Essex Superior Court following a messy trial where his client was found guilty. When he retold the story to those who would listen, he often portrayed the attorney as a quivering bowl of jelly whose wife had to come and rescue him from a men's room bathroom stall. When Pickering left the profession to become a teacher, the sergeant wrote him off and assumed he would never see or hear from him again.

But now Pickering advanced toward the sergeant and only stopped when the pair were inches apart from each other. Both men eyed each other suspiciously during several awkward moments of silence. McCam was surprised at Pickering's brazenness and wondered if the aggressive attorney he once knew was back in the saddle. Rather than find out, the sergeant decided to defuse the situation.

"Tim, listen, I'm sorry for disrupting your class, but I needed to move quickly on this guy," the sergeant whispered as he pulled Pickering aside by the arm.

"That was not right, what you just did. You embarrassed the kid and probably ruined his good name for the remainder of his career here at Brighton," Pickering seethed.

McCam smiled in a patronizing manner. Tim always did have a flair for the dramatic. "Career? This jackass is going down sooner rather than fucking later for killing his girlfriend. His 'reputation' at this glorified community college is going to be the least of his worries."

Pickering stood up straight and looked past the sergeant to Carmen. The technician was now scraping underneath his finger-nails. It was clear that she was collecting evidence for DNA analysis. The professor turned his attention back to the detective.

"Yet here we are, just like the Jiminez case, running roughshod over a defendant," Pickering loudly announced, knowing that the reference to the Jiminez case would anger the sergeant.

McCam laughed out loud, trying to mask his displeasure at the reference to the very public case he lost a few years ago. "Well, maybe his court-appointed attorney can ask you to testify at trial about how we didn't coddle him after we arrested him."

McCam glared momentarily at Pickering before signaling the conversation was over by turning his back on the attorney and walk-ing back to Carmen.

"Carmen, do not say a word if they question you!" Pickering barked.

McCam stopped in his tracks and glanced over his shoulder at Pickering. "Counselor, do you represent this young man? Because if not, I suggest you shut the fuck up right now and go back to teaching your flunkies about the basics of criminal law."

Pickering cocked his head slightly to the right as his eyes darted back and forth between Carmen and the detective. He saw how the young man appeared desperate for guidance. After a moment of reflection, Timothy smiled and then walked past McCam.

"That is just it, sergeant. Carmen Vaughn is *my client*."

The sergeant bristled at the realization he had overplayed his hand and goaded Pickering to step into the legal fray. However, before he could respond to Pickering's announcement, his cell phone buzzed. McCam stepped back and answered the call. After a brief conversation, he turned his attention back to the professor and smiled cockily at his former coworker.

"Well, counselor, we're going to take a walk with *your client* to his car," McCam announced. "We've got something we'd like to share with the two of you."

Before Pickering could respond, one of the uniformed troopers hauled Carmen to his feet, forcefully seized his left arm, and gestured for him to walk to the front entrance of the building. McCam and Pickering closely followed. The remaining officers, technician, and security guard followed.

"A perp walk, McCam? Is that really necessary?" Pickering quietly hissed.

"What have we done wrong?" the sergeant replied, feigning horror as the group exited the building. "He's walking under his own power, and he's not in handcuffs . . . yet."

"What the hell is that supposed to even mean, Dennis?" Timothy demanded.

The detective ignored the question and instructed the group to turn right down a cement pathway that led to the campus parking lot. The dean, who had witnessed the entire argument between the trooper and one of his professors, gestured for Pickering to step away from Carmen and speak with him immediately. Pickering brushed him off and continued to walk with Carmen and the troopers.

As he stepped into the lot, Pickering saw three unmarked cruisers, a tow truck, and a black Honda Accord surrounded by yellow caution tape. Two technicians from crime scene services were pouring through the interior of the car while a third was taking pictures of the open trunk. A plain-clothed detective was standing near the back of the Accord, arms folded and eyeing Carmen with disgust. Pickering recognized the detective as Trooper Brian Eriksen.

"So, how did you get into my client's car without the keys?" the professor demanded as they continued walking to the vehicle.

McCam smirked and looked over at the attorney. "Your genius client left it unlocked. C'mon, Tim, I want you and Mr. Vaughn to see what Trooper Eriksen found inside the trunk of the car."

"Keep your mouth shut, Carmen. Not a word," Pickering warned his client as the two, as well as McCam and one of the uniformed troopers, advanced toward the Honda.

"Brian!" the sergeant barked triumphantly. "Please tell Mr. Vaughn what you told me a few moments ago regarding what you found inside his trunk."

Eriksen broke out in a wide smile, pulled a pair of rubber gloves out of his coat pocket, and quickly slid them on. He softly called over to a nearby technician who handed him two evidence bags. He waited until McCam, Pickering, and Vaughn were within five feet of the rear of the trunk and then signaled for them not to approach farther.

"Located at the back of the trunk on the left-hand side, I found a roll of duct tape," Eriksen announced triumphantly as he reached into the back of the trunk, removed a roll of duct tape, held it up for Pickering to see, and then dropped it into one of the clear evidence bags.

Pickering showed no emotion as his mind rapidly explored several scenarios as to how he could successfully suppress the evidence in a future court hearing.

"Interesting," McCam announced to no one as he looked over at Pickering and shook his head in disappointment. "I do believe Ms. Russo's body was bound with duct tape."

"Stop it, Dennis," Pickering uttered in a low tone of contempt. "You and I both know you're trying to get a reaction out of Carmen. He is in custody, and you are trying to secure an incriminating response without Miranda. It'll never stand up in court."

The sergeant brushed off the attorney's warning with a wave of his hand and continued with a theatrical flair. "Did you find anything else, Trooper Eriksen?"

"I did," Eriksen immediately answered. "Near the front right corner of the trunk, I found a gold necklace and cross with a ruby birthstone. I took a picture of it and sent it to Ms. Russo's father. He immediately called me and told me that it was the necklace he gave Jillian on her sixteenth birthday," Eriksen announced as he once again leaned into the trunk, removed the piece of jewelry, held it up, and then dropped it into a second evidence bag.

Pickering was standing directly next to Carmen. He rested his right hand on the young man's shoulder, leaned into him, and whispered instructions to him to remain silent and not to show any emotion.

"Well, I don't know about you, professor, but at this point, I believe I have probable cause to arrest your client," McCam sneered as he approached Carmen, spun him around, and slapped handcuffs on the young man's wrists. He then took him by the arm and started to lead him to a nearby unmarked cruiser. Pickering followed.

"Where will you be taking him?" he demanded.

"Haverhill Police," McCam answered without looking back at the professor.

"Haverhill?" Pickering asked, somewhat surprised.

"Yes. Haverhill. Don't worry, Tim; we won't ask him any questions without you being present. You do remember how to represent a client, don't you?" the sergeant demanded as he guided Carmen into the back of his cruiser and then slammed the door.

Vaughn looked about the cruiser in stunned silence, unsure of what exactly was happening. He opened his mouth to speak, but the professor banged on the cruiser window and loudly barked, "Shut up!"

The interior of the cruiser, with its hard-plastic seats, lack of lighting, and caged windows, made Carmen feel claustrophobic. Worse, the handcuffs were too tight and burned his wrists. He felt his heart start to race, and he gasped for air as he realized that his life was now hanging in the balance. He wanted to call his mother so she could reassure him that everything would be okay, but he knew that was not going to happen anytime soon. As he reviewed every horrific scenario of what the future held for him, he reached the same conclusion every time. Carmen Vaughn was going to prison for the murder of Jillian Russo.

Pickering watched in disgust as the cruisers, crime scene services, and the tow truck all drove out of the campus parking lot together. He turned around to see the campus dean with his arms crossed and shaking his head in disappointment at the professor. Timothy sneered at the dean, turned away, and examined the parking lot one last time. As he slowly calmed down from the excitement of the afternoon, he suddenly realized he had just committed to representing Carmen Vaughn. He looked down at the ground, spat, and then stared up at the gray clouds in the sky. In his mind, he rehearsed how he was going to tell his wife that he had broken his promise to her and would once again return to the arena of criminal litigation.

NINE

"Are you fucking kidding me, sergeant?" First Assistant Geoff Walker growled as he slammed his fist against the desk. "I told you no criminal charges without my authorization, and you went behind my fucking back!"

McCam laughed and brushed off Walker's rage. "Come on, Geoff. We recovered enough evidence from the trunk of that Honda to sink him three times over."

"Bullshit!" the prosecutor roared.

McCam raised his hands in protest before continuing. "We found in the trunk duct tape that matched what was used to bind Jillian's body and her necklace. Those two items alone are going to put him away for the rest of his life. With everything else we already have on Vaughn, there's no way a jury won't convict him of murder."

Walker chewed on McCam's proclamation for a moment before taking a deep breath to calm down. After a moment of silence, he finally addressed the sergeant. "Have you been able to locate the last known location of Jillian before she disappeared?"

The sergeant nodded in earnest. "Haverhill Police scoured the area around the train station where Jillian was last seen. They were able to locate time-lapse footage from a security camera outside of a neighborhood salon. She was recorded standing at the intersection of Granite Street and Gardner Way for approximately five minutes before we suspect she encountered Mr. Vaughn."

The first assistant district attorney scowled at his detective for several moments before letting out a loud sigh. "You're still out of line, Dennis. You could have left that kid with another trooper while you called me to get the okay to arrest."

"With Pickering slithering around the scene? Not a Goddamn chance," McCam retorted in slight anger.

Walker clasped his hands together, leaned back into his office chair, and smiled broadly. "Well, you've got a problem, my friend. Your team somehow managed to draw Timothy Pickering out of retirement."

"I'm not concerned," McCam quickly replied as he tried to mask his own concern about the retired attorney entering the case. "He's a washed-up scumbag lawyer who had a mental breakdown in a court-house bathroom. I highly doubt he poses any threat to this case."

"Stop right there, Dennis," Walker interrupted, once again grow-ing angry. "You should be fucking concerned. Before he switched over to molding the minds of college students, he was one of the best criminal litigators in the state, and he wasn't afraid to try a case."

"I'm not concerned," McCam repeated.

"Really? You're not concerned he may have found clarity and is back on top of his game?" Walker pressed. "This won't be his first rodeo when it comes to handling a murder case, sergeant. If he's in this to win, I promise you, Dennis, he will go after every mistake you made, every loose end you didn't tie up, and every bias you ignored to establish reasonable doubt to a fucking jury."

"Let him, Geoff!" Walker exclaimed. "He hasn't tried a case in years! Do you really want to roll the dice on how solid your case currently is with Timothy Pickering on the other side?"

"Absolutely," the sergeant confidently replied.

"Then you're a fool," the prosecutor announced. "The mere fact that Trooper Eriksen threatened to turn Vaughn over to ICE custody is not going to help your case. By the time Pickering is done cross-ex-amining, your partner is going to look like a jack-booted thug. Want me to walk you through how the rest of your case might go?"

McCam seethed as he mentally conceded that his bravado most likely drew Attorney Pickering into the case.

Walker looked down at his watch and then clicked his tongue in frustration. It was already six o'clock on a Friday evening. He leaned over his desk, picked up the handset to his phone, and punched three numbers on the dial pad. After a brief delay, he spoke into the receiver. "Vicky, I know you're still in. Could I trouble you to please come down to my office as soon as you get this message so we can discuss the Russo case?"

Geoff hung up the phone and looked once again at Dennis. He groaned loudly and then continued his conversation with the investigator. "You made the tactical decision to arrest Vaughn on a Friday afternoon, Dennis. That means the earliest he appears in Haverhill District Court is Monday morning. Your 'washed-up scumbag lawyer who had a mental breakdown in a courthouse bathroom' will be spending the weekend with Carmen identifying witnesses to interview for his defense."

"Let them," McCam sneered. "Timothy Pickering can't save this little shit's ass."

Walker stared directly at the sergeant, rose out of his chair, leaned forward, and growled. "Dennis, you better have crossed your fucking T's and dotted your God damned I's. Every damn felony case Pickering has handled as a defense attorney always has—and I do mean always—included Adrian Watson as his private investigator. I guarantee those two will be up at the Middleton House of Corrections before the end of the weekend."

"So what?" the sergeant retorted as he shifted uncomfortably in his seat. He was growing annoyed that Geoff Walker was treating his case as a law school exercise in hypotheticals and what-ifs.

"So what?" the prosecutor sneered. "You and your team better not have made any fucking mistakes during this investigation. If there is even a hint of a fuck up, Watson is going to be breathing down your neck before Pickering pounces."

McCam looked away from Walker and stared at a picture of Salem Common hanging on the office wall. As much as Pickering was a pain in the ass, the sergeant had to concede that Watson was a whole different animal. If anyone had the ability to derail a case through hard work and determination, it was Adrian fucking Watson. His ability to find witnesses law enforcement missed, uncover evidence favorable to the accused, and generally shred the government's cases were all well-known and commonly reviled amongst the law enforcement community.

The sergeant's thoughts were interrupted by a loud knock on the door, followed by Victoria Donovan entering the room.

"Perfect!" Walker exclaimed as he sat back down behind his desk. "Your timing couldn't have been better. Vicky, I'm pleased to tell you that the case of *Commonwealth v. Carmen Vaughn* is officially assigned to you."

"What? Why aren't you handling this case, Geoff?" McCam demanded as his face flushed with anger. He quickly composed himself and turned in his seat toward the female prosecutor. "No offense, Vicky, but I was hoping Geoff would be the lead prosecutor for this case."

"Why?" Walker asked. "Vicky is perfectly capable of prosecuting this case, and you've known for more than a week that she would be heavily involved with this case."

Victoria shifted from side to side in heeled shoes as she stood there, listening to the two men discussing her qualifications. From her perspective, it was both humiliating and degrading. After a brief but heated exchange, the first assistant loudly declared his decision was final. He stepped out from behind his desk, picked up a rather thick file, walked over to the female prosecutor, and handed it to her.

"Here's the Vaughn case file," Walker announced as he glared at McCam one last time. The sergeant was staring down at his lap and silently shaking his head in opposition. Walker ignored the quiet protest and turned his attention back toward Victoria. "I want you to copy all investigative reports, forensic test results, warrant applications, and crime scene photographs before you leave for the evening. Please have all copied materials delivered to Attorney Pickering's place of residence by tomorrow morning. I want the judge to know at Monday's arraignment that we have already started to share the discovery with the defendant."

"Yes, Geoff," Vicky responded quickly as her eyes darted between Walker and McCam.

"Please contact the Essex Sheriff's Department first thing Monday morning as well. I want to start monitoring all outgoing calls Vaughn makes to his family and friends. Pickering will likely tell him to keep his mouth shut while on a jail phone, but I suspect this young man is not bright enough to follow instructions."

"Absolutely," Victoria replied robotically.

Geoff looked again at McCam, rolled his eyes, and directed his attention back to his prosecutor. "I would strongly advise that you and Sergeant McCam's investigative team meet with the medical examiner to determine the exact cause of Jillian's death and exactly what his thoughts are on how Mr. Vaughn may have disposed of the body. Sergeant McCam has an interesting theory as to where he would have disposed of the body if he was the killer. Please take some time to hear the good sergeant out as I think he's on to something."

"One more thing," McCam announced as he rejoined the conversation at hand. "For once, use your fucking head and keep Trooper Eriksen off the stand."

"Excuse me?" Victoria replied, taken aback at the comment.

McCam eyed her in silence for a moment before noting to himself that his previous reservations about her abilities were correct. "Allow me to explain," he declared condescendingly. "Eriksen is not exactly the type that will warm up to a jury in a case like this. The last thing we need is Pickering turning this case upside down because of something stupid he may have done during a previously attempted interview with Vaughn. I know you are fond of this young man, but do not let that feeling cloud your judgment as we move forward on this case. Keep him off the stand."

Donovan nodded in understanding. She waited in silence for a moment before Walker thanked her and casually waved at her, signaling she was dismissed. The prosecutor turned on her heels and left the first assistant's office.

She silently fumed over how McCam and Walker had treated her as she glided down a long hallway to her office. She quickly reigned in her anger and reminded herself that if she could secure a conviction in this case, she could use it as a springboard to a judicial appointment. However, she also knew McCam was right. Trooper Eriksen was a potential threat to the case and her long-term plans. She had begged him several times not to get too involved in the case and to take a back seat. Instead, he stubbornly refused and positioned himself as one of the lead investigators. She reminded herself that this was probably God's way of punishing her for getting romantically involved with a Massachusetts state trooper.

For the next two hours, Victoria sat inside her small office and poured through the police reports, crime scene documents, and other material from the Vaughn case. When she finally finished, she flipped open her laptop and started to prepare a list of documents and materials that would be turned over to the defense pursuant to Massachusetts Rules of Criminal Procedure, Rule 14. Afterward, Donovan picked up the case file, left her office, and strode down the hallway to the copy room.

Once finished, she pulled all the copied documents out of the printer feeder, examined them to ensure no pages were missing, and set them aside on a nearby table. As she was returning the original documents to her case file, Donovan froze, stood up straight, and turned her attention back to the copied packet. She quickly began to rifle through the pages until she found a two-page document prepared by crime scene services. She clenched her jaw as she read a fingerprint analysis, which revealed that a pair of latent prints recovered from the adhesive side of duct tape used to bind the victim's wrists did not match the fingerprints on file for Carmen Vaughn.

Donovan looked up from the report and stared at the wall for a fleeting moment. Afterward, she walked to the entrance of the copy room, looked up and down the hallway, and listened for any sign that her coworkers were still in the office. Instead, the prosecutor was met with an eerie silence. Satisfied she was alone, Victoria turned around, walked over to an industrial size shredder, and put the defendant's copy of the fingerprint analysis into the device. There was a loud roar from the machine as it destroyed the document.

Victoria smiled to herself. She left the copy room, returned to her office, and sat back down in front of her laptop. She quickly pulled up the Word document outlining the items that were to be turned over to Timothy Pickering. She studied the document momentarily before typing once again. In a section identifying scientific reports and test results, Donovan quickly entered, "*Scientific Testing—Fingerprints. No fingerprints were recovered; therefore, no analysis report exists.*"

She leaned back in her chair, studied the entry, and smiled to herself. After a moment of reflection, Victoria quietly giggled and declared that McCam could go fuck himself if he thought she could not secure a conviction against Carmen Vaughn.

TEN

FRIDAY, MARCH 15

Pickering's vehicle quickly rolled into the driveway of his Newburyport residence on Lime Street and came to an abrupt stop. He stared in silence at the three-story federalist-style brick structure that had been built in 1795 by an up-and-coming seafaring merchant. It was already well past eight o'clock in the evening, and he was over two hours late for dinner with his wife Elizabeth and his two children, Catherine, age fifteen, and Hannah, age thirteen. Rather than race inside to join his family, Timothy sat in the driver's seat of his vehicle and reflected upon the events of the afternoon and early evening after he left Brighton College.

After Carmen had been hauled away, Pickering jumped into his car and drove immediately to the Haverhill police station. Despite his repeated requests, the shift commander, as well as Sergeant McCam, refused to let Pickering speak with his client until Carmen was processed, fingerprinted, and tossed in a holding cell. Once finally granted access, Timothy explained to his student that he was going to be transferred to the Middleton House of Corrections, where he would remain until the following Monday. At that time, he would be brought before a judge in the Haverhill District Court. He also repeatedly stressed to Carmen to keep his damn mouth shut while in custody and not speak to anyone about his case.

Carmen was beside himself. He was shaking and broke down crying twice. He begged Timothy to somehow convince the Haverhill Police Department to release him so he could go home to his mother. All Pickering could do was simply repeat "no" over and over and assure Carmen that he was going to do his absolute best to help him out once they were in front of a judge on Monday.

After spending a considerable time unsuccessfully trying to calm Carmen down, Pickering asked for the contact information for his mother and assured the young man that he would call her as soon as he left the police station. Timothy also promised that he would visit Carmen at the county jail at some point over the weekend.

The call to Carmen's mother was equally difficult and heart-wrenching. At first, she thought that Timothy was a prank caller who was playing a cruel joke on her. After reassuring her that he was not, she broke down and started shrieking and wailing. She kept asking Timothy to repeat the circumstances of her son's arrest, what the allegations were against him, and what the different outcome could be. As the conversation continued, Maria's emotions swung like a pendulum between rage and fright. She screamed incoherently into the phone before chanting in Spanish short prayers to a family patron saint.

Eventually, Pickering was able to get Maria to calm down and listen to him. After reassuring her twice that he would indeed visit her son at the jail, she asked if she could go with Pickering to see him. When he told her no, she began to shriek again and mumble incoherently. Realizing that the conversation was not going to be productive, Timothy ended the call. However, before he hung up, he agreed to meet Maria in the parking lot of the jail in the morning.

Pickering sighed and leaned forward until his forehead rested on the steering wheel of his car. He felt his breath start to shorten and a tight, throbbing pain radiate from his right shoulder across his chest. He knew the last thing he wanted to do was return to the world of criminal litigation, yet he had unceremoniously inserted himself in what was expected to be a high-profile murder prosecution. Even worse, he was keenly aware that his wife would vehemently object to his actions.

The professor silently swore under his breath, pushed open his driver's side door, exited his vehicle, and walked slowly to a side entrance to his home. He quietly ascended a small flight of granite stairs, pushed in a brick red door that was decorated with a large brass knocker, and stepped into a small mudroom. He sighed again, unslung his briefcase, and dropped it to the floor. He removed his coat and hung it on a nearby wall rack. He stepped into the adjacent room, the kitchen, and listened. It was oddly quiet.

Since Catherine and Hannah were both teenagers, there was a good chance they decided to go out with their friends rather than wait around for their uncool father to finally return home. Oddly, Elizabeth was nowhere to be found either. He called out her name twice as he walked through the kitchen to the dining room, but there was still no answer. He stopped at the refrigerator, opened it up, and retrieved a bottle of beer. He popped off the cap, took a gulp of the beverage, and started toward the dining room. As he rounded a corner, he saw his wife seated at the dining room table with her arms folded across her chest. Her light blue eyes glared icily at him.

Timothy looked down at the table she was seated at. For the first time, he noticed an exceptionally large package with the Essex County District Attorney's office logo emblazoned across the front of it. Next to it was a glass of white wine. He started to swear but caught himself. Instead, he took another gulp of his beer, hoping the liquid would quell his churning stomach.

Timothy had met Elizabeth during their freshman year at Providence College in Rhode Island. They were both history majors and shared a fascination with the heritage of New England. By sophomore year, the two were madly in love and spending almost all their spare time together. After the pair completed law school and graduate school, respectively, they quickly married and moved to the seaport community of Newburyport.

Unlike Timothy, Elizabeth utilized her history degree and served as an independent consultant to several New England preservation groups, museums, historic sites, and parks. She routinely assisted them with exhibit designs, identifying historical documentation, program development, and preservation efforts. Of course, she commanded exorbitant hourly rates from her clients, which allowed the family to enjoy the benefits of living in the downtown area of Newburyport.

Standing at five-foot-eight in height, Elizabeth was fair-skinned and wore her brown hair at shoulder length. Tonight, she had it pulled back into a ponytail. She typically greeted others with a warm smile, but tonight, there was none of that. Instead, Pickering's wife cleared her throat, leaned back in her chair, and clenched her jaw as she studied her husband for several moments in silence. All Timothy could do was shift uncomfortably from side to side as she carefully studied him. Finally, she took a gulp of wine, placed the glass back down on the dining room table, and spoke.

"Tim, you can imagine my disappointment this evening when not only did you miss dinner with the girls, but you didn't even give me a courtesy of a call to tell me that you would be late," she distantly announced.

Pickering nodded in silence as Elizabeth's voice started to shake with anger as she continued to speak. "But you can't imagine how fucking surprised I was when a Massachusetts state trooper showed up at our front door to drop off a package of discovery for you. I told him that he had to be mistaken, as my husband no longer practices law."

He continued to nod like a fool as she took another sip of wine, stood up, and stepped behind her chair. "Do you know what the trooper told me, Tim, when I said that to him?" she hissed.

"No," he nervously replied.

"He laughed," Elizabeth shouted as she kicked a dining room chair. "The fucking trooper laughed and told me that my husband, Professor Timothy fucking Pickering, was representing a student who is accused of murdering his girlfriend and then dumping her body in the Merrimack River. Did I hear that story correctly, Tim? Are you representing a damn killer?"

Tim felt his heart racing rapidly, and his eyes darted around the room as he tried to craft in his mind an appropriate response to his wife's question. After a moment of foolishly stammering, he simply stated, "Yes."

"Jesus Christ, Tim," she bellowed as she threw up her hands in exasperation. "Are you kidding me? Why? Of all people in the entire fucking legal community throughout the Greater Boston area, why are you representing this idiot?"

"It was a snap decision, and I didn't think it through," Pickering protested.

"You're damn right you didn't think it through," Elizabeth hissed as she repeatedly jabbed a finger in the air at her husband.

"Liz, the state police dragged this kid out of my classroom and were about to steamroll all over him. The kid has an alibi and a fucking shot at getting off. I was only going to help him out only until the court assigned him an attorney."

Pickering's wife eyed him with utter disbelief. After she regained her composure, she started to mockingly laugh at him. She picked up the package, walked around the table, and swung the package at him. As it struck him in the chest with a loud thud, Pickering clumsily grabbed the package from her. He looked down at it and saw it had been opened. He looked back up at Elizabeth with a hurt look.

"Tim, I opened the package to see what the hell you had gotten yourself into. Alibi? Your genius of a client sent dozens of threatening text messages to the victim the night she disappeared. Oh, and there's more."

"Is there?" Tim replied as he desperately tried to remain calm. He felt his face become hot and flush with embarrassment. He realized Carmen Vaughn had played him as a fool.

"His cell phone records place him at the same location where she was last seen alive," Elizabeth chided.

"Fuck," he replied as he took a large gulp of beer before tossing the package back onto the dining room table.

"So, what are you going to do, Tim?" Elizabeth demanded coldly.

"I'm not sure," Pickering replied.

Elizabeth's eyes again grew wild, and she slapped the dining room table. "What do you mean you don't know what you're going to do? This student clearly gave you some bullshit alibi, and you are still hesitating to kick him to the curb. Why, Tim? Why are you doing this?"

He looked around the room, place his beer down on the table, and then sat down. "Where are the girls?"

"Don't change the subject," she barked.

Given his daughters had not yet emerged to greet their father led Pickering to conclude that the two girls had in fact gone out for the night or, more likely, Elizabeth had sent them out so they would not hear their parents arguing. Timothy sighed, ran his hand across the top of his head, and finally addressed his wife.

"I have no idea why I took on the case. Maybe I felt bad for him, or perhaps I felt I had to do something to save face in front of my students. Either way, it was stupid, and now I'm neck-deep in this case."

His wife snorted in contempt and sat down across the table from him. "No, you're going to go to the jail tomorrow and tell that young man you are not representing him. End of story."

Timothy could hear his wife breathing loudly through her nose in anger. Her face was bright red, and she was completely on edge. She took another gulp of her wine and then stared intently at her husband. Pickering shifted uncomfortably in his chair for a moment before responding to his wife.

"I have to at least hear him out before I decide to withdraw from the matter."

"Bullshit," Elizabeth snarled as she leaned in toward him. "You're going to drive your stupid ass to that fucking jail tomorrow. You are going to get out of your piece of shit car, walk inside that facility, and tell that miserable prick that you are not representing him."

"Elizabeth, I need to—" Pickering started to interject before his wife again slapped the table, rapidly stood up from her chair, and started to walk out of the dining room. She stopped at the doorway, turned around, and started to walk toward her husband. She only stopped advancing when she was inches away from him. She stooped down, narrowed her eyes, and whispered in a menacing tone.

"I will fucking not go back to that day I had to carry my emotionally destroyed husband out from a damn bathroom stall inside of a superior courthouse. Do you understand what your breakdown did to your daughters or me?"

The last thing Timothy wanted to do was revisit the events of that day or its aftermath. He felt his stomach tighten and his heart start to race as his mind sought an appropriate answer to Elizabeth's question. Part of him wanted to damn her for bringing up the past. On the other hand, he knew the impact his breakdown had on the family. For almost a year, his daughters and wife were forced to deal with the depression, mood swings, and constant battles to reestablish his confidence and self-identity. There were countless days where Timothy would struggle simply to get out of bed by eleven in the morning and other days where he would simply sob in his home office. Worse, he easily lost his temper and continuously snapped at his family, forcing them to walk around the house on eggshells to not set him off.

After a moment of silence, Timothy nodded his head in agreement. Elizabeth studied him for a moment and stepped back from her husband. She folded her arms again and looked out to the kitchen. She wiped a tear away from her eye and sniffed loudly. Finally, she broke the awkward silence.

"I mean it, Tim. I am not going to put the family through that time again. I don't want to know if your getting back into the game of criminal litigation is to satisfy your fucking ego because you have some warped sense of nostalgia or you think you can be the white savior to this kid. I do not care, and I do not want to know. But I am warning you right now, you better not come home tomorrow and tell me that you are still representing that kid. Because if you do, I promise you there will be hell to pay."

ELEVEN

SATURDAY, MARCH 16

Pickering watched as the heavy metal door slowly ground open and came to a halt with a loud clang. A deputy sheriff stationed near the doorway quickly motioned the professor to step forward and hand his briefcase to him. Afterward, the professor was directed to a nearby metal detector and x-ray machine. Girlfriends, family members, and, on the rare occasion attorneys, often smuggled drugs, booze, cell phones, weapons, and sex toys into Middleton House of Corrections. As a result, the Essex County Sheriff's Department took no chances and searched every person who entered the facility. A second guard instructed Pickering to remove his belt, coat, and shoes and place all three on the x-ray machine's conveyor belt so they could be scanned for any hidden contraband.

Pickering watched as the two guards rifled through his briefcase and opened his case file on Carmen Vaughn. He started to protest but quickly gave up, recognizing his efforts had fallen on deaf ears. The first guard looked up and politely explained that they were not reading the contents of his files but merely searching for anything that could be converted into a weapon, such as paper clips, binder clips, and pens.

Once finished, the two sheriffs returned Pickering's belongings to him and ushered him down a wide hallway to a glass-encased security control room. Timothy heard a bang on the glass, looked to his left, and saw a short guard gesture to a nearby telephone mounted on the wall. He picked up the phone and was instructed to provide identification, proof he was an attorney and a list of the clients he was visiting. After five minutes of completing the paperwork, Pickering was granted permission to see Carmen.

Beyond the control room, a second metal door slowly slid open with a loud squeal. Waiting for Pickering on the other side of the door was a large, well-built deputy sheriff wearing black tactical gear. He greeted the attorney with little more than a curt nod and a quick gesture of his hand to follow him. The two walked through a common area, stepped through the doorway, and entered an open asphalt lot that was enclosed by ten-foot chain-link fencing and several layers of coiled razor wire. The guard guided Pickering to an electronically locked gate in the fence line and then barked into his radio.

"Control, six, open!" the guard demanded.

There was a loud clack followed by a soft electric hum as the door creaked open. The two men passed through the fence line and walked to an administrative building located at the far end of the asphalt lot. To the left of the structure was a large garage where prisoners being transported to or from the jail were received. To the right was an infirmary where sick inmates would allegedly receive medical treatment from a half-competent medical staff.

The main building Pickering was being escorted to was often viewed as the hub of inmate activity. It contained an intake area for newly arrived prisoners, a cafeteria, a records department, a family visiting area, and several educational classrooms. Unfortunately, the building was rarely, if ever, kept up by the sheriff's maintenance team. The restrooms were notorious amongst staff and visitors alike for clogged and overflowing toilets. To complicate matters, just about every summer, the building's air conditioning system failed, causing the interior room temperature to swell to over one hundred degrees. It was also quite common on any given day for a sour smell of human waste and body odor to permeate throughout the halls of the building.

As he stepped into the facility, Pickering tried to ignore the overwhelming foul stench as it filled his nostrils. He and his escort continued down a drab, windowless hallway until the pair arrived at yet another heavy metallic door. As the door crept open, the guard gave another quick nod, mumbled something about having a nice day, and walked away.

The professor shrugged to himself, stepped through the doorway, turned right, and found himself in yet another long hallway. To his immediate left was the inmate processing center. Inside were over a dozen Dominican, white, and black prisoners who had just arrived at the facility and were being questioned by a squad of deputy sheriffs about their health, criminal background, and immigration status. Once questioning was complete, the prisoners were ordered to strip naked for physical cavity searches and then ceremoniously handed faded orange jumpsuits and cloth flip flops.

To Pickering's right was a row of three rooms that were no more than eight feet by eight feet in size. Inside each cramped chamber was a pair of cheap plastic chairs and a wooden table. These rooms were designated as the sole locations where lawyers could meet with their clients in alleged privacy to discuss their cases. Unfortunately, the walls were paper-thin, the acoustics poor, and anybody walking past the rooms could easily ascertain the purpose and topics of the meeting.

A sergeant who was seated behind a desk in the intake room looked up from his computer and greeted the professor. After a moment of small talk, he directed Pickering to the far-left attorney-client room. Pickering entered, walked behind the table, looked around the tiny room, quickly sat down, and leaned back in his chair as he waited for Carmen. He studied the table for some time, making a note of the gang symbols, profanities, and cartoon-like characters that had been carved into it.

Timothy's thoughts wandered to his argument with his wife the previous evening. She was adamant that he was to withdraw from Carmen's case or there would be hell to pay. To emphasize her point, she sentenced her husband to a night of sleeping on the couch. Yet, despite his wife's anger, he still harbored a slight reservation about abandoning his client.

His concentration was broken when the meeting room door swung open, and Carmen hobbled in with his wrists and ankles bound with shackles. Flanking him on either side were two correctional officers. He was wearing a bright orange jumpsuit and a white t-shirt underneath. His hair was disheveled, and he smelled of vomit. He appeared terrified, and it was obvious he had gotten no sleep the night before.

The guards motioned for Carmen to sit down in the vacant plastic chair across from Pickering so they could remove his restraints. Once the shackles were taken off, one of the deputy sheriffs informed Pickering that his client was not to leave the room under any circumstances. The two guards then backed out of the room and shut the door behind them.

Pickering studied Carmen for several seconds as he internally debated how to best approach the coming conversation with the young man. Finally, he spoke. "I know it's been less than twenty-four hours since you arrive here in Middleton, but how are you holding up?"

Carmen started to speak but stopped as tears welled up in his eyes and he gasped for air. After a moment of quietly sobbing, he regained his composure, slumped back in his chair, and looked over at Timothy. "When can I see my mother?"

Timothy quietly nodded, acknowledging that he heard the question. "It's the jail's policy that family members can't visit or talk by phone with new inmates for at least forty-eight hours. Sometimes longer. I suspect the earliest you are going to see your mother is Monday when we appear in Haverhill District Court for arraignment on the charges against you."

"What are the charges?" Carmen quietly asked, knowing what the answer would be.

"First-degree murder," Timothy replied matter-of-factly. "The government believes you choked Jillian to death and then tried to conceal your actions by dumping her body into the Merrimack River."

"Professor, I didn't kill her, I swear!" Carmen blurted out as Pickering withdrew a file from his briefcase. "As I told you, I had no contact with her after she left the club. I took an Uber home and—"

Carmen's protest came to an abrupt end when Timothy removed Carmen's file from his briefcase and then slammed it down onto the wooden desk with a loud thud. He stared at Carmen before exhaling in disgust.

"You are a lying mother fucker!" he sneered at his client.

"What? What the fuck are you talking about?" Vaughn blurted out, somewhat confused and becoming defensive at the same time.

Timothy began tapping the file with his right index finger as he looked directly at Carmen. "You see this fucking file here? Inside this file are the police reports and other materials the Essex District Attorney's office has already given me. It was hand-delivered to my house in Newburyport last evening by a fucking Massachusetts state trooper. Do you know what these reports say, Carmen?"

"No," Carmen responded sheepishly as he looked away from his professor.

"They say you're a fucking liar," Pickering roared as he stood up from his chair, leaned toward his client, and rested both of his hands on the table before him. "You told me in my office you took an Uber home and that you had no contact with Jillian after she left."

"That's right!" Vaughn protested as his eyes darted nervously around the tiny room.

"Bullshit!" Pickering hissed. "Last night, I read two reports telling me that you never got in an Uber. Instead, you drove your own fucking car to the Centro nightclub. When Jillian left after the two of you got into a pissing match, you found out she was going to Haverhill, and you followed her."

"How do you know that?" Carmen responded, almost sounding incredulous.

"How?" Timothy replied with a condescending tone. "Your cell phone registered on every fucking tower along Route 495 between Lawrence and Haverhill. The police even have cell phone records of you being in the same general area as Jillian immediately before she disappeared."

Carmen sat in shock with his mouth wide open as the professor continued. "Because the police have your phone, they now know you called her no less than a dozen times after she left Centro and texted her sixty-two times in the space of one hour. You and I both know, some of the messages you sent her are threatening."

Carmen started to answer, but Pickering held up his right hand and gestured for the young man not to talk. After a moment of awkward silence, he continued speaking in a low, angry tone. "Carmen, what are you, some type of possessive sick stalker? Who texts someone sixty-two times in one hour? What is that, one text a minute?"

"I . . . I don't know. I guess." Vaughn stammered as he started to physically shake in his seat.

"The police also have images of Jillian from nearby security cameras immediately before she disappeared," Pickering continued. "They're currently looking for surveillance images that will place you in the same area. I guarantee they're going to find pictures of you strolling around downtown Haverhill around the time she disappeared."

"But I didn't kill her!" Vaughn exclaimed as he started to weep again.

"Not my concern anymore. You lied to me, Carmen. I'm out of your case," Pickering retorted as he started to place the file back into his briefcase and prepared to leave. "If I were you, when you talk to your mother, I'd ask her to pack you a toothbrush and a bar of soap because you are going to jail for the rest of your life."

"No, professor, please!" Carmen begged. "I was too embarrassed to tell you what happened. Please, don't leave me. Please, I will tell you what happened, but I didn't kill her. I swear on my mother's life I didn't kill her."

Pickering studied Carmen carefully. The young man's face was buried in his hands as he sobbed uncontrollably and repeatedly blurted out, "I didn't kill her! I didn't kill her." Carmen again gasped for air and started to gag and dry heave. Eventually, he slumped back into his chair and began to shake and whimper softly.

Elizabeth's warnings to walk away from the case screamed inside Pickering's head, yet he could not help but feel a slight sense of pity for Carmen.

"Shit," Pickering cursed as he dropped his briefcase to the floor, sat back down, and retrieved the file. He knew Elizabeth was going to cut his balls off and hang them from the nearest tree once she discovered what he was about to do.

He banged the table again with his fist and pointed directly at Carmen. "Stop your crying! You do not cry inside this jail; do you understand me? You have one chance . . . one . . . to tell me what happened. If I think you are bullshitting me, this conversation will be over. I will walk out of this room, and you will be on your own. Are we clear, Carmen?"

"Yes, sir," Carmen replied with a loud sniffle as he avoided eye contact with Pickering.

"Start talking," Pickering replied angrily as his mind raced through the possible explanations he possibly could give his wife if he decided to remain on the case.

Carmen nodded as he took a deep breath. "Everything I told you about how we got to the club is true, except I drove over with Jillian. I didn't want to take an Uber, so we all rode to the club in my car."

"The car the state police searched at the college?" Timothy asked as he started writing down notes on a legal notepad.

"Yes," Carmen quickly answered, his voice shaking.

"All right, what happened next?" Pickering demanded as he looked up from his notes to gauge Carmen's body language and demeanor.

"Everything I told you about what happened inside the club is also true," he replied.

"Go on," Pickering replied as he eyed his student momentarily and then resumed taking notes.

Carmen nodded in understanding. "After Jillian got into the Uber and left the club, I went back inside Centro. One of Jillian's friends was riding me hard about how Jillian was cheating on me with an older man. I asked her if she knew where Jillian was going. She said downtown Haverhill because the guy supposedly lived somewhere around there."

"So, you decided you were going to confront the two of them?"

Tim asked as he again looked up from his notepad and how Carmen reacted to the question.

"Yes. Well, no. I wanted to confront the guy more than her," the student replied as he shifted slightly in his chair.

"Were you looking for a fight?" Pickering pressed.

"Yes, I was," Carmen conceded.

"So, you did what, jumped in your car and drove to Haverhill?"

"Yes." Carmen sighed. "I was repeatedly texting and calling her as I drove toward the city. I'm surprised I didn't drive off the fucking road."

"Did she respond to your messages?" Pickering asked with mild curiosity.

"She never answered my calls, but she did respond to my texts."

"What did she say?" Pickering asked as he withdrew from Carmen's case file the police reports detailing the text communications between Carmen and Jillian.

"Something along the lines of 'leave me alone,' 'fuck off,' and 'don't talk to me,'" Carmen noted as he looked away from Timothy in embarrassment.

Pickering read the police report in silence. After he reviewed Jillian's text messages that corroborated what Carmen had just described, he put the report down on the table and resumed the conversation. "Which exit did you get off?"

"I don't remember the exit number, but the sign said, 'Downtown Haverhill.'"

"What happened next?" Timothy asked as he furiously scribbled notes on his legal pad.

Carmen furrowed his eyebrows and rubbed his eyes as he tried to recall the details of the evening. "I parked my car, got out of my vehicle, and walked past some of the bars along Merrimack Street. I then backtracked to Railroad Square."

"Why were you walking around?" Pickering asked as he gauged just how truthful Carmen was to him.

"I don't know," the young man replied as he shrugged his shoulders.

"Maybe I was hoping to see her. Jillian's friends said the guy lived somewhere near Washington Street."

"Did you ever go up Railroad Square to Wingate or Granite Streets?" the attorney asked as he removed a second police report and reviewed a paragraph detailing Jillian's last known whereabouts.

"I don't remember. I know at one point I was near the back of the Chit Chat Lounge, but I turned around and went back to my car."

"The Chit Chat is a block away from Wingate Street and two blocks away from Granite," Pickering announced with some concern. "Jillian's last known location was somewhere between those two streets."

Carmen shrugged his shoulders. "I don't know what to say. I didn't see her."

"Were you still texting her?" Timothy calmly asked.

"I was," Carmen admitted softly.

"Did she respond?"

"No."

"What did you do next?" Pickering asked again.

Carmen leaned back in his chair. He looked exhausted and in anguish as he had to retell the events of the evening with his professor. "I walked around for another fifteen or twenty minutes, mostly up and down Washington Street. I then gave up and drove back to school."

"What time did you leave downtown Haverhill?"

Carmen paused for a moment before answering. "Definitely after 1:30 in the morning."

"Who saw you return to campus?" Timothy inquired.

"No idea. Maybe campus police. I can't say," Carmen replied matter-of-factly.

"Your roommate didn't see you?" the professor asked with a tone of surprise. He found it unusual that Carmen did not cross paths with his own roommate.

"He wasn't there when I got back around 2:30 in the morning," Carmen announced.

Pickering thought for a few moments about what Carmen had said, scribbled a few notes, and then continued with his questioning. "Tell me about the duct tape found in the trunk of your car."

"I bought a couple of rolls of duct tape to keep my car from falling apart. The rear bumper, door mirrors, and my muffler were basically held up by duct tape," Carmen answered confidently.

Pickering nodded before continuing. "What about the necklace? What can you tell me about that? How did that end up in the trunk of your car?"

"I have no idea, professor, how that got inside my trunk," he replied with a raised voice. Carmen rocked back and forth in his chair and started to become emotional yet again. "I'm in that trunk a lot, and that necklace was never there. Never."

"Don't lie, Carmen," Pickering growled softly.

"I'm not!" the student snapped back. "Jillian never went inside my trunk or left any of her belongings in it. Hell, she never took that necklace off."

"You do understand, Carmen, that the police seized your vehicle after you were arrested," Timothy quickly retorted with a stern tone. "They towed it to their facility in Danvers and are processing the interior for any forensic evidence that can be used to convict you. If they find anything, it is going to be the final nail in your coffin. I'm going to ask you only once—are you telling me the truth when you say you have no idea how the necklace ended up in your trunk?"

"I swear on my mother's life that I have no idea how that necklace ended up inside my trunk," Carmen replied as he stared directly into Timothy's eyes.

The professor clenched his jaw and mulled over what Carmen had just told him. He immediately recognized that it was going to be an almost impossible task to secure an acquittal. He wondered to himself if that was the excuse he needed to walk away from the case so he could reestablish peace with Elizabeth.

However, Pickering also realized he needed to verify his student's story and comments before he developed any possible exit strategies. Naturally, he knew just the man who could help him. He looked directly at his client.

"Carmen, before I explain what is going to happen when you appear in court on Monday, I'm going to go over with you what needs to be done immediately. I've got to go out and hire a private investigator to corroborate your version of events, find witnesses who may be favorable to you, and start looking for weaknesses in the government's case."

"Do you have a particular private investigator in mind?" Carmen asked hopefully.

"I do." Pickering nodded with a slight grin. "He's one of the best, and if we're lucky, he may give you a fighting chance."

TWELVE

Adrian Watson slumped down into his worn yet sturdy leather chair, placed a Blue Moon beer bottle onto the floor, and lowered a hot plate of nachos smothered in cheese and spicy salsa onto his lap. He picked up the remote, turned on his television, and scrolled through the menu in search of the latest episode of his favorite science fiction show, *The Orville*.

As he was about to start the show, there was a knock at his front door. The private investigator looked back over his left shoulder, cursed, and contemplated whether to ignore the early Sunday afternoon disruption. After a brief delay, there was a second longer and louder knock. Adrian swore again, put the plate of steaming nachos onto the floor next to his beer, stood up, and walked to the front door of his residence.

"You better be not selling solar panels!" he barked in annoyance as he unbolted the locks and pulled open the door. As it swung back, he saw Timothy Pickering standing before him. Watson stared at him for a moment and chuckled softly with contempt. "You have a lot of balls visiting me unannounced on a Sunday afternoon."

"You have something better to do? Perhaps watching *Star Trek* version 2.0 on this fine St. Patrick's Day?" Pickering replied with mock horror.

"It's called *The Orville*, and it's an amazing show," Adrian retorted.

"Oh, I'm sure it is, but I'm not here to nerd out with you," Pickering answered as he looked around and closely examined the outside of Adrian's home. The structure was a classic nineteenth-century farmhouse. Based upon some of the features, the professor surmised it was probably built just before the American Civil War. To the immediate left of the front door was Cobbler's Brook. The stream gently flowed past the structure, passed underneath River Road, and emptied into the Merrimack River, which was located directly across the street from Watson's homestead. Pickering turned around and stared at the river.

"I always forgot what an amazing view you have," he noted as he admired the sunlight dancing across the water's surface.

"It's great, but I roll the dice every spring during flood season," Watson replied as he gestured at Cobbler's Brook. "That little waterway has caused more havoc on my basement than I care to admit."

Pickering nodded as he glanced over toward the stream. "Well, you decided to buy a house that's literally ten feet away from something that can quickly turn into a raging river."

"Thanks," Watson replied with a hint of annoyance. "Where were you ten years ago when I was looking for advice on purchasing a house?"

After a moment of awkward silence, Timothy looked at an open field that was up the street from Adrian's home, surveyed it for a moment, and then looked back at the private investigator. "I didn't realize you were so close to the crime scene."

"I got to play a spectator the day the girl washed ashore," Adrian announced. "I even saw crime scene services processing the body."

"Oh?" Pickering blurted out in surprise.

Watson studied the professor carefully for a moment, shook his head back and forth in disappointment, and then motioned Timothy to follow him into the house. "Come on inside. Something tells me you want to talk with me about this particular case."

Timothy entered the front hallway behind Watson, turned left, and followed the investigator into a dining room. The room had a pair of large six-over-six windows that looked out to the Merrimack River. The wide pine floors, rustic table, wood benches, and historic colors on the walls all gave the room a feel of genuine authenticity. A large fire roared in the hearth in the corner.

"So, what makes you think I'm here on the Russo murder?" Tim asked cautiously.

Adrian stared knowingly at Pickering for a moment before answering. "Because the mother of your newly acquired client visited our office a little over a week ago. She mentioned you might be representing her son."

"Well, here I am," Pickering calmly replied.

Watson motioned for the attorney to sit down on one of the table benches and went to the living room to retrieve his beer.

"Tim, do you want a beer?" Watson asked loudly.

"What do you have?"

"Blue Moon."

Watson heard Pickering gag. "I'll take that as a no?"

"No . . . no, a Blue Moon is fine," Timothy responded with some trepidation. Watson re-emerged into the dining room with two open beer bottles. He handed one to the professor, walked around the table, and sat down across from him. He studied the attorney for a moment, took a gulp of his beer, and then placed the bottle down on the table. He rotated the bottle on the table as he addressed Pickering.

"To be honest, Tim, I was surprised to hear you were taking on this case," Adrian stated softly as he looked up at Pickering. "I thought you were permanently retired. I know we haven't spoken in over a year, but I figured I would have at least received a courtesy call from you letting me know you were back in the game."

"Well, if you know about the case and my role in it, you know why I'm here," Timothy responded as he took a gulp of his own beer.

Adrian chuckled softly. "You need an investigator, Tim, and I'm the best around."

"I see we're still humble," Pickering quipped.

"It's not humility; it's the truth, Tim," Adrian retorted with a slight tone of defiance in his voice. He examined Pickering for a moment, and then sighed in frustration. "I don't know, Tim. I worked for you for almost a decade, and I got some great results for you."

"You did," Pickering conceded as he interrupted the investigator.

"And I paid you well for your services. I suspect I helped pay for this house."

Adrian held his hands up in protest. "I'm not complaining, Tim, but we were a team! Suddenly, you shut down your practice after you have some crazy breakdown. Rather than ask for my help, you decide to disappear across the state so you can play professor at some small unknown school that you and I both know will eventually shut down because they can't afford to pay their bills."

Pickering clenched his jaws slightly at the slight but chose not to say anything. The private investigator continued. "A lot of the other attorneys refused to work with me after you closed up shop. I eventually had to get a job as an investigator for the public defender's office. That was a tough hit, Tim."

"From what I understand," Pickering interjected as he struggled to keep his temper in check, "you raised your fees for your services. Several lawyers I spoke to over the past couple of years said you wouldn't budge when they asked you to be more reasonable."

"I wouldn't, and I stand by that," Watson snapped. "You can pay for a Yugo, or you can pay for a Mercedes. I'm a Mercedes."

Pickering laughed slightly in surprise. "Yes, yes, you are a Mercedes, as you always reminded me. Listen, Adrian, I understand you are upset, and I guess we never had a chance to clear the air. I am sorry if you felt that I abandoned you; that was not my intention. But I need you now. A kid has asked me for help, and I don't know if he's bullshitting me or not."

"So, you need me to detect bullshit," Watson quipped before taking a large gulp of beer from his bottle and setting it on the table.

"I do," Pickering replied with a curt nod. "But if the kid's story is true, I need the best to help me win this case."

"Why did you take this case? I mean, why now?"

"I don't know," Pickering exclaimed with a loud sigh. "Maybe I just felt sorry for him. I didn't like how Dennis McCam and another trooper were bullying him when they dragged him out of my classroom and arrested him in front of half of the campus."

Watson studied the attorney for several minutes in silence. He then picked up his beer bottle and took another large swig. Afterward, he swirled the liquid around inside the bottle and looked over at Pickering.

"What does your wife think of this?" he asked as he studied Tim's body language.

Tim shifted uncomfortably in his seat and avoided eye contact with the investigator. He sighed and then answered the question. "She's absolutely rip shit, Adrian. She told me on Friday to abandon this kid and let someone else represent him."

"Then why haven't you abandoned this kid?" Watson pressed.

"My gut is telling me I should help him out."

Watson snorted with disappointment. "You're the only one who can rescue this poor Hispanic kid, Timothy Pickering? A public defender or some other attorney can't help Carmen out?"

"I didn't say that," Pickering replied softly, still avoiding eye contact with the private investigator.

"But you were thinking it," Adrian announced as he raised his voice and swept his arms widely above his head. "The noble college professor rushing to the aid of one of his poor, misunderstood Hispanic students at the risk of destroying his marriage and family."

Pickering stammered for a response but could not find an appropriate answer. He wondered if Watson was right. Was he simply acting as Carmen's white knight? The investigator continued.

"Does Elizabeth even know you're here right now?"

Pickering shook his head in the negative. Adrian cursed softly to himself before taking another sip of his drink and pointing the bottle at the attorney. "That's on you, Tim. If you are going to handle this matter beyond the arraignment, you need to come clean with your wife. There is far too much publicity on this murder for you to hide it from her. You're only digging a deeper hole for yourself."

"I know," Pickering admitted. "I have to let her know what I'm doing, but I need to know I turned over every stone for this kid before I walk away from the case."

There was an awkward silence for a moment as Watson contemplated Pickering's response. Rather than press the issue further, the investigator decided to redirect the conversation back to the Carmen Vaughn matter.

"McCam is involved?" Watson asked with great interest.

"He's one of the lead investigators. Victoria Donovan is apparently the prosecutor handling the case," Pickering replied.

"She hasn't tried a case in several years," Watson noted. "Has she even seen the inside of a courtroom recently?"

"Walker is mentoring her on the case, but if I had to guess, she's going to use this trial as a springboard to a judicial appointment," Tim noted.

"Of course, she will," Watson replied with a contemptuous chuckle. "She's wanted to become a judge since she was in high school."

"What do you think, Adrian? I need you to level the playing field against these bastards. You up for seeing if Carmen has a fighting chance?"

"Assuming the kid is telling the truth," Watson quickly countered.

"Assuming," Pickering repeated.

"I don't know, Tim," the investigator reluctantly stated. "It's tempting, but I'd have to submit a lot of paperwork to my boss in Boston just to get permission to work on a criminal case not handled by our office."

"How long will that take?" Tim asked as he cocked his head slightly.

"A couple of days."

"A couple of days? That's it?" The professor laughed as he chided the investigator. "Come on, Adrian, what do you need to come on board this case? If he is a bullshit artist, then it is a quick walk in the park. I can walk away from the case, and Elizabeth can calm down. But if he is truly innocent, then we have the opportunity to do something good once again."

Watson leaned across the table and coldly stared at the attorney. "That's what this is about? It is not about leaving any stone unturned. It's about your desire to redeem yourself. I know that last rape case tore you up inside, but let us be serious for a moment, Tim. You and I both know criminal defense work is a very ugly, soul-wrenching job. If you are looking for redemption, this is not the case to do it."

"Okay, then let's go with the explanation of Tim is just bored and wants back in," Pickering shot back with slight annoyance.

"Maybe someone else would accept that as a reasonable explanation, but I won't," Adrian shot back. "Why should I get involved? I'm not going to join the team for the sake of a reunion."

"It's about money?" Pickering chortled. "What do you think it's going to cost for you to run a thorough investigation?"

Adrian reflected for a moment on Pickering's response. In the end, financial compensation could persuade him to examine the matter. "To start, I'm going to need five thousand dollars. This is a murder case, not an assault-and-battery allegation. I am going to be spending a considerable amount of time looking into the facts of this case, interviewing witnesses, and reviewing any discovery you send me."

"Of course," Pickering replied instinctively.

Watson continued, "I expect that my retainer will need to be replenished as the case progresses. Oh, and just to remind you, I also charge additional fees for testifying in court."

Pickering eyeballed Watson for a moment and then looked around the room. "Are you putting an addition onto this house? Five thousand dollars?"

"That's the going rate for my services, counselor." Adrian shrugged.

"Just so you know, I'm representing this kid pro bono. I—" Timothy argued as he attempted to reason with the investigator.

"That's your mistake, Tim," Watson interrupted. "I remember a time when you would have charged this kid and his family $50,000 easily."

Pickering glared at Watson. "You know, Adrian. You are right. It was a mistake. I am not sure what is going on here, but I am not your cash cow, and I never was. I paid you for your services because you did your job very, very well. The fact that your investigative services practice collapsed after I shut down my practice is not my problem."

The investigator rolled his eyes and looked away from the attorney in disgust.

Annoyed, Pickering continued. "I've heard there's a retired DEA agent who's now offering his services as a private investigator. From what I have been told, he is just as good as you and about half the price. Nice seeing you, Adrian. Enjoy your knockoff *Star Wars* show."

Tim stood up, turned around, and started to walk to the front door. Watson sighed, muttered to himself, and called out to his former partner. "Tim. Wait. You are right. I have been pretty pissed at you. You were a major source of business for me, and when you closed your office, I just could not compete with the other investigators out there. I refused to lower my prices, and other investigators came in and undercut me. What is worse, some of them were just as good, if not better, than me. Hell, that DEA agent you mentioned solved a case I couldn't crack despite my best efforts. Word got out I was overpriced and underperforming. I started twisting in the wind, and without much work, I had no choice but to get a job at the public defender's office. They pay me shit, and I am barely making ends meet. I'm sorry for giving you a hard time, but yes, money is tight."

Pickering held up his hand and gestured for Adrian to stop talking. "I am sorry that happened to you. I truly am. However, I do not care about the other investigators. I honestly believe that you are the best man for this task. But I do not want you distracted by any hard feelings you have toward me or what happened after we parted ways. If you do not think we can work together, I'll leave now and find someone else."

Watson exhaled and then nodded quickly. "I can handle this case, Tim. It would be nice to work with you again. I'll start on the paperwork immediately to get approval from CPCS to work with you."

"Good. It's settled then," Pickering responded as he advanced on the investigator and held out his hand. Watson quickly shook it and then gestured for him to return to the dining room table.

As the two sat down, Adrian looked across at the attorney and asked, "Do you have discovery yet?"

"I do."

"What do you have?"

"Police reports, forensic results, preliminary autopsy report, and photographs of the crime scene," Pickering replied.

Watson paused for a second. "Are the photos from crime scene services or from ADA Donovan?"

"Why would Donovan be taking pictures?"

"Tim, the body washed up five hundred feet from my house. I was present with other spectators when Assistant District Attorney Donovan arrived at the crime scene. I saw her yell at a few troopers, walk over to the body, pull out her phone, and take several photographs of the body. I am 100 percent positive she took pictures of the victim."

"Odd. That's a complete violation of crime scene protocol," Pickering announced.

"I know." Watson nodded in agreement.

"What happened after she took the pictures?" the attorney inquired.

"She stepped away from the body and appeared to be texting someone," Adrian stated.

"Think she sent the images to someone?" Pickering pressed.

"Possibly," Adrian replied after a moment of careful reflection.

"Was she alone when she examined the body?" Pickering asked as he mentally reviewed possible arguments to the court regarding a tainted crime scene.

"No. There was a pair of state troopers with her."

"We are going to need to file a discovery motion after our client's arraignment tomorrow. I'll email a draft affidavit over to you later today to review and add any information you believe might be helpful."

"More than happy to," Watson replied.

"Good," Pickering replied with a curt nod. "Although I am representing this kid for free, I'm going to be filing a motion with the court asking for the state to pay your private investigator's fees. I will ask for the five thousand you requested, but as you know, judges are cheap. I may only get half."

"Do your best, Tim," Adrian pleaded with the attorney.

"I will. However, I want you to work first on determining whether this kid's story is bullshit. If it is, this is going to be a noticeably short case and not much money for you. On the other hand, if he is even remotely telling the truth, I will keep asking the court for additional funding. If they say no, I'll pay your bill."

Adrian tried to protest, but the professor quickly cut him off. Afterward, he inquired, "When do you think I can review discovery?"

"I've already made a copy for you," Pickering replied as he withdrew a small, black flash drive from his pocket and pushed it across the table to the investigator. "Find out if this kid's story is bullshit, Adrian. I don't want to waste your time or mine if he is full of shit."

"I'll review what you gave me tomorrow when I get into office. Is there anyone you would like me to speak with first?"

Timothy thought for a moment. "Yes. Speak with the kid's mother. She might be able to provide some background information as well as potential witnesses who may be helpful. Also, check in with the people who were with our client the night the victim disappeared. Finally, check in with the Centro nightclub to see if any of their employees saw or heard anything."

"Well, let's get to work, counselor."

The pair spent the next two hours poring over police reports and preliminary witness statements. As the two men continued examining the mounting evidence against Carmen, Adrian peppered Timothy with a variety of questions and action items designed to explore weaknesses in the case. Eventually, after several more beers, a few unanswered questions, and a general plan as to how best to explore the truthfulness of Carmen's story, both men decided to call it for the afternoon. Adrian walked Timothy out of the house and to his vehicle, which was parked on River Road. As they crossed Watson's lawn, the professor stopped and glanced reflectively at his investigator.

"You're the Mercedes of investigators?" he quipped.

Watson smirked slightly.

"I think you are," Pickering continued. "But I have to ask—why didn't you become a police officer? I mean, with your investigative talents, you'd be heading up a detective division by now."

Adrian looked contemplatively at the attorney and nodded in gratitude. He then gazed out toward the Merrimack River as he addressed the attorney's question. "You know, Tim, I never really talk about what led me to become a private investigator instead of a cop. After all these years, I guess I never told you."

"No, you didn't," Pickering noted. "I never really pressed the issue, but in a profession where over 90 percent of all investigators are retired cops, state troopers, or federal agents, you stand out from the crowd."

Adrian clenched his jaw, relaxed the muscles, and then answered the question softly as he looked down at his lawn. "I was a junior in college when my younger brother got into trouble. The police treated him so badly. I swore I'd never become a cop."

"Not George?" Pickering asked, recalling Adrian's younger brother, who was a known Lawrence heroin junkie.

"No, no," Adrian replied as he brushed the question off. "It was my youngest brother, Victor. He was only seventeen years old and was walking home from a party on Jefferson Street in Lawrence. He saw a police cruiser tailing him because he was a black kid in a pre-dominantly white neighborhood, and he had weed on him. Victor panicked and ran."

Timothy could already envision what happened next. "Did the cop chase him?"

"Of course, he did. He lit up his cruiser like a Christmas tree and tried to run Victor down. However, my brother jumped out of the way at the last minute, and the cop drove his vehicle straight into a telephone pole."

"Holy shit, that must have pissed the cop off," Pickering exclaimed.

"It did," Adrian replied matter-of-factly. "A backup officer found my brother a block away, hiding underneath a porch and brought him back to the accident scene. The cop who smashed up his cruiser immediately started to kick his ass. It took another officer and two spectators to get him off my brother."

"I . . . I'm so sorry, Adrian. I had no idea," the attorney stammered.

"That's not even the worst of it," Adrian replied, his voice starting to shake. "After they transported my brother to the Lawrence police station, the same cop dragged Victor out the transport van by his hair and pepper-sprayed him in the face at point-blank range. He then hauled my brother into the booking room, shut off the internal surveillance camera, put on a pair of hard knuckle gloves, and proceeded to beat my brother to a pulp. Afterward, he sprayed him a second time with mace, dragged him to an eyewash station, and washed his face with scalding hot water."

"Oh my God," Timothy replied in horror.

"The Lawrence Police tossed him into a holding cell and left him there until he was taken to the district court the next morning," Watson announced as he visibly fought back tears. "My dad and I went to the court to be there for him. When Victor appeared before a judge, my father could not even recognize his own son. For the first time in my life, I saw him break down and cry."

"What was he charged with?"

Adrian chuckled softly for a moment. "Resisting arrest, assault and battery of a police officer, and possession of marijuana. Thank God Victor was appointed a decent public defender. The attorney worked his ass off to prove that my brother was innocent of the charges against him."

"The charges were dismissed?" Pickering calmly asked.

"They were," Adrian replied with a curt nod as he struggled to regain his composure. "But it took four months for the charges to go away. The district attorney's office tried to cover for the cop, and the *Lawrence Star* decided to portray my brother as some black street thug who was a threat to public safety. It wasn't until Victor's attorney uncovered evidence that the cop had been previously fired by the Boston Police department for excessive force that everything went away."

"Holy hell," Timothy blurted out. "Did Victor ever sue the police for violating his civil rights?"

"He did," the investigator quickly answered. "But a judge dismissed Victor's claim against the city after the cop was fired. He never collected a dime, and to this day, he still suffers from the injuries of that night."

"I'm so sorry, Adrian. I had no idea."

"Do you know what the worst part was?" Adrian asked rhetorically. "The Lawrence police, the Essex District Attorney's office, and the *Star* never apologized for what they put my brother through."

The was a long, uncomfortable pause between the two men. Adrian swept his foot back and forth across the grass a few times before looking over at Pickering. "Do you think this kid is innocent?"

"I don't know, Adrian," Pickering replied with a loud sigh. "The kid swears he didn't do it."

"Well, let's see what we can find out," Adrian answered with a loud sigh. "The last thing I want to see is another kid even remotely go through what Victor experienced."

THIRTEEN

Timothy Pickering stood at the bottom of the cement and brick stairway and looked up the steep incline toward the front entrance of the Haverhill District Court. The building sat on a high ledge that was only accessible by ascending the stairs before him. Oddly, until 2018, there was no handicapped entrance to the facility. If a disabled person wished to access the courthouse, court officers would have had to carry the person up the stairs to a portico that was bordered with wood columns that were decorated with white peeling paint.

The building itself dated back to the 1960s and served as the court of justice for the city of Haverhill as well as the Massachusetts towns of Boxford, Georgetown, and Groveland. It typically handled about half the criminal caseload in comparison to the Worcester, Lowell, or Lawrence District Courts, but it had its own fair share of domestic violence, theft, narcotics, and firearm-related offenses. When he practiced law, Pickering always enjoyed handling criminal matters in this courthouse because he felt justice was well served inside. The courthouse staff, prosecutors, and judges were professional; defendants were treated with respect and courtesy; and crime victims always received the necessary attention they required.

The college professor occasionally hoped to visit the courthouse between semesters simply to say hello to the staff and judges. Unfortunately, family and professional commitments prevented such joyful reunions. Nevertheless, as he stood at the base of the outdoor staircase, he felt his stomach start to gurgle and his breath shorten. He took a long, painful breath and surveyed his surroundings. He immediately noticed at least a dozen local and regional news vans parked along each side of the roadway in front of the courthouse. Most of the news teams had already raised the satellite dishes affixed to the top of their vehicles while reporters rapidly scrambled to prepare for today's hearing. Several cameramen negotiated with each other over who would go inside the courtroom to film the arraignment of Carmen Vaughn. Surprisingly, none of the television news personalities approached him. Pickering imagined it was because they did not even know he was Vaughn's attorney—yet.

He took another deep breath, looked reluctantly up at the portico, and started to slowly climb the stairs. When he reached the landing, he found several men and women standing in a single line in front of the main entrance. The group was waiting to pass through a metal detector before being granted access to the courthouse. Pickering unslung his leather bag, opened a pouch, and started to fumble through it as he tried to locate both his legal and driver's licenses. According to Massachusetts court rules, an attorney could bypass security screening upon presenting a bar membership card and photo identification to a court security officer.

As he dug through his bag, he sensed someone approaching him from his left side. Pickering stood upright, glanced to his left, and saw Harriet Jenson of the *Lawrence Star* walking briskly toward him. She had a slight smile and an air of misplaced confidence about her. Pickering noticed that Harriet had gained significant weight since the last time he saw her. It was also clear that she was under the misimpression that she still had the body of a nineteen-year-old. She was wearing an open blouse that exposed her ample cleavage and a skirt that was two sizes too small and three inches too short. She complemented the ensemble with knee-high suede boots, a layer of cheap makeup caked on her plump face, and a hairstyle that was likely last seen in 1987. Pickering shuddered and quickly tried to avoid any contact with her by resuming his advance toward the courthouse entrance. Unfortunately for the attorney, she quickly fell in next to him.

"Timothy Pickering!" she exclaimed, her voice dripping with

insincerity. The professor ignored her as he desperately reached for the door handle. She called out his name again.

He sighed, rolled his eyes, and turned around to face her. "Yes, Harriet?"

"I guess the rumor is true," she gushed. "I received a few tips over the weekend that you had come out of retirement and were representing Carmen Vaughn. Word is he's your student?"

"Who told you that?" Pickering replied with a tone of concern. "Wait, let me guess. Was it Sergeant McCam? Perhaps it was one of the Haverhill police officers that booked Mr. Vaughn?"

"I don't give up my sources," Harriet huffed.

Pickering bit his tongue and chose to remain silent. He knew damn well Jenson routinely burned her sources and tried to pit law enforcement against the defense bar when it suited her needs. He studied the reporter quietly for a moment and then simply asked, "What do you want, Harriet?"

"Well, can you tell me about your client and what your defense strategy is going to be?" she pressed.

"You're kidding, right?" Pickering replied curtly.

"No," Harriet replied with an aggravated tone in her voice.

"I'm not telling you shit."

"Really, Tim? I mean, I'm more than happy to share your client's side of the story," the reporter replied with a subtle hiss.

"No, no, you won't," Timothy replied as he momentarily stared down Harriet, turned around, and started to enter the courthouse.

"Excuse me?" she barked as she started to pursue him into the courthouse.

Pickering stopped, spun around, and walked back toward the reporter. "No matter what I would tell you, you will spin it against my client." He growled as he closed with inches of the woman. "There's no scenario in which I am going to share anything with you before the arraignment. So back the fuck off and stop wasting my time."

Pickering turned his attention back to locating his credentials at the bottom of his briefcase. When he finally found them, he entered the courthouse and presented the two identification cards to a young Hispanic court officer. The guard motioned Pickering to bypass the metal detector positioned to the right of the entranceway and proceed into the interior of the courthouse. Harriet desperately tried to pursue the attorney but was stopped mere feet beyond the entranceway and ordered to be screened. As he walked farther into the building, Pickering heard Harriet Jenson unleashing a string of insults at him. The attorney smiled to himself and continued to walk down a long hallway decorated with dim fluorescent lighting, concrete cinder-block walls, asbestos floor tiles, and worn wood doors.

Every aspect of Haverhill District Court's interior, including the water bubblers, bathrooms, and décor, were Cold War relics. In fact, as he walked down the hallway, Timothy spotted no less than three old nuclear fallout shelter signs affixed to the walls. When he reached a flight of stairs, he descended to a lower level. He walked quietly past the Essex County District Attorney's satellite office on his right and the Haverhill Probation Department on his left. He continued down the passageway until he reached a large metal door. He pulled on it, only to discover it was locked. He pressed the white button on an intercom located to the right of the door. There was a moment of silence followed by a loud crackle. A female voice over the intercom simply asked, "Yes?"

Pickering leaned toward the device and spoke into it, "Attorney Pickering here to see my client, Carmen Vaughn."

"One moment," the voice replied. Several seconds later, a young female court officer with brown hair and a welcoming smile pushed open the heavy metal door and greeted him. She escorted him through a small office into the "lockup," a series of holding cells for defendants awaiting to appear before the court. The lockup of Haverhill District Court more closely resembled a dungeon than it did a courthouse holding area. To Pickering's right, a series of old, rotted, and unsteady wood benches lined the wall. Over a dozen metal ankle shackles and handcuffs were strewn across the seats. To his left were three consecutive jail cells with heavy iron bars and mesh screens. The lockup's old, worn cement floor was painted battleship gray while fluorescent ceiling lights repeatedly flickered on and off.

"Attorney Pickering, your client is in the last cell on the left," the guard stated cheerfully before turning around and leaving the room. Tim walked over to Vaughn's holding cell and immediately realized that with the metal screen covering the front of the holding cell, he could barely make out who was inside.

A shadow approached the iron cell bars and called out, "Professor Pickering? Is that you?"

Timothy immediately recognized Carmen's voice. "Yes. I am here. How was your ride over from Middleton?"

"Not the best ride," Carmen responded, his voice trembling with fear. "They jammed a bunch of us into a windowless van."

"Sorry to hear that," the professor replied sympathetically, choosing not to tell the young man that his experience was the standard operating procedure for the Essex County sheriff's office.

"How's it looking up there?" Carmen asked.

"It's a circus," Pickering conceded. "The media is crawling all over the place. I spoke to your mother by phone as I drove over here. She will be here with two of your uncles, your grandparents, and four cousins. They're going seated in the front row nearest you."

The young man reflected for a moment before inquiring about Jillian's family. "Will her parents or sisters be there?"

"I expect they will," Timothy answered softy. "You absolutely do not look at them. Carmen. Don't speak with them or do anything that is going to piss them off or give the media something to hang their hat on. Absolutely no courtroom outbursts. Do you understand?"

"Yes, sir," Carmen replied, his voice growing with despair.

"Any other questions?" Pickering pressed as he looked around the lockup to see if anyone was eavesdropping on their conversation.

"I'm not getting out today, am I?" Carmen asked after a moment of hesitation.

"We've been over this," Pickering retorted with a tone of slight exasperation. "You're charged with murder, and you're not entitled to bail. There is no judge on this planet, let alone the liberal state of Massachusetts, that would even remotely entertain releasing you before this case goes to trial."

"I know," Carmen replied with a loud sigh. "I guess I was just hoping for a miracle."

"I understand, but there's no miracle waiting for you upstairs in that courtroom today. I'm sorry about that."

Carmen leaned up against the iron bars. He rubbed his eyes for several seconds before continuing to pepper Pickering with questions. "So, I'm going to be held without bail?"

"You're not going anywhere but back to Middleton House of Correction," Timothy patiently answered. "I've explained that to your mother as well. She's prepared herself for the worst."

"Did you speak with the private investigator?"

"Yes," the attorney whispered as he looked around the room once again. "He's waiting for his boss to give him the okay to work on this case. Once he gets that, which he will, he's going to start interviewing the people you were with the night Jillian disappeared."

"All right. Good."

"At some point, you're going to be brought upstairs into the courtroom. When you enter the courtroom, look at the judge, not the cameras, and do not say anything other than, 'Yes, Your Honor,' and 'No, Your Honor.' Do you understand?" Timothy pressed.

"Yes, Professor Pickering," Carmen softly answered.

"All right," Pickering replied as he tapped the cell bars as a sign of reassurance. "I'm going to check in with the prosecutor. I expect Assistant District Attorney Donovan will be handling your arraignment. Sit tight, and I'll check in with you as soon as I have an update."

"Thanks . . . and, professor?"

"Yes, Carmen?" Pickering responded.

"Could you tell my mom that I love her, and I'm sorry for putting her through this?" Carmen asked as he broke down and started to sob.

Pickering leaned forward and tried to reassure his client. "Carmen, we'll get you through this. You just have to have a little faith."

The attorney stepped away from the holding cell and started to walk back to the court officer's office. As he did, the female guard emerged from her room with wrist and ankle shackles dangling from her hands.

"Sorry, counselor. I have already received word from the clerk upstairs. The judge wants to arraign your client now, so I'll be bringing him upstairs to courtroom one. You can follow me if you want."

The attorney nodded and watched as the court officer heaved and pulled the heavy iron door to Carmen's cell open. Pickering's client slowly stepped out into the open area. He was visibly shaking and gasping for air. Timothy stepped forward and gently put his hand on the young man's right shoulder. Carmen looked over at him, his eyes wild with fear.

"Carmen, look at me," Timothy assured with a calm voice. "You're going to be fine. Keep your head held high and remember what I told you. Okay?"

"Yes . . . yes, professor," he replied, his voice trembling.

After the court officer snapped the restraints onto Carmen, she led the two toward a large wood door. She yanked the door back with a hard jerk, revealing a very steep stairwell that led up into the prisoner's dock of courtroom one. Timothy looked up the stairs, which more closely resembled a vertical ladder, and braced himself. He knew that as soon as he ascended the stairs, he would be returning to the arena of legal combat.

The court officer cupped Carmen's left arm, issued a series of instructions on how to safely climb up the stairs, and then nudged him forward. Timothy followed closely behind. The trio slowly ascended the stairs and emerged into a holding area that was enclosed on three sides with low wooden walls and white painted railings mounted on top of them. To Pickering's immediate left were a judge's bench and the clerk's desk. In the center of the courtroom were the probation officer's desk as well as tables for the prosecution and defense. At the back of the room was the public gallery. It was jammed with noncustodial defendants who were waiting for their cases to be called, reporters, attorneys, police officers, and, of course, morbid curiosity seekers.

Pickering continued to scan the audience and saw Carmen's mother and other family members seated in the front row closest to him. Four rows back and seated in the corner of the courtroom was Adrian Watson. The private investigator gave a quick nod to the defense attorney.

He continued to survey the room and noted that Sergeant McCam and Lieutenant Lammoth were also present and had taken up seats on the right-hand side of the public gallery. Seated next to them was a young female victim witness advocate. Serving as an advocate with the Essex District Attorney's office was a difficult and emotionally draining job. It was the advocate's responsibility to act as a liaison between prosecutors, law enforcement, and crime victims, as well as provide emotional support and guidance to family members who had lost loved ones to heinous crimes.

Sitting adjacent to the victim-witness advocate was a middle-aged couple. Pickering presumed they were Jillian's parents. Even from his position, some two-dozen feet away, he could see that the dark rings that had formed underneath the woman's eyes. She occasionally leaned into the advocate and silently sobbed. Jillian's father glared coldly at Pickering, never once taking his eyes off him.

Pickering's focus was interrupted as he heard the rapid whirl of cameras snapping images. He quickly shot a harsh glare across the courtroom toward the media pool and saw Harriet Jenson directing a *Star* photographer to take pictures of his client. Timothy leaned over to Carmen, instructed him to sit down on the bench behind them, and then reveled in Harriet's disappointment as the young man disappeared.

A short, thin Italian gentleman quietly approached the holding area, unlocked the security door, and gestured for Pickering to step out. As he did, the man extended his hand.

"It's good to see you, Tim," Robert Ferrar, clerk of the Haverhill District Court, stated as he clasped hands with Pickering.

"Thank you, Bobby. How have you been?" Tim eagerly replied.

"Good, good Tim," the clerk responded with an eager nod of his head. "Are you doing all right? How's that teaching job going?"

"That teaching job got me a trip here," Pickering replied with a soft chuckle.

"Tim, I just wanted to let you know that I'll be calling your case first," Robert announced softly. "Judge Williams wants to get you out and away from this circus as quickly as possible."

"Thanks. I appreciate that, Bobby. Please tell the judge I send her my best."

"Of course, my friend. Of course," the clerk replied with a slight bow. "So good to see you, Tim. We really missed you."

Prior to being appointed to the bench, Paula Williams was the town manager for the neighboring community of Boxford. She was an old-school judge who used her street smarts and common sense to craft fair resolutions for those who appeared before her. She also had an insatiable love of golf and her dog.

As the clerk walked away, Pickering saw Assistant District Attorney Donovan enter the courtroom with a junior prosecutor following in tow. Victoria stopped to confer with Sergeant McCam before walking past Harriet without even acknowledging her. She entered the bar enclosure and strode quickly over to Pickering.

"Attorney Pickering. So nice to see you again," she purred. "I trust you received the discovery package I had delivered to your house Friday night?"

"I did, thank you. That was kind of you." The professor paused for a moment before continuing. Elizbeth was still not speaking to him because of his decision to take on Carmen's matter. "So, you will be handling this matter?"

"Yes. Will that be a problem?" There was a sudden change in Donovan's tone following Pickering's inquiry.

"Oh, no. I just wanted to make sure you were the point person on the matter," Pickering retorted as he held up his hands as a sign that he did not want a confrontation. "I look forward to working with you, Victoria."

"Is your client going to do the right thing and plea?" Donovan pressed.

"We're kind of getting the cart before the horse, aren't we?" Timothy snapped back. "I mean, I just received discovery. I am going to need time to review it. I'm sure there will be motions filed after that and—"

"Fine!" Donovan interrupted with a huff and a tone of exasperation in her voice. "I get it; you need to do your job. Just let me know when your client decides to plead guilty to the charges against him. I don't want to put the victim's family through an unnecessary trial."

Pickering noted Donovan was already trying to avoid going to trial. He brushed the momentary outburst aside and assured her that he would keep her apprised of any developments.

Moments later, there was a loud bang as a court officer swung open a door next to the judge's bench and yelled, "All rise!" Everyone in the courtroom stood up in unison. Pickering swung around to face the bench. After a brief delay, a blond woman wearing a black robe entered the courtroom, stepped up onto the bench, and stood behind her chair.

The court officer cleared his throat, looked out toward the courtroom audience, and barked a second time. "All persons having business before the Honorable Justice Paula Williams are admonished to draw near and give their attention, for the court is now in session! God save the Commonwealth of Massachusetts and this Honorable Court!"

"Be seated," Judge Williams instructed as she repeatedly gestured with her hands for everyone to take a seat. The clerk and judge conferred for a few moments before Bobby called Carmen's case. As he did, a lone television news cameraman activated his device and zoomed in on the judge.

"Calling the matter of Commonwealth v. Carmen Vaughn, docket number 1936CR2012."

A bald male court officer motioned for Carmen to stand up and step toward the edge of the enclosure where Pickering was waiting for him. Immediately, the cameraman spun his camera and focused on Carmen. Several photographers started taking snapshots of the pair. The clerk continued and loudly announced the charges against Carmen.

"Mr. Vaughn, you have been charged with the following offenses pursuant to Massachusetts general laws: Count one, murder. Count two, kidnapping. Count three, assault and battery. A not-guilty plea has been entered on your behalf, and Attorney Timothy Pickering has entered his appearance on your behalf. Your Honor?"

"Thank you, Mr. Clerk," Judge Williams replied as she looked over at the prosecutor's table. Cameras continued to whir in the background. "Attorney Donovan, is the Commonwealth seeking bail in this matter?"

"We are requesting the defendant be held without bail, Your Honor. He is charged with a capital offense and therefore is not entitled to bail under General Laws 276, section 58."

"I'm familiar with the bail statute, Ms. Donovan," the justice dryly noted as she looked over her glasses at Carmen's attorney. "Attorney Pickering, so nice to see you."

"Thank you, Your Honor," Timothy replied with an awkward smile.

"Attorney Pickering, is your client asking to be released on conditions of bail? I mean, he is charged with a capital offense," Judge Williams inquired.

"No, Your Honor. Currently, we are not contesting the Commonwealth's request that Mr. Vaughn is held without bail. However, as the court is aware, bail is set without prejudice and can be re-argued if there is a change in circumstances. If there is some change, I will notify the court and request a hearing."

"That's fine, counselor," the judge replied as she scribbled notes onto a bail order. "Attorney Donovan, could you please provide a summary of the facts of this case that the government is relying upon so I can enter the appropriate grounds for holding Mr. Vaughn without bail?"

"Certainly, Your Honor." Victoria cleared her throat, opened her file, and removed a preliminary police report. "Your Honor, I will be summarizing from a Massachusetts State Police report from Trooper Brian Eriksen. According to the report, the defendant and the victim were in an on-again and off-again relationship since high school. This was a relationship that was often contentious and marked by occasional violence. According to the government's investigation, there were at least two instances prior to the matter before the court, where the defendant physically assaulted Jillian Russo after she attempted to terminate the relationship. In February 2019, Carmen Vaughn and Jillian Russo were once again romantically involved. On the night in question, February 23, 2019, the couple, as well as four to five college friends, went to a nightclub in Lawrence. While there, Jillian informed the defendant she was dating another person and no longer wanted to be romantically involved with the defendant. A verbal argument ensued, and Ms. Russo left the club. She then took an Uber to meet her new boyfriend in Haverhill. To this date, we have been unable to identify who this boyfriend is. However, we do know from security surveillance footage obtained from a Haverhill business she ended up in the downtown area. Furthermore, based upon data retrieved from area cell towers as well as the defendant's own phone, it is the Commonwealth's position that Mr. Vaughn followed the victim to Haverhill. He was able to locate her, assault her, and forcibly drag her to his car. At some point after that, it is the Commonwealth's position that the defendant took Jillian Russo to an unknown location and beat and choked her to death. He then panicked and attempted to dispose of the body. However, prior to doing that, Mr. Vaughn removed a necklace from the victim as a memento of their relationship. He then bound the victim's hands, legs, and ankles with duct tape. Afterward, the defendant wrapped Jillian's body in a plastic tarp and secured it with duct tape. Although the exact location is unknown at this time, it is believed Carmen Vaughn transported the body to some waterfront location between Bradford and Groveland and disposed of the body by throwing it into the Merrimack River. The body was eventually recovered when it washed ashore in the town of Merrimac. Within days of this incident, the defendant was identified as a potential suspect. Approximately two weeks after Jillian Russo's disappearance, a search warrant was obtained for the defendant's vehicle. A search of the trunk resulted in the recovery of the victim's necklace, as well as a roll of duct tape that was consistent with what was used to bind Ms. Russo's body after her murder. Mr. Vaughn was subsequently arrested and charged with the offenses before the court."

"Thank you, Attorney Donovan," Judge Williams stated as she feverishly jotted down notes onto her bail order. After a moment of silence, the judge looked over at the prosecutor and asked a single question. "Ms. Donovan, I just have one question, and it is asked merely out of curiosity. Were any fingerprints or forensic evidence of the defendant recovered from the interior of the duct tape used to bind the victim's body?"

"No, Your Honor," Donovan lied with a convincing smile. "Unfortunately, no identifiable forensic evidence was recovered from the duct tape."

"Very well," Judge Williams replied as she continued to scribble notes onto the bail form. "Based upon the Commonwealth's presentation, I believe there is a sufficient basis to hold the defendant without bail, and as a result, I will be entering that order. Ms. Donovan and Mr. Pickering, what will the next court event be?"

Before Pickering could answer, Victoria interjected. "Your Honor, I obviously intend to indict the defendant within the next thirty days on the offense of first-degree murder. I would respectfully request that this matter be scheduled for a status hearing within the next thirty days."

The professor smirked knowingly and looked up at the judge. "Your Honor, Massachusetts Rules of Criminal Procedure 3(f) clearly states the defendant is entitled to a probable-cause hearing. It is clear Ms. Donovan is attempting to circumvent the rules to avoid having to demonstrate that a crime was committed and that my client was the one who committed the crime. I would respectfully request this matter be marked for a probable cause hearing within the next thirty days."

"I agree, Mr. Pickering," the judge quickly noted as she tossed paperwork toward the clerk. "This matter will be scheduled for a probable cause hearing on April 25, 2019, in courtroom two. Thank you both for your time this morning. Mr. Clerk, call the next case, please."

"I apologize, Your Honor," Timothy interrupted as he looked back at Watson. The investigator appeared to have watched the court proceeding with keen interest. "I have one final matter. I have filed a motion for funds for an investigator. I would need your approval on the motion so I can start my own investigation of the underlying facts of this case."

"You're not appointed to represent the defendant in this matter, are you, Attorney Pickering?" Judge Williams asked inquisitively. "If you are privately retained, I am unsure how I can authorize funds for your investigator at the taxpayer's expense."

"I'm representing Mr. Vaughn pro bono, Your Honor," Pickering loudly announced.

"Ah," the judge replied as a low murmur echoed through the courtroom. "Well, that's different. I see you're requesting five thousand dollars for your investigator?"

"Given the nature of the case, yes," Pickering conceded. "My investigator is going to have his hands full."

Judge Williams looked over her glasses and smiled knowingly at the professor. After a moment of reflection, she nodded in agreement. "Very well; it's approved, Mr. Pickering. Call the next case."

As many spectators stood up to leave the courtroom, several cameramen tried to secure parting images of Carmen. Pickering watched as Assistant District Attorney Donovan led a pack of journalists out into the courthouse lobby. He had no doubt she was about to issue some form of a scathing statement against his client. Ignoring the media circus, Pickering turned back to his client and whispered a few instructions to the young man before he was led back down to his holding cell in the basement. Afterward, the attorney looked back at the court gallery and saw Watson gesturing to meet him in the hallway.

Timothy followed his private investigator out into a small narrow hallway located adjacent to the courtroom. Watson silently motioned for him to follow him down a flight of stairs to a rear exit. After looking all around to ensure no one was following him, the investigator pushed open the door and stepped out into a parking lot behind the building. Pickering's curiosity was piqued, and naturally, he followed. Once outside, the pair walked to the back of the parking lot. Watson looked around. Satisfied that no one was within earshot, he finally addressed the attorney.

"Tim, Donovan lied," he blurted out.

"What? What do you mean she lied? What are you talking about?" Pickering demanded, shocked at the investigator's allegations.

"She lied about there being no fingerprints recovered off of the duct tape," Watson replied with a strained voice.

"I have no clue what you're saying, Adrian."

"Listen to me," the private investigator retorted. "Judge Williams asked Victoria if any prints or forensic evidence was recovered from the duct tape. She answered no. When she said that, Sergeant McCam and Lieutenant Lammoth looked at each other in shock and then had a very heated discussion. Afterward, they stood up and stormed out of the courtroom."

"What? I never saw any of that," Pickering responded with horror.

"You didn't see it because you were too busy representing your client at the arraignment," Watson snarled. "I'm telling you, Tim; the sergeant and lieutenant were sitting very quietly in the audience until Donovan made that representation."

"C'mon, Adrian," Pickering snapped as he brushed Adrian's response aside. "You and I both know she could get into a lot of trouble if she gets caught lying to a judge. Especially in a murder case."

The private investigator snorted. "You and I both know how often prosecutors lie to the court and get away with it. We are talking about Victoria Donovan, Tim! For the past decade, she has been looking for every opportunity to advance her career, even if it is at the expense of a defendant. She has repeatedly thumbed her nose at the defense bar as long as I have known her. You think lying to a judge is beneath her?"

Pickering contemplated for a moment before grudgingly nodding in agreement. "Jesus, you could be right, Adrian."

"I am right," the investigator replied with a slight grin.

"Possibly," Pickering quickly responded.

"So, what's the game plan, counselor?" the investigator pressed.

"We've got to start looking into whether or not there's evidence favorable to Carmen," Pickering announced as he contemplated what his next move should be. "If the district attorney's office is sitting on a fingerprint that doesn't belong to our guy, then it's a game-changer."

"Where do you want me to start?" Watson asked as he proudly held up a letter from the public defender's office authorizing him to work with Pickering.

"Well, that was fast," the professor mused.

"I'm good," Watson announced with a wink.

"If Donovan is sitting on a piece of evidence favorable to Carmen, it's highly unlikely she's going to turn it over to us if we simply walk up to her and ask for it," Pickering contemplated out loud. "We need to gather corroborating evidence that a fingerprint analysis report exists, bring it to the judge, and then force her to disclose it. I need you to sniff around and see if you can gather any information from third-party sources that may know about the prints. Start with the Merrimac Police. There's a possibility that they received copies of forensic reports since the crime took place in their jurisdiction."

Watson grinned broadly. "You know the Merrimac Chief isn't going to just hand over the information simply if I ask."

"I thought you two were buddies," Timothy jibed.

"We are. We go fishing together every now and then."

"I never understood the joy in fishing," Pickering reflected thoughtfully for a moment.

"I didn't expect you would. Most boys don't," Watson replied with a slight chuckle.

The professor ignored the sarcastic jab and continued. "I think if the Merrimac chief hears that exculpatory evidence was possibly hidden from us, he may help us out. What do you think?"

"He'll bite. He is too honest and fair of a guy not to," Adrian replied with confidence. "I'm going to have to play up the 'we've been screwed over awfully hard and we need your help, chief' card, but I think I can pull it off."

"Very well," Pickering replied. "Do it. In the meantime, I have a few connections inside the Essex District Attorney's office that are not fans of Victoria Donovan. I'll reach out to them and see if I can get any other leads."

"Very well, Tim," Adrian announced as he confidently cocked his head to the side. "We have a game plan."

"It's a game plan that's based on your hunch, Adrian," Timothy replied as he poked Watson squarely in the chest with his index finger. "You better be right."

"I'm telling you, Tim, McCam's reaction to Donovan's claim was wild," Watson replied with a wide grin.

"Well, investigate it. But don't forget about your other tasks," Pickering demanded, growing annoyed at Watson's display of confidence. "Start interviewing Jillian's college roommates and witnesses at the nightclub."

"Absolutely, counselor," Watson replied, ignoring Pickering's growing irritation. "We've got our work cut out for us."

"Well, we've got thirty days until the probable cause hearing. That's thirty days to try to possibly turn this case around."

FOURTEEN

Victoria Donovan walked away from the impromptu press conference held on the portico of the Haverhill District Court with a sense
of satisfaction. She smiled to herself, knowing that the reporters she
had just spoken with, especially the useful puppet Harriet Jenson,
would lap up her talking points about the dangers of domestic
violence, the lost innocence of Jillian Russo, and the culpability of
Carmen Vaughn. She re-entered the courthouse, glided past the
security checkpoint, and hummed softly to herself as she strolled
toward the satellite office in the basement of the courthouse. As she
approached the entrance to the office, Victoria was already reciting
the title "Judge Donovan" over and over in her head.

Upon entering the office, Victoria saw three state police detectives waiting inside the office for her. The room was closer in size
to a large walk-in closet and had no less than five desks, two photo-
copiers, several file cabinets, and an assortment of chairs displaced
throughout the office. A lone district court prosecutor sat at his desk
in the far-right corner, silently reading the *Boston Herald*. Sergeant
McCam was leaning against a file cabinet while Trooper Eriksen and
Lieutenant Lammoth were huddled around a water cooler near the
back of the room. Everyone fell silent as Victoria entered.

"Well, I thought that went better than I expected," Victoria
gushed. "I honestly expected Timothy Pickering to put up much
more of a fight."

There was an odd, awkward silence that was finally broken by
Lieutenant Jacqueline Lammoth. The trooper turned to the district
court prosecutor, who was engrossed in a political editorial. She

tapped his desk twice to get his attention, and as he looked up, she gestured to the office door.

"You," she hissed softly. "Out!"

The prosecutor casually looked around the room, placed his newspaper into a desk drawer, stood up, and walked directly out of the room without speaking to anyone. Donovan eyed the lieutenant with mild curiosity as the office door slammed shut.

"Problem, Jackie?" she asked coyly, knowing full well what the lieutenant was about to bring up.

The lieutenant inched closer toward the prosecutor and shot an icy glare at her. "Yes, I have a problem. You lied to the judge and Vaughn's attorney that no fingerprints were recovered from the scene. Are you fucking kidding me?"

"The information is not relevant at this time," Donovan dismissively replied, seemingly unconcerned with the issue.

"Did you really attend law school?" Lammoth snapped. "This is Discovery 101. You and I both know that the fingerprints did not come back to Carmen Vaughn. That is exculpatory evidence, and you need to share it with Attorney Pickering."

"Interesting," Donovan mused out loud. "I didn't hear you or anyone from your team object when Geoffrey Walker ordered Sergeant McCam not to disclose the existence of fingerprints a few days ago."

Lammoth bristled at the slight. "That's different, and you know it. We were in the middle of an investigation, not post charge. There is no justification for you to sit on this evidence, Victoria."

Sergeant McCam quickly interjected, growing concerned at Donovan's nonchalant attitude. "You do realize that Pickering is going to find out about these prints, right? This information is going to come out, one way or another."

"You're overacting, sergeant," Donovan defensively replied.

"No, I'm not," McCam responded with a raised voice. "The last thing I fucking need is this case dismissed or overturned on appeal because you sat on exculpatory evidence."

"That's not going to happen," Donovan shot back as she tossed a pen onto a nearby desk. She looked agitated. Her face was flushed red, and her eyes were growing wide with anger. "We have this son of a bitch dead to balls, even without those fucking prints, and I will be damned if I'm going to let Attorney Timothy fucking Pickering derail this case by distracting a jury with a non-issue."

Jacqueline Lammoth's mouth gaped open in horror as she stared speechless at Donovan. After she was able to regain her composure, she addressed the prosecutor's bold statement. "You are not thinking clearly here, Victoria. You need to disclose this evidence. If you don't—"

"If I don't, what?" Victoria snarled. "The evidence is overwhelming against Carmen Vaughn. We have the victim's necklace and damn duct tape used in the aftermath of the crime recovered from the defendant's vehicle. Those two pieces of evidence alone are going to nail the defendant's ass to the wall. Now you are asking me to throw a bone to Pickering? I'm not going to do it, not yet."

"What do you think is going to happen, Victoria?" Sergeant McCam demanded as he struggled to keep his temper in check. "Timothy Pickering will just walk into your office and beg for a plea deal? He is a fucking trial attorney. I do not care if he has been teaching at some half-ass glorified community college for the past three years; he's going to take this case to trial. Did you even bother to notice Pickering's private investigator seated in the audience?"

"No," Donovan sourly stated.

The sergeant rubbed his temples with his hands and then continued. "Adrian Watson, one of the best fucking private investigators in the state, was sitting in the audience today watching your damn presentation. There is a more than certain probability he is already working on this damn case!"

"So what?" Victoria replied as she shifted uncomfortably and stepped slightly backward. "I'm not going to be intimidated by some half-ass mall cop."

"This is a mall cop you need to be gravely concerned about," Lammoth answered angrily. "What happens when you call a member of crime scene services to the stand? Do you really want to roll the dice and hope Adrian Watson didn't unearth the information you're sitting on?"

"He'll miss it," Victoria replied with slight confidence.

"You are a fucking crazy bitch if you think he will miss anything," McCam interjected. "Allow me to fill you in on what will happen next if you continue to go down this path."

"Please do," the prosecutor sarcastically replied.

The sergeant cleared his throat. He desperately wanted a cigarette and a beer. "Adrian Watson, one way or another, will uncover the ugly fact that you sat on exculpatory evidence. Maybe he will interview someone from crime services or a courthouse employee. Perhaps he will do something cute and speak with one of the local cops who may have overheard something he should not have. Maybe one of our victim-witness advocates will leak the information to him. Adrian Watson is far too talented of an investigator not to uncover this information. When he discovers what you did, and he will, Adrian Watson will immediately notify Timothy Pickering."

Victoria looked away from the troopers and softly muttered to herself. She knew she could only bluff for so long. Mentally she was terrified. She knew that if Timothy Pickering or his investigator discovered what she had done, there would be hell to pay. The disclosure that evidence favorable to the accused was hidden would prove embarrassing to the district attorney's office and could lead to her firing. Worse, Victoria knew she could face sanctions from the Massachusetts Board of Bar Overseers, including suspension or disbarment.

Victoria felt her stomach gurgle as her stress level rose. She quickly steadied herself and recalled that prosecutors were rarely, if ever, sanctioned for misconduct. Victoria slowly convinced herself that the odds were in her favor and the likelihood of being caught by Adrian Watson was slim to none. But even if her actions were discovered, she knew the consequences were minimal. Massachusetts judges, as well as the bar association, rarely punished prosecutorial misconduct. Similarly, the *Lawrence Star* and other media outlets routinely provided cover for law enforcement missteps.

Lammoth snapped her fingers twice to recapture Victoria's attention. The prosecutor turned back around, folded her arms, and simply asked, "Are you finished, lieutenant?"

McCam cursed loudly, threw his hands up into the air, and chastised Victoria. "Do you really want to go down this road? Victoria, it's better to get ahead of this now before it's too late."

"You're assuming I'd put someone from the crime lab on the stand who will testify about the prints," Donovan purred.

Lammoth and McCam both let out simultaneous loud groans of frustration. Trooper Eriksen, who had been quiet throughout the entire argument, shifted uncomfortably from his vantage point at the back of the room. Lammoth crossed her arms and studied Donovan in silence. Afterward, she coldly addressed the attorney.

"I do not understand why you are risking this case, and your career, over such a minor piece of evidence."

Donovan clenched her jaw and glanced back and forth between all three troopers. After a moment of reflection, she addressed them. "Each of you knows this is a serious case, and the district attorney himself is watching this matter. We are all aware that Timothy Pickering is an exceptionally talented litigator who will turn the forensic results of this fingerprint against us. He may even argue that the print belongs to a police officer at the crime scene. Hell, when I arrived at the crime scene, Eriksen was slobbering all over the body. For all we know, the print is probably his. I believe there is no need for this matter to be derailed and—"

McCam quickly straightened himself up and kicked a chair adjacent to him. It slid across the room, crashed into a metal desk with a loud, hollow thud, and tumbled over onto the floor.

Lammoth silently shook her head at Victoria, unfolded her arms, and stepped toward the prosecutor. She studied Victoria and then pointed at Eriksen. "Now we know the real reason why you don't want to turn over the prints. You're protecting your boyfriend."

"Excuse me?" Victoria retorted with a sense of mock horror.

"Oh, cut the shit, Donovan," McCam growled. "The entire office knows you and Eriksen have been in a dating relationship for at least the past six months. Neither of you even bothered to be discreet about it. I saw the two of you snuggling and pawing each other inside the Museum Square Parking Garage at least twice over the last week and a half. You're both worse than a pair of teenagers."

"Tell me, Victoria," Lammoth continued as she once again stepped even closer to the prosecutor. "Have you disclosed your romantic relationship to Attorney Pickering yet?"

"Of course not; it's none of his business," Donovan replied as she struggled to conceal her growing fear of Lammoth.

"No, you didn't," the lieutenant repeated calmly as a thin smile spread across her face. "Let us not fool anybody here, Victoria. You are required by ethical rules to disclose any significant or romantic relationship with a witness."

Donovan looked past Lammoth and glared at Eriksen. "You see? This is exactly the reason why I told you to stay off this fucking case. You see the shit I have to deal with because of you?"

"I'm sorry, ethical and discovery rules are now 'shit'?" McCam quipped.

"That's not what I mean," Victoria replied as she nervously stepped back from Lieutenant Lammoth and leaned against a nearby desk.

"You have some serious reflection time ahead of you, Ms. Donovan," Lammoth declared as she put on her jacket and slung a purse over her shoulder. "Allow me to provide you with some guidance. You are going to disclose to Attorney Pickering before the next court date your relationship with Trooper Eriksen. You are also going to turn over the fingerprint results within the next two weeks. If you do not do both, I'm going to the district attorney himself to have you removed from this case. Am I clear?"

"Perfectly clear," Donovan muttered sheepishly.

"If I were you, I'd also get an ethical opinion from a source other than yourself as to whether or not you should even be handling this case," Lammoth growled as she started to leave the office. She gestured for McCam and Eriksen to follow her.

As they stepped out into the basement hallway, Lammoth stopped in her tracks and turned back to Eriksen. "You better talk to your little honey and remind her I will fucking bury her if she does anything to fuck up this case. Do you understand me, trooper?"

"Yes, lieutenant," Eriksen instinctively replied.

"Good," Lammoth replied and then gestured in the direction of the prosecutor's office. "Get your ass in there and start talking some sense into her now."

"Yes, ma'am."

Eriksen immediately spun around and stepped back into the office. He saw Victoria staring out an office window located near the back of the room. He carefully approached her until he was standing directly along her left side. He looked over at her and noted he she was physically shaking and struggling fight back tears. She loudly sniffled several times before taking a deep breath and shuddering as she exhaled. Eriksen placed his right arm around her shoulders and tried to comfort her.

"Vicky, listen, it's going to be all right." He softly stated as he tried to calm her down. "There's no way I'm going to let the lieutenant throw you under the bus."

Donovan looked over at the trooper. Her eyes were bloodshot, and her nose red. "Really? Do you not think Lammoth will fuck me over if the need arose? God, you're far more of an idiot than I thought."

Eriksen gulped, backed away from his girlfriend, and shrugged slightly. "At some point, you've got to give Pickering a bone so we can move past this issue before it jams you up. I have made sure there is enough evidence against this guy to sink him, regardless of fingerprint results. You and I both know that."

Donovan turned her head and glanced at the trooper. She had a wild look of terror across her face. "This is not going to end well, Brian. It is going to blow up in our face very quickly."

Brian smiled thinly as he caressed Victoria's hair. "It may, but I doubt it. Focus on the bigger picture, Vicky. One way or another, that fucking kid is going down. I promise you that is going to happen, and then we will come out of this entire damn mess looking like fucking heroes."

FIFTEEN

Carmen awoke from a fitful sleep in the predawn hours as the metal door to his cell ground open. He sat up and looked wearily around his current living quarters. The cinderblock walls were painted a dull, eggshell white and were decorated with unknown stains, gang-related graffiti, and mold. There was a single, narrow window that looked out to the free world. Beneath it was a cold, metal toilet that doubled as a sink. Carmen's bed was nothing more than a hard metal slab with a thin mattress and a threadbare wool bedsheet.

His cellmate also woke up and looked around for a moment. Afterward, he quickly slumped onto his mattress and pretended to be asleep. As Carmen's eyes adjusted to the early morning light, a correctional officer dressed in a blue tactical uniform stepped into the cell. The man was approximately six-foot-two in height, well-built, and bald. He was armed only with a radio, which he carried in his left hand. The guard looked around the room in silence for a moment and then stepped back out of the cell.

Carmen thought the encounter was odd. For the brief time that he was incarcerated inside the Middleton House of Corrections, he had already become accustomed to the daily routines of prison life. At least three times a day, there would be a lockdown where prisoners were confined to their cells so guards could conduct a headcount of all prisoners directly under their care. Meals and exercise were closely supervised, and calls to loved ones and attorneys were strictly limited to thirty minutes. Jail visits were permitted but only occurred twice a week and were held under the watchful eyes of several deputy sheriffs.

While Carmen expected random room searches for weapons and illegal contraband to occur, a pre-dawn visit to his cell seemed highly unusual. Nevertheless, as the guard left the cell, Carmen turned toward his cell wall, lay down on his right side, and started to close his eyes to sleep.

However, he could not shake the feeling that something was not right. He quietly rolled onto his back and again looked over toward the doorway of his cell. He was shocked to see that now standing in the entranceway were three guards, all glaring at him in silence. Suddenly, the largest of the three rushed forward, grabbed Carmen by the throat, physically dragged him out of his bed, and tossed him onto the cold concrete floor. Before he could shout in protest, the other two guards came to their companion's aid, shoved a dirty sock deep into his mouth, grabbed his legs and arms, and dragged him out of the cell.

Carmen gagged and dry heaved as he struggled to spit the sock out of his mouth. Twice, the large guard smacked him in the back of the head and told him to be quiet. When the group reached the center of the common area of the jail block, the guards hauled Carmen to his feet. One of the guards held up a roll of silver duct tape and shook it.

"Look familiar, Carmen? We hear you're a fan of duct tape," the large guard emotionlessly announced as he tore off a piece of the tape and slapped it across Carmen's mouth. The other two correctional officers had iron grips on the young man's arms, preventing him from removing the tape or fighting off his assailants.

The large guard stepped back and gestured with a nod of his head for the other two correctional officers to take Carmen away. The two dragged Carmen out of the holding block and into a long, dimly lit hallway. The young man struggled to break free, but the guards' grip was too tight. The trio rounded a corner and came to a large, heavy metal door that opened with a loud metallic click. As Carmen was pulled through the door, he realized he was being brought outside to the courtyard.

In the early dawn light, Carmen was hauled across a patch of grass and a pair of basketball courts to a white building located in the center of the courtyard. As they closed in on the building, Carmen was convinced he was about to be killed. He felt his stomach churn and his heart race. Adrenaline pumped into his blood and his muscles tightened as he prepared to fight for his life. He swung his feet in front of him and tried to plant them firmly into the ground in a desperate effort to either slow or halt the guards' advance. However, the pair simply picked up his legs with their free hands and carried him up a flight of stairs into the building. Carmen violently twisted his body to break free, but the effort was futile. He tried to scream, but with the sock and tape muffling his voice, he could only let out soft gurgles and grunts.

Carmen was carried down a dark hallway and then up a flight of stairs toward the second floor. The guards breathed heavily as they struggled to bring Carmen to the top of the stairs. Once they reached the landing, they turned immediately into a room and tossed him onto the tiled floor with a loud thump. Both men stepped back and silently stared at their prisoner.

Carmen quickly struggled to his feet, ripped the duct tape off, and pulled the sock out of his mouth. He wretched, doubled over and vomited. Afterward, he wiped his mouth, stood up, and tried to assume a defensive stance. However, before he could, one of the two guards rushed him and body-checked him, causing Carmen to unceremoniously stumble backward onto the floor.

As he sat on the floor, he looked about the room. There were several desks with computers on top of them. Along one of the walls was a display of handmade weapons—shanks—that were seized from prisoners before they could cause some form of bodily damage. The other two walls were adorned with posters about investigatory and administrative protocols. In the corner of the room, there was a large metal rack that housed nonlethal weapons and body armor. Carmen quickly realized he was either inside the office of the prison's detective unit or riot control.

Either way, he quickly concluded he was in grave danger.

As he struggled to get back on his feet, there was a loud squeak as a chair rolled backward. An older bald correctional officer peered out from behind one of the computer desks, carefully studied Carmen for a moment, and finally spoke.

"I wouldn't get up, son. It's bad enough that you already vomited on my floor once; I don't want to have you clean up more than you already need to."

"I want to speak to the shift commander. Now!" Carmen demanded as he looked wildly around the room. In addition to the man who just spoke to him and the two guards, three additional correction officers entered the room.

The bald man stood up. He was wearing a white shirt, gold lieutenant bars on his shoulders, and blue pants. Around his waist was a utility belt that carried a collapsible baton and mace. He walked over toward Carmen, crouched down, and stared intently at the young man. "Son, I *am* the shift commander."

Carmen let his head drop down to his chest in defeat. He brought his left hand up to his head and began to rub his eyes. He knew what was going to happen next, but he wanted to hear it from the shift commander. "What do you want from me?"

The man snorted slightly as he eyed Carmen as if he was some insignificant insect. "Carmen, tell me, did you kill Jillian?"

"My attorney told me not to speak to anyone or answer any questions," the young man shot back.

The shift commander smiled as he stood back up, reached across his chest, retrieved his collapsible baton, and snapped it open with a loud metallic click. Carmen again looked around the room nervously as all the other guards repeated the same action. The commander crouched back down and prodded Carmen's throat with his baton.

"Carmen, let me explain this to you. At this very moment, you are at an especially critical crossroad in your fucking miserable life. If you want to do the right thing, things will go easy. If you do not, well . . ." the shift commander trailed off as he looked at his guards and then glared knowingly back at Carmen.

"I didn't kill Jillian," Carmen protested but was quickly interrupted by the shift commander.

"Now, Carmen, let's not be too hasty," the officer stated in a soft, icy tone. "I want to give you the full picture before you make a decision. Tell me, what is Jillian's relationship to me as well as two of my officers in this room?"

Carmen was taken aback by the unusual question. Nevertheless, he felt he had no choice but to respond. He reflected for a moment and then looked around at all the correctional officers. "I honestly have no idea."

"That's right; you don't," the shift commander replied in a mocking tone as he gestured back to the other correctional officers with a sweep of his hand. "I was Jillian's uncle, and two of my men in this room were her cousins."

"Oh, shit," Carmen muttered to himself as his thoughts wandered back to Jillian when she was alive.

"Yes, oh shit," the shift commander replied with a quick wink. "So, you can imagine when her father asked us to check in on you to make sure your current accommodations were less than acceptable, we gladly accepted."

"He wouldn't!" Carmen blurted out, trying to comprehend why Jillian's father would arrange for this encounter.

The shift commander continued, "At first, I seriously contemplated how to best convince you to spare the Russo family of an ugly, drawn-out trial. I thought about forcing you to write out a confession to the crime that I could deliver to the district attorney's office. Would you do that for me, son?"

"I'm not going to do that," Carmen spat. "I won't confess to something I did not do."

The shift commander grimaced for a second and looked back toward a short, fat corrections officer standing directly behind him. The guard was slapping his extended baton rhythmically into his free hand.

"I told you, Patrick; he wouldn't agree to that," the shift commander loudly announced.

"Lieutenant O'Rourke. Let me convince this little shit," Patrick sneered as he took a step toward Carmen.

"I won't do this," Carmen replied with a sense of desperation in his voice. He started to shudder softly and sob. "I won't confess to something I didn't do!"

O'Rourke studied Carmen for a moment as two more correctional officers moved closer to the prisoner. "No, Carmen, you and I both know you won't admit to what you did. You're too much of a fucking coward to do the right thing."

"What happens now?" Carmen demanded as he noticed the correctional officers starting to close in on him.

"Well, that's simple, Carmen," the shift commander replied as he pressed the tip of the baton into Carmen's temple, causing the young man to turn his head away. "If you're going to drag my sister's family through a long, ugly, protracted trial, then my men get to use you for softball batting practice."

"Fuck you!" Carmen hissed at the correctional officers.

O'Rourke laughed. "Don't worry, Carmen. We won't touch your pretty face. The last thing I need is your jackass attorney breathing down my neck because you have visible injuries and bruises. But my men are going to hurt you in a bad way. When this is all over, I am going to write a disciplinary report that will describe how you assaulted my men and that it took all of us to subdue you."

"That's bullshit," Carmen replied with horror.

"Perhaps," O'Rourke replied calmly as he looked back at the display of shanks on the wall. "I think I'll report that we also seized a razor blade or sharpened toothbrush from you as well."

"Whatever happens, I'm going to report it to my lawyer so he can sue your ass."

"You're assuming you are going to have contact with attorney— what's his name?" O'Rourke inquired of a nearby correctional officer.

"Pickering," Patrick responded with disgust.

"Ah yes, Attorney Pickering. Carmen, you are not going to be having contact with Attorney Pickering for some time because I am going to throw you into a hole somewhere in the sub-basement of this miserable facility. After that, I am going to transfer you to D block. Do you know what the D block is, Carmen?"

"No. I don't."

"It's where I keep all my gangbangers and violent offenders," the lieutenant proudly announced. "You're going to be up-close and comfortable with the Latin Kings, Gangsta Disciples, the Asian Boyz, and MS-13. Trust me, Carmen. I will take every measure to ensure they give you a proper welcome."

Carmen tried to articulate a response to the lieutenant's threat, but he could only stammer and occasionally whimper. After a moment of struggling to regain his composure, he swallowed loudly and looked directly at Lieutenant O'Rourke.

"You can't touch me. There are security cameras everywhere. I'll tell my attorney, and he'll get the footage."

O'Rourke chuckled loudly as he stood up straight and looked around the room. The remainder of the correctional officers also burst out laughing. The lieutenant returned his attention to Carmen. "Son, the strange thing is about the time we pulled your ass out of your cell, there was a computer system failure that caused all of the security cameras between your cell block to this office to go offline. I have already notified our IT department of the malfunction, and they assured me that the issue would be resolved by lunchtime today. Unfortunately for you, those cameras aren't going online anytime soon."

"I didn't kill Jillian. I loved her, and the last thing I would ever want is for her to be hurt," Carmen desperately argued to no avail with the officers.

O'Rourke silently nodded and then stepped back from Carmen. "I'm not surprised, Carmen. But I will be damned if you think you can hide behind some warped presumption of innocence bullshit."

The lieutenant gestured to the two correctional officers closest to him. The pair rushed forward with batons raised as Carmen struggled to stand up so he could defend himself. As he struggled to his feet, the first guard swung his baton in a swift downward motion and connected with Carmen's knee. There was a sharp, searing pain that ran from Carmen's kneecap up through his thigh. He yelped in pain and collapsed back onto the tiled floor. The second guard stepped up and drove the tip of his weapon into Carmen's ribcage. As he gasped for air, yet another correctional officer stepped into the fray, drove his knee into Carmen's jaw, and then slammed the butt of his baton into his collar bone.

"Careful, Patrick!" O'Rourke barked from a safe distance away from the beating. "Avoid the face. I don't want that pretty face touched!"

The remainder of the correctional officers surged forward and started to repeatedly club, kick, punch, and beat Carmen. He writhed in pain with each blow that landed on his body and begged the officers to stop. Realizing his pleas were useless, he desperately tried to fight back, only to be punched in the ribs or stomped on the groin. From the corner of the room, Carmen could hear O'Rourke bellowing orders and instructions on how to best hurt him.

After what seemed an eternity, the attack stopped. Carmen was desperately gasping for air and repeatedly coughed up blood. The room was spinning, his vision was blurred, and his legs and torso were throbbing with raw, blinding pain. Nevertheless, Carmen struggled to stand back up. He clawed at a nearby chair to help him regain his footing. When the chair slid away and he crumpled back to the floor, the correctional officers merely laughed. Again, Carmen tried to stand, this time using a nearby desk. As he pulled himself up, a correctional officer came up from behind, swung his baton, and struck Carmen behind the kneecaps. The pain ran up Carmen's body to his lower back, and once again, he tumbled to the ground.

Carmen refused to give up and was determined to stand before his assailants. He scraped yet again at the desk and pulled himself up to his knees. The entire lower half of his body trembled and shook with pain. After much difficulty, he was finally able to stand on his own. He tried to stand upright and turned to face his attackers.

As he turned around, Lieutenant O'Rourke closed in on him. He grabbed Carmen by the top of his orange prison jumpsuit, pulled him close to him, spit in his face, and then heaved the prisoner toward the desk behind him.

Carmen crashed onto the desk and rolled, head over heels, off it. As he landed on the floor, the desktop monitor landed on top of him. Carmen felt everything start to go black, and he slipped into unconsciousness as the beatings once again resumed.

SIXTEEN

Over the next two weeks, Carmen Vaughn's case moved excruciatingly slow. Pickering split his time between conducting legal research, reviewing discovery that trickled in from the Essex District Attorney's office, and teaching his classes. The professor did his best to ignore the inflammatory and occasionally bigoted news articles that Harriet Jenson and the *Lawrence Star* churned out in the days after Carmen's arraignment.

Unfortunately for Pickering, several self-proclaimed social justice warriors at Brighton College read the articles and began to vocally question why the school would employ a professor who would represent a person accused of murdering his girlfriend. Although the school was not pleased with Pickering's decision to represent Vaughn, they assured him that a small student mob that had no understanding of due process or the presumption of innocence would not dictate the terms of his employment.

However, Pickering's wife was not as forgiving. At first, he tried to delay telling Elizabeth that he was still representing Carmen. However, as news reports from the *Star* trickled in, it was impossible to keep his wife in the dark. When he finally confided in her that he had not withdrawn from the case, she exploded in a fit of rage. Two hours later, Timothy had checked himself into a room at the Essex Street Inn.

Of course, Carmen's future at Brighton College was all but finished. Less than two days after his arraignment, his mother received a certified letter from the dean of students informing her that Carmen had been suspended indefinitely pending the outcome of his criminal matter. He would not be allowed to complete his semester courses or take his final exams. The same day, a campus police officer called Carmen's mother and announced to her that her son's belongings and personal property had been removed from his dorm room and could be picked up at the campus police chief's office. As she left with her son's belongings in a cardboard box, the department curtly informed Maria that Carmen was banned from campus and would be promptly arrested for trespassing if he dared to set foot on the property.

But Carmen's academic future was the least of his worries. As the police reports, witness statements, and forensic studies poured in, Pickering realized that the likelihood of securing an acquittal on behalf of his client was growing more and more remote. Even after a casual review of the prosecution's evidence, it was clear Carmen had all the necessary requisites to commit the murder of Jillian Russo—motive, opportunity, and capability. He called Attorney Donovan twice to inquire whether fingerprints were recovered off the duct tape from the scene or if a report existed. On both occasions, the prosecutor firmly asserted no tests were conducted, and no report existed. The professor desperately scrambled to identify potential legal loopholes, evidentiary issues, or even grounds for a reduced charge. Each time, he came up empty. Even his connections inside the district attorney's office were unable to provide him with any hints or leads.

He began to question his judgment about representing one of his own students and whether the decision was worth the risk of being permanently separated from his wife and children. As the days passed, Pickering fought harder and harder not to slump back into a mild depression.

To complicate matters, Adrian Watson was having little success of his own. Photographing and mapping the last known location of Jillian Russo proved to be routine and non-eventful. The Merrimac chief of police gladly provided access to his department's investigative reports, but he had no information about undisclosed fingerprints that he could share with the private investigator. Likewise, the interviews of Carmen's friends and family for potential leads proved to be fruitless. The government's civilian witnesses were even worse. Assistant District Attorney Donovan identified five individuals from Merrimack College who were friends with Jillian and could provide information on the events leading up to her murder.

The first two, a male sophomore and a female junior, were both familiar with the contentious, on-again-off-again relationship between Jillian and Carmen. However, neither responded to Watson's repeated requests to meet and discuss the case. The next three were Jillian's roommates, who were at the club with her immediately before her disappearance. The first two informed Watson that they had already spoken with the Essex District Attorney's office and had been told they were under no obligation to speak with the investigator. It was a lawful but common tactic utilized by prosecutors to discourage witnesses from cooperating with any independent investigation led by a criminal defense team. In short, the pair told Watson to fuck off. Surprisingly, the final witness, Emily MacKay, agreed to speak with Adrian. The two agreed to meet on a Friday afternoon at a Dunkin' Donuts about a mile down the road from Merrimack College in Andover, Massachusetts.

Watson was the first to arrive and grabbed a table at the back of the donut shop. Emily entered the establishment shortly afterward. She was a short, slightly overweight blond woman with bright green eyes, pale skin, and a friendly smile. After getting a coffee and a donut, she greeted Adrian and sat down at his table. The investigator immediately noted she was outgoing and showed little hesitancy to speak with him.

At first, the two made small talk over her time at Merrimack College, their respective hometowns, and the weather. After several minutes of light conversation, Watson gradually steered the meeting to Jillian Russo and the circumstances surrounding her death.

"How did you know Jillian?" Watson initially asked.

"Jillian and I were roommates, and we shared the same bedroom inside our dorm," Emily quickly answered. "We quickly became close and had discussed continuing as roommates our sophomore year of school."

"How was Jillian as a student?" the investigator asked as a follow-up question. It was his intention to gradually shift the conversation toward romantic life.

"Overall, she was a great student. It seemed as if As and Bs came easy to her."

"How did she get along with her classmates?"

"Honestly, she got along with mostly everyone," Emily answered after a moment of reflection. "Her professors loved her, and other students always greeted her as we walked between classes. I don't think she ever had any problems with any of the other students."

"How about her romantic life with Carmen? Was it just as good as her academic life?" Watson pressed.

"She was an emotional train wreck," Emily noted rather quickly as her demeanor appeared slightly sour. "To be honest, Jillian's relationship with Carmen was toxic at best."

"How so?" Adrian asked, his curiosity slightly piqued as he jotted down notes onto a yellow, coffee-stained legal pad.

"They continuously argued, broke up, and made up almost on a weekly basis," she noted. "They repeatedly hurled insults at each other in person, on social media, and through text messages. Honestly, it was horrifying to watch it."

Watson nodded in understanding before asking a follow-up question. "Did you ever see Carmen act violently toward Jillian? Did he ever hit her, shove her, or threaten her?"

Emily paused for a moment to look down at the floor and contemplate the question and how to best answer it. After biting her lip, she looked back up at the investigator. "Not really. I mean, Carmen would often raise his voice with her and wave his arms around while they argued, but I never saw him slap or punch her."

"Did you ever see Jillian attack him?" Watson pressed.

Emily shrugged her shoulders and sighed loudly. "I seem to remember she threw her cell phone at him once in front of me, but other than that, no, I never saw her strike him either."

"Were you aware that Jillian had previously pressed charges

against Carmen for allegedly attacking her?" Adrian asked as he studied Emily's demeanor.

The college student shifted uncomfortably in her chair for a moment and looked away from him. She appeared to be somewhat embarrassed. "I was."

"Did she ever tell you what happened?" Adrian asked as he leaned slightly forward in his chair. The investigator picked his drink and took a sip of it as he awaited her response.

Emily continued to avoid eye contact with the investigator as she struggled with the question. She nervously chewed on her fingernails and fought back the urge to become visibly upset. "She never told me, but one night, after we drank way too much vodka, she told our other friends and me that she made up a criminal charge against Carmen to teach him a lesson."

"What did you think of that?" the investigator asked as he continued to observe Emily's behavior during the conversation. Occasionally, he scribbled notes without looking down at his pad of paper.

"Honestly," she replied before pausing to reflect for a moment, "I thought it was fucking nuts. But I chalked it up to the nature of their relationship and Jillian's attitude toward it."

"I'm sorry, I have to ask," Adrian asked with a slightly nervous laugh. "Why did you remain friends with Jillian if she had this much drama in her life?"

"That's a fair question," Emily conceded. "She was always nice to me, and she always looked out for me. I don't have too many friends back home, and it was nice to have someone who cared about me in my life."

Watson considered Emily's comment for a moment and then resumed the conversation. "You chose to remain friends with Jillian after she told you she made up a criminal charge?"

Emily's face became flush with shame. She silently nodded in the affirmative. Adrian continued speaking. "Perhaps Jillian liked to control the relationship with Carmen?"

"She absolutely did," Emily replied as she tried to regain her composure. "If she didn't get her way, she would go elsewhere to get the attention she desired."

"What do you mean, elsewhere?" the investigator asked as he cocked his head slightly to the left.

Emily nervously scratched her arm before continuing. "Jillian started dating a second guy shortly after she arrived at Merrimack College."

Adrian leaned back in his chair and eyed the student carefully. "Tell me about him."

"I don't know much because I never met him. Hell, Jillian never showed me a picture of him. All I know is that he was older than her, and he lived in Haverhill. At the end of our first semester, she was hooking up with him a few times a week. Ironically, she once told me that the other guy was pretty controlling."

"Excuse me?" Adrian blurted out in surprise.

"Jillian told me he was pretty rough with her," Emily responded, looking around anxiously.

"How so?" Adrian demanded as he furiously scribbled notes.

"She told me they'd often get into arguments, and sometimes he would grab her or push her. On one occasion, she told me that he choked her during an argument."

"Did you ever see any of this?" Adrian asked as he continued to write.

"Nope. Never," Emily replied sadly.

"Did you ever see Jillian with any injuries such as bruises, scrapes, cuts, or scratches?" Watson asked as he put down his pen and looked back up at the student.

Emily softly exhaled before continuing. She looked cautiously around the Dunkin' Donuts for a moment and then returned her attention to Adrian. "Before she disappeared, Jillian showed me a pair of large bruises on her upper arm. She told me that this other guy gave them to her."

"When you say, 'Just before Jillian's disappearance,' do you remember when?" he inquired.

"About two weeks before she died," she replied with a slight tremble in her voice.

"Emily," Watson replied with a tone of concern in his voice, "did you ever call the police or encourage her to call the police?"

The student nodded rapidly as tears started to roll down her cheeks. "I did; several times, Mr. Watson. I begged her to get help."

"What was Jillian's response?" Adrian asked, already knowing what the answer would be.

"Each time she told me she was in control of the situation, and there was no need for the police to be involved."

"Did you ever call the police?" Adrian replied after Emily finished speaking.

"No, because I foolishly didn't want to upset Jillian," Emily said as she wiped her eyes and cheeks of tears.

"Did this guy have a name?" Adrian asked as he resumed taking notes.

"I think it was Eric or Ethan. He lives in Haverhill," Emily announced.

Watson continued to write in silence for several seconds and then looked up at her. "Do you know how they met?"

"From what I understand," she replied as she struggled to recall the exact details, "Emily met this guy in a Lawrence bar a week or two after the start of the school year. I think it was at the Claddagh Pub in Lawrence. The relationship took off pretty quickly after that."

"Did Carmen know about this guy?" the investigator asked.

Emily laughed slightly. "You know, she rarely hesitated to remind Carmen about this guy, knowing it would set him off."

"Tell me, did this other boyfriend come up when all of you went to Centro the night Jillian disappeared?"

"Of course," Emily replied with a shrug of her shoulders.

"When?"

"About an hour after we arrived at the club," she answered.

"This place doesn't check IDs, does it?" Adrian inquired with a slight smile.

"No," Emily replied with a curt shake of her head.

"You guys were all drinking alcohol that night?"

"Most of us were," she admitted. "Carmen wasn't because he was our driver."

"Who went to the club besides you, Jillian, and Carmen?" Adrian asked as he once again put his pen down and took another sip of his coffee.

"Jillian's other roommates, plus two of Carmen's friends," she replied matter-of-factly.

Watson made a quick note to himself to reach out to Carmen's friends once again as they were still unresponsive to his repeated requests to meet. Afterward, he turned his attention back to Emily and smiled at her. "When she told him about the other guy, what exactly did she say?"

Emily chuckled slightly. "She started off by telling told Carmen that he was a boring, immature ass."

"How did he react to that?" Adrian inquired, curious as to what Carmen's response was.

"He was upset because she said it loud enough for everyone around us to hear it," she announced calmly.

"So, he was embarrassed?"

"Hell yes," Emily replied with a raised voice.

"What happened next?" Adrian asked.

Emily snorted slightly and continued. "She ramped it up and announced to anyone who could hear how Carmen meant nothing to her. She even threw out there that this guy was fucking her better than Carmen ever could."

Watson winced slightly in disbelief. "I take it Carmen blew up?"

"Of course," she replied as her mood shifted toward anger. "They got into a heated argument in front of all of us."

"Did you ever see him hit or shove her?"

"No, but he got up in her face—like real close, inches away. He was definitely puffing up, and it looked like he wanted to smack her, but he never did," Emily replied as she became more animated.

"What about Jillian? How did she respond to this?" Adrian asked as he noted Emily's increased excitement.

"Well, Carmen started shouting at her, calling her a slut and a whore," she replied with a wild wave of her arms. "She shoved him away, grabbed her stuff, and started to leave."

"Did the bouncers or bartenders ever step in to put a stop to this?" Adrian asked with a hint of curiosity.

"No, they didn't," Emily replied with a click of her tongue. "There were a lot of people in the club, and security was nowhere to be seen."

"While this argument is going on, were there a lot of people watching?"

"Yes," she simply replied.

"Carmen must have been pretty embarrassed by this fight," Adrian wondered aloud.

"I would be," Emily responded.

"Did Carmen let Jillian leave?" he asked as a follow-up question.

She shook her head in the negative. "As she walked away, he grabbed her arm and spun her around toward him. It was the first time I ever saw him put a hand on her."

"Go on," Watson replied, listening carefully to the college student.

"She broke away from his grip, shoved him, laughed, and walked outside."

"Carmen, of course, followed," Adrian announced as he rested his chin on his hands and once again started to study Emily's demeanor.

"Yes, they were outside for about ten minutes. I guess Jillian got an Uber and left to go see this other guy," Emily speculated.

"You never went outside the Centro nightclub to see what was going on?" he asked, curious why she did not check on her friend.

"No. I thought it was just more drama between Jillian and Carmen, and I wanted nothing to do with it. I stayed at the bar to drink," Emily admitted.

Adrian nodded in understanding. "What happened afterward?"

"Carmen came back inside," she proclaimed. "He was really upset, and we tried to calm him down. However, one of our other roommates fucked things up."

"How so?" Adrian replied, somewhat interested as to what the answer would be.

"She started nagging him about how Jillian was cheating on him with an older guy and that he needed to do something about it."

"How long did Carmen stay in the club after that?" Adrian inquired. He reflected upon Emily's last statement and concluded he too would have stormed out of the bar after the roommate's comment.

"Maybe five minutes, tops," Emily answered. "He ran out saying he was going to find Jillian."

"Did you guys try to stop him?"

"His friends did, but I didn't."

"Too much drama?" the investigator quipped.

"Too much drama," Emily responded with a hint of remorse.

"Did you see Carmen again that night?" Adrian replied as he once again started writing.

"No," Emily replied as she looked down at her cell phone, which was repeatedly buzzing. After she silenced the device, she returned her attention to the investigator. "The next time I saw him was at his arraignment at the Haverhill District Court."

Watson looked up from his notes. "You were at his arraignment?"

"Yes. I was there to support Jillian and her family."

"I understand," Adrian replied as he closed his notebook, put his pen down, and prepared to wrap up the meeting. He noticed Emily look around the shop once again and then leaned forward to speak with him.

"You never asked me if I thought Carmen killed Jillian," she whispered.

"Well, it's not my job to ask what you think. Besides, the—"

"I don't think he did it," she interjected, her voice shaking slightly.

Watson studied the young woman for a moment. She was staring intently at him. "Why?" he asked, never looking away from her gaze.

Emily nervously smiled and then continued. "After the arraignment, a victim-witness advocate told me that I was a witness in Jillian's case. She asked me to go downstairs to the district attorney's office and leave my contact information. When I got there, a prosecutor told me to take a seat in the hallway and wait. I was probably ten feet away from the office."

"I don't understand why you're telling me this," Adrian replied as he took a large gulp of coffee.

"I'm telling you because I heard the entire argument between the woman prosecuting Carmen and the state troopers who are involved in the case," Emily countered with a tone of concern in her voice.

Watson choked on his coffee and looked at Emily in bewilderment. "What? What do you mean, argument?"

SEVENTEEN

SATURDAY, APRIL 20

Geoffrey Walker eyed his breakfast greedily for a moment before seizing a piece of thick bacon and shoving it into his mouth whole. As he chomped on it, he picked up a large mug of black coffee and drank the hot black liquid with a loud gulp. After he set the mug back down on the table, he reached with one hand for a second piece of bacon as the other guided a fork to a thick pile of French toast slices. As he continued to devour his meal inside Duffy's Diner in Bradford, Massachusetts, Sergeant McCam approached the booth and silently sat down across from his boss.

"Jesus Christ, Geoff, will you slow down? You're going to choke on your food," the trooper protested with grim horror as he watched Geoff devour his breakfast.

Walker simply waved the sergeant off and continued to scoop large cuts of French toast into his mouth. After several moments of this behavior, Walker put his fork down, wiped his mouth with a paper napkin, took another large sip of coffee, and then looked across the table at his sergeant.

"Well, Dennis, this must be pretty fucking important if you felt it was necessary to disturb my Saturday morning breakfast."

"It is," the trooper responded with a tone of concern. "It's the Vaughn case."

"Oh, for Christ's sake, this case again?" Geoff barked as he picked up his fork to resume eating. "Let me guess; you don't like how Donovan is handling the matter?"

"No, to be honest, I don't," McCam coldly replied.

Walker shook his head and chuckled to himself softly before

taking another bite of his breakfast. After swallowing, the prosecutor pointed his fork directly at the sergeant. "You just don't like the fact that she's getting all the media attention, and you and your investigators are off on the sidelines. Or perhaps you're uncomfortable with her pushing your team harder than they're used to."

McCam stiffened slightly as his superior lectured him and raised his hand to interject. "Perhaps you might want to hear me out before you decide to take potshots at my detectives or me."

Walker picked up another piece of bacon and chewed on it as he studied McCam. As salty bacon grease ran down the back of his throat, he gestured for the sergeant to continue.

"Donovan is screwing around on this case," McCam announced.

"How so?" Walker interrupted, growing annoyed at the direction the conversation had turned.

The sergeant took a deep breath and continued, "Victoria is hiding exculpatory evidence from the defense. She lied to a Haverhill District Court judge and Vaughn's defense attorney when she announced no fingerprints were ever recovered."

"You're making more out of this than is needed, Dennis," Walker replied softly as his attention wandered back to his breakfast.

"How so?" McCam retorted with a tone of contempt.

Walker once again put his fork down onto the table, folded his hands, and looked across the booth at the sergeant. "Dennis, let us assume, as you say, she lied to the judge and defense counsel about the existence of prints. So what? That can be easily rectified when Donovan tells the court she was mistaken and discovered that a print that does not belong to the defendant was recovered from the duct tape."

McCam was stunned and at a loss for words following Walker's declaration. He stammered for a moment, paused, and then collected his thoughts. Afterward, he resumed the conversation. "Geoff, come on. You want to put your reputation and your office's reputation on the line for Victoria Donovan's antics? Do you really want to do that?"

"You're being over-dramatic, sergeant," Walker announced with a wave of his hand. "This happens all the time, and the court rarely slaps our wrists for the occasional misstep. Besides, is this finger-print really that powerful a piece of evidence that it could lead to Vaughn's acquittal? I highly doubt that."

"You have got to be kidding me," the investigator shot back. "You are truly serious that you want to sit on exculpatory evidence?"

"Come on, Dennis; you were chomping at the bit to arrest this guy even before I approved of his arrest. I guess you were right. The evidence is so overwhelming that with or without this print, no jury is going to let him off the hook."

Walker's words stung, and McCam was silently chastising himself for arresting Vaughn so quickly. "What happens when the case gets overturned on appeal?" the sergeant fired back in disgust.

"I highly doubt any appellate court would overturn the convic-tion in light of the strength of our case," Walker brushed the ques-tion aside as he eyed a small piece of syrup-coated bacon resting on his plate.

"Geoff, I understand all that," McCam pleaded. "I believe this kid is guilty as they come, and we've got him dead to rights. But Pickering will make this an issue if we don't fix this problem before it gets much worse."

"The issue will be resolved, Dennis. Do not worry about this," Walker replied as he looked back up at his sergeant. "In due time, we will disclose that piece of information to the defense."

"Why not now?" McCam demanded as he leaned across the table toward the prosecutor. "Listen to me, Geoff; every day that goes by is another day that Pickering and his bullshit investigator build a case that makes us look incompetent. I do not want us sitting on poten-tially exculpatory evidence. It's just not right, and it could come back to bite us in our collective asses."

Walker laughed before waving a waitress over to refill his coffee cup. "Dennis, you've been around long enough to know what Rule 14 of the Massachusetts Rules of Criminal Procedure states. The gov-ernment must disclose exculpatory evidence at or prior to a pretrial conference. We have not even had that hearing yet, so I would argue turning over a potentially exculpatory fingerprint report is, at this time, premature. Besides, are we not looking for an accomplice?"

"You're really going to hide behind a convoluted court rule rather than do the right thing?" the trooper demanded before falling silent. Recognizing the argument was quickly becoming futile, he made one last plea to his superior. "Geoff, please, at least take Victoria off the case. She lied to the court and a defense attorney. Who knows what else she is capable of? I am warning you she is going to fuck this case up. She is not playing on the level, Geoff."

"I'm sorry, Dennis, but no," Walker replied with a tone of frustration. He was growing tired of McCam's overtures. "The district attorney believes she is more than qualified to handle this case, and this is an excellent opportunity for her."

Dennis' jaw dropped, and he slowly slumped back into his booth seat. He remained silent for a moment, looked around the restaurant, and then finally back at his boss. "Holy shit, Geoff. You're cutting Victoria slack because you know she wants to use this case as a springboard to a judicial appointment."

Walker held his hands up in protest. "I didn't say that Dennis, but you should know that the district attorney passionately believes that it is in the office's long-term collective interest to ensure Ms. Donovan is fully supported as she moves forward with this case. If you want my advice, I suggest you get with the program, shut the fuck up, and enjoy the fucking ride."

EIGHTEEN

MONDAY, APRIL 22

Timothy Pickering stared through the glass window and looked toward the Middleton House of Correction's inmate processing center. Unlike his first visit, the attorney-client room he was assigned offered a far better view of the interactions between newly arrived inmates and the correctional staff. He watched with curiosity as a facility nurse walked about the room, questioning each incoming inmate about any infectious or communicable diseases they may have been exposed to or possibly carried. Nearby, a guard wearing a tactical jumpsuit eyed each prisoner suspiciously while his partner, a two-year-old German Shepherd, softly growled at them. Two more guards sat behind computer stations and collected contact and personal information from each of the prisoners before directing them to another location for a cavity search.

The professor found the entire process disorganized and woefully inefficient. However, his random musings on prison management were interrupted when Carmen Vaughn arrived. Pickering stepped back from the metal and glass door as a correctional officer led his client inside the room. He noticed that Carmen was limping and occasionally winced in pain. After a brief conversation with the guard, they were left alone to speak.

Timothy gestured for Carmen to take a seat on one side of the old wooden table while he sat down on the other side. He watched as his student groaned in discomfort and struggled to slowly lower himself down into the seat.

"How are we doing, Carmen?" Timothy asked with concern. He noticed that Carmen's demeanor suggested that he had already given up all hope.

"As good as can be expected," his client responded softly and somewhat unconvincingly.

Pickering studied the young man for a moment before withdrawing a case file from his briefcase and dropping it on the table. "You don't look good, Carmen. What's going on?"

Carmen looked up at his attorney. His eyes were red and puffy. "I'm not good, professor. A couple of guards dragged me out of my cell a few days ago, carried me into an office, and beat the shit out of me."

"Wait, what?" Pickering exclaimed as he bolted up from his chair, walked around the table, and seized Carmen's right arm. He pushed back the orange sleeve of his jumpsuit and inspected his arm. The underside of the forearm up to the elbow was swollen and discolored with multiple large bruises. Pickering immediately recognized the injuries as defensive wounds caused when a person raises his arms to protect his body or head from blows or to fend off an assault. Timothy then seized the front of Carmen's jumpsuit and pulled it open. Carmen's chest was a checkerboard of black and blue bruises. More than one of the bruises was shaped like a boot tread. There were multiple contusions, and it appeared the entire right side of Carmen's rib cage was swollen.

"Holy mother of God," Pickering stated as he stumbled back in shock. The attorney at first wanted to vomit, and he felt a sour taste start to form in his mouth. However, the initial nauseous feeling was quickly replaced with a boiling rage. Timothy struggled to regain his composure but failed. He turned away from his client so he could desperately regain his composure. After several seconds of breathing loudly through his nose, Pickering turned back to his client.

"What else have they done to you, Carmen?" he asked coldly and with a menacing stare. His face was quickly becoming a deep red.

Carmen looked down and started to button his jumpsuit back up. His voice quivered and revealed a deep fear. "Professor, they have me in a cell block with gangbangers and drug dealers. There are fights almost every day, the guards wake me up at all hours of the night to inspect my cell, and I was threatened twice today by two white guys who want to avenge Jillian's death."

"As soon as this meeting is over, I am going directly to the sheriff's office and demand an internal investigation. You need to tell me who the fuck did this to you so I can hang them by their balls," Pickering demanded as he banged the table twice with his fist.

"No, professor," Carmen replied softly as he avoided eye contact with his lawyer.

"What?" Pickering replied incredulously.

"Professor Pickering," Carmen announced as he shifted in his chair and flinched in discomfort. "No, we need to focus on you getting me out of here. The guards are just a distraction right now."

Admittedly, Timothy was impressed with the foresight of Carmen's response. However, the professor was not as forgiving. "Carmen, I want you to think very carefully. We can't let these bastards get away with this."

"We're not letting them get away. Get me off these charges, and then we will deal with the assholes who did this to me. I need you to focus on getting me out of this fucking shithole."

Pickering took a deep breath and reluctantly nodded in agreement. He sat back down, reached across the table, and rested his hand on top of Carmen's. "Son, listen to me. I warned you when this ride started it was going to be ugly. It could get a whole lot worse. Are you sure you don't want me to file a request for an internal investigation?"

"Yes, professor," Carmen mumbled as he shifted awkwardly in his chair.

"Carmen, look at me," the attorney ordered as his client looked up from the table at him. "I can make things exceedingly difficult for this facility. Please, just give me the word, and I will come down on them like the wrath of God."

Carmen stared blankly at his lawyer for several seconds and then shook his head in the negative. "No, professor. I just want you to focus on getting me home to my mother. Please, Professor Pickering, that's all I want."

Pickering looked away and muttered a slight objection. Afterward, he gazed once again at his client. "Carmen, you're going to get through this. One way or another, we are going to get you through this. This is going to be a long, drawn-out fight, and I need you to keep yourself together while you are in this shit hole. Do not do anything that is going to come back and bite us in the ass. Do not give them an opportunity to tack on additional charges or produce a witness who could testify against you. Do you understand?"

"I do, professor," Carmen replied softly.

"You're keeping your mouth shut and not talking about your case?" Pickering demanded.

"Of course."

"That means you are not talking about the case on the phone with your mother?" Timothy inquired.

"Absolutely not. I know that the police are listening to my calls," Carmen quickly replied.

"That's right," Pickering reminded his client. "Anything you say on a call to your mother or your friends is recorded by the people who work at this jail. I promise you the police are listening to those calls in the hope that you will say something that will jam you up. So be smart."

"I will. I promise," Carmen replied with a curt nod.

"I guess you're wondering why I'm here," Pickering inquired as he tapped Carmen's file with his index finger.

"I assumed it was to prepare for the probable cause hearing we have coming up," Carmen speculated.

"That's part of it." Timothy grinned and opened the jacket of the case file. "I wanted to review with you some of the discoveries I've received from the government. However, there is another, more important reason why I came to see you. My investigator has dug up a few pieces of information that could be extremely helpful to your case."

"Really?" Carmen replied, sounding somewhat surprised and mildly hopeful.

"Yes. Really. Let me give you the real good news first," Pickering replied with a slight smile and leaned toward his client. "Mr. Watson has discovered that a fingerprint was recovered from the duct tape that was wrapped around Jillian's body."

"And?" Carmen asked breathlessly.

Timothy paused momentarily for dramatic effect and then continued. "The fingerprint belongs to someone else, but we don't know who. It appears that the government is trying to hide that piece of information from us."

Carmen's mouth dropped as he attempted to process what Pickering had just told him. After several seconds of awkward silence, he lowered his head into his hands and started to weep softly. He then took a deep breath, composed himself, and looked back up at his attorney.

"What does this mean? Is this good news?"

"It's very good news, Carmen," the professor responded. "It means that I can argue that someone else is responsible for the murder of your girlfriend."

Carmen let the attorney's words sink in. He finally felt as if he had a slim chance of beating this nightmare. Nevertheless, a burning question still nagged at him. "Professor, is it possible that the prosecutor could argue someone helped me commit the crime and the prints belonged to that person?"

Pickering cocked his head slightly and contemplated the question. "That is an excellent question, Carmen. I suppose it is possible, but realistically, such a scenario is unlikely."

"Why?"

"The government has not provided me with any evidence suggesting that they think that an accomplice helped you kill Jillian," Pickering explained. "If they believed that you had help, they would not be sitting on this piece of evidence. I believe they are hiding this information because this fingerprint hurts their case."

"So, what do we do next?" Carmen cautiously asked.

"We are going to bring it to judge's attention when we're in court this Thursday," Timothy announced.

"What do you think the judge will do?" Carmen pressed.

"In a best-case scenario, the judge could punish the government for not sharing this information with us and dismiss the case," Pickering answered. "The worst-case scenario is the judge does nothing and lets some other judge down the road address the matter."

"What do you think will happen?" his client repeated.

"Too soon to tell," Timothy replied before withdrawing a report prepared by Watson and waving it in front of his client. "I need to review with you the other information my investigator uncovered."

"All right," Carmen quickly replied, his mood continuing to improve. "What's the other information you want to discuss with me?"

"Tell me about Jillian's other boyfriend."

Carmen shifted a third time in his chair and looked uneasily across the table at Pickering. "What do you want to know about him?"

"First, let me tell you what Mr. Watson and I know about this guy," the attorney replied as he passed Adrian's investigative report across the table. "Mr. Watson recently interviewed one of Jillian's roommates, Emily MacKay."

"I know her. She's pretty nice," Carmen noted as he started to review the report.

"She is." Pickering nodded in agreement. "She was the only one of Jillian's friends and roommates who would talk to us. Your friends weren't much better."

Carmen looked up from the report and visibly scowled as Pickering continued. "She told us that Jillian started dating this guy shortly after she arrived at Merrimack College last Fall. She does not know the guy's name, but she believes it may be either Eric or Evan. Do either of those names sound familiar?"

"Yeah, yeah!" Carmen exclaimed as he reeled in pain. Carmen clutched his side momentarily and then continued. "It's definitely one of those two names, although I'm fairly sure his name was Eric. I would always ask her who this guy was. Most of the time, she would refuse to tell me. Occasionally she let his first name slip."

"You ever hear a last name?" the attorney asked.

"No. Never."

"We believe he's an older gentleman who lives in Haverhill," Pickering announced.

"Jillian mentioned once he was older than her, but I don't know by how much. I do know he lived in downtown Haverhill. That is the other thing Jillian used to always tell me when she would talk about this guy. She said he lived in an expensive condo in the downtown area of the city and that it overlooked the Merrimack River."

Timothy looked down at his legal pad and began to scribble a few notes on it. "Is it safe to say the reason you went to the Washington Street area of Haverhill the night Jillian disappeared was that this other guy lived in the general area?"

"Yes. I finally wanted to see who this guy was," Carmen conceded.

"Carmen, have you ever seen this person before?" Pickering inquired. "We're trying to figure out who this guy is. Any chance you've seen him in person or on social media?"

"Nope. Not even on Snapchat or Instagram," Carmen calmly admitted.

"Then, assuming you found Jillian with another guy, how would you know if he was the right guy?" the professor asked, curious at what Carmen's response would have been.

"I wouldn't. But I would find out."

"Punch first, then ask questions?" Pickering demanded.

"Yes."

The attorney nodded in response. At least Carmen was truthful with him. He took a few more notes and then looked back up at his client. "Did you know this guy was smacking her around?"

Carmen breathed in deeply and exhaled. He clenched his jaw and then relaxed it. "I did."

"How?" Timothy asked calmly.

"I often saw bruises on her wrists, shoulders, and one on her neck. I would always ask her about it, but she would always lie and tell me she got them from bumping into things or playing sports. I knew she was full of shit."

"Any black eyes?" Pickering asked as a follow-up question.

"No, but her best friend told me she once saw Jillian with a black eye," Carmen announced softly as he shook his head back and forth in disgust.

Pickering sat up in his chair. "Best friend? Who?"

"Her name is Sandy Minerva. She lives in the Point section of Salem. Jillian and Sandy have been best friends since they were both in third grade. She's the one who first told me Jillian was cheating on me and was afraid that the new guy was smacking her around."

The attorney was stunned and struggled to respond to Carmen's announcement. However, after regaining his thoughts, he finally addressed his client. "Wait, do you know if Sandy has met this guy?"

"Yes. I think she has," Carmen replied after a moment of reflection.

"Have you had recent contact with her?" Pickering pressed.

"No, not since I was arrested."

Timothy slid his notepad and pen across the table to Carmen. "Write her address and phone number down if you know them. Mr. Watson needs to speak with her as soon as possible."

"Why?" Carmen asked with curiosity.

"Because neither the district attorney nor the police has spoken with her. Hell, they may not even know Sandy exists. We need to get to her before they do."

"I understand, sir," his client stated and started to write down Sandy's contact information.

"Carmen, I want you to listen to me carefully." Pickering leaned forward and whispered to his client. "It's possible that the night Jillian was killed, she was with this guy. There is someone else's fingerprint on the duct tape that was used to wrap up her body before it was tossed into the Merrimack River. Do you understand where I'm going with this, Carmen?"

His client appeared to relax slightly. "Yeah, I do, Professor Pickering. Thank you."

For the next two hours, Timothy Pickering and his client reviewed the evidence the government had provided to date, including autopsy reports, witness statements, photographs, and chain of custody documentation. It was rather routine, but Carmen showed a legitimate interest in the material presented to him. From time to time, he would ask Tim to explain how certain statements or reports were relevant to his case or how the evidence would be used against him.

Toward the end of the meeting, Pickering shared with Carmen photos from the crime scene, including those taken by crime scene services of Jillian's body. The young man struggled to look at the images and kept pushing them away. The professor urged his client to look at each image only because they would be paraded before a jury at a future trial, and he needed to be prepared for that moment.

After several attempts to have Carmen view the images, Timothy gave up and put the packet away. However, as he did, one of the pictures caught his attention. He studied it carefully for several minutes before looking up at his client.

"Carmen, tell me about Jillian's necklace, the one they found in the trunk of your car."

"Her father bought it for her sixteenth birthday. It was a gold cross with a red stone set in it."

"Did she ever remove it in your presence?"

"Never. She always said it was her favorite gift from her dad."

"Was there ever a time Jillian lost the necklace, and as a result, her dad bought her an identical replacement necklace?" Pickering asked as he continued to study the image.

"No, not that I know of."

"Was there ever a time she did not wear that necklace that you know of?"

"No, professor. Even when we went to the beach, she kept it around her neck," Carmen replied, unsure where his attorney was going with this line of questioning.

Timothy suddenly held up an image and showed it to his client. The picture was of Jillian's bloated face, bruised neck, and upper torso. Hanging around her neck was a necklace with a gold cross and a ruby stone set in it.

"Carmen, this picture was taken by the Massachusetts State Police crime scene services the day Jillian's body washed ashore along the banks of the Merrimack River. Is that the necklace?"

Carmen was stunned. He looked at the picture, then Pickering, and then back at the picture. "Yes, professor, it is."

"So, tell me, Carmen, do you have any idea how this necklace ended up in the trunk of your car a week or two after it was found on Jillian's body?"

NINETEEN

Victoria Donovan's office was not particularly large, but it did have its perks. Unlike many of the junior prosecutors assigned to the Essex County District Attorney's office in Salem, Massachusetts, Victoria's workplace had windows that overlooked the North River. She was also isolated from many of her coworkers, thereby allowing her to come and go as she pleased. Finally, she was only a few doors down from the district attorney himself. This created an opportunity for Victoria to have an unusual level of access to the county's chief law enforcement officer—a benefit that would be especially useful when the Vaughn matter concluded, and she submitted her judicial application to the Massachusetts Trial Court.

Attorney Donovan arrived early to her office this morning to review the latest police reports on a sexual assault investigation she had been preparing to present to a grand jury later that day. She had struggled internally over whether the eight-year-old victim of the case should testify. On the one hand, the experience would likely be traumatic for the young girl. On the other hand, her testimony would send a message to the defendant that the government was taking the accusations very seriously. More importantly, she knew that if the accused became aware of the victim's cooperation, it was highly likely that he would instruct his court-appointed attorney to seek a resolution of the matter as quickly as possible so as to avoid a harsher sentence that would result after a trial.

Victoria's review of the case was interrupted as Geoff Walker knocked on the open door of her office, stepped inside, and sat down in a chair across from her. He silently stared at her for a moment before leaning back in the wooden chair. He folded his arms across his rather bulging stomach and then shook his head in disappointment.

"Is there a problem, Geoff?" she reluctantly asked. She felt her stomach tighten as she mentally speculated whether Walker was there to confront her about her conduct.

"I'm not sure, Vicky. Perhaps you could enlighten me," the first assistant replied with a slight wave of his right hand. "Why don't you tell me where we are on the Jillian Russo matter?"

"We're almost done with the grand jury presentation," Victoria instinctively replied. "I expect to have Sergeant McCam testify on Wednesday regarding the items seized from the defendant's vehicle. If all goes well, we should have an indictment for first-degree murder handed down by Friday."

"Good," Walker replied with a quick nod. The fact that Donovan had started to present her case to the grand jury meant Pickering and his client were no longer entitled to a probable cause hearing. With that door closed, the case could be quickly transferred to the Essex County Superior Court in Salem, where Walker could more closely supervise the matter.

"What about discovery?" Walker continued. "Does Mr. Pickering have everything he's entitled to?"

Donovan shifted uncomfortably in her seat. "He should."

The first assistant cocked his head slightly to the side. "What do you mean he should? It is a yes or no question, Vicky. Either yes, he has all the discovery, or no, he does not. Which is it?"

"Yes, yes, he has everything," she replied with a nervous stammer. In her gut, she knew where Walker was going with this line of questioning, and her mind raced to prepare a battery of excuses and deflections.

Geoff leaned forward in his chair and coldly eyed Victoria. "I don't believe you."

"I don't understand. Everything I've received I've turned over to Attorney Pickering," Victoria stuttered in protest.

"Really?" Walker casually declared as he whimsically looked

around Victoria's office. "I want you to think long and hard about that answer before you say another word."

Victoria started to answer, but Geoff held up his hand and quickly snapped at her. "Victoria, Sergeant McCam interrupt my breakfast at a Bradford diner this past Saturday to tell me that you are still sitting on the fingerprint results that were lifted off of the duct tape."

Victoria struggled to keep from appearing on the defensive and raised her hands as if to surrender. "I didn't think it was appropriate to disclose the results just yet, Geoff. In no way was I trying to play hide-the-ball."

"Really? Is that what you want me to believe?" he retorted, sounding somewhat incredulous.

"Geoff," Victoria protested, fearful that her legal career was about to unceremoniously collapse in a scandal, "I was planning on disclosing that information to Timothy Pickering when his client's case was transferred to the superior court."

Walker reflected upon her words for a moment and then smiled thinly. "I gave McCam a similar excuse when he came to me on Saturday."

"It's not an excuse," she announced coldly.

"It's an excuse!" he shouted before checking his temper. After a deep breath, Geoff continued. "You've had this case for over six weeks. You have known about the fingerprint report for most of that time. I do not know why you are sitting on the results, but we both know you are. If I had to guess, I'd say you're either trying to stack the deck so you can secure a conviction, or covering for your boyfriend who, from what I've been told, may have tainted the crime scene."

"I'm not sitting on the forensic results," Victoria responded as a sense of dread washed over her.

"Very well," the first assistant replied calmly as he leaned back in his chair, "please show me the minutes that documents that you shared the fingerprint results with the grand jury."

The color drained out of Victoria's face as she sat in silence and was unable to respond.

"You did present the forensic reports on the fingerprint to the grand jury, didn't you, Victoria?" Walker demanded as he dipped his head forward and rested it on the tip of his fingers. "Please tell me you presented that information, Victoria because you are required to share it with a grand jury."

"No. I didn't," Victoria admitted softly.

"God damn it!" Walker roared as he leaped out of his seat, took a step forward, and leaned in across Donovan's desk. He slapped her desk several times to emphasize the seriousness of the situation. "It's bad enough that you want to fucking hide exculpatory material from Attorney Pickering. Now you have taken it up a notch and intentionally concealed that same piece of information from a grand jury investigation! Do you really want Timothy Pickering waving around a motion to dismiss due to prosecutorial misconduct?"

"That won't happen," she replied, recoiling in fear as Walker continued to slap her desk.

"Oh really? His fucking investigator is already asking around about whether prints exist or not. It's only a matter of time before you get caught."

Donovan nodded in silence as she fought back tears. Walker continued. "This is what you are going to do. You are going to fucking go back to that grand jury on Wednesday and present the forensic results of the prints that were recovered from the duct tape. Then you are going to hand-deliver the test results to Attorney Pickering the next time you see him in court."

"I understand," Victoria conceded, trembling at the thought that she was about to be fired for her actions.

"When is the next time you will see Attorney Pickering in court, Victoria?" Walker demanded.

"Thursday in the Haverhill District Court," she whispered meekly.

"Then, on Thursday, you are going to hand him the print results. Once that is done—and only when it is done—you will see me. I will then decide whether you can ask the grand jury to hand down an indictment of first-degree murder against Carmen Vaughn. Am I clear?"

"Yes. Yes, I understand," Donovan replied as she avoided eye contact with her superior and looked at a corner of the office.

Walker straightened up and took a step back away from her desk. "Victoria, you have let your ambitions get ahead of your responsibilities. If it were up to me, I would have yanked you off the case as soon as I learned you were hiding exculpatory evidence. However, the district attorney has repeatedly stated he wants you to handle this matter. Unsurprisingly, he is unaware of this fuck up. I strongly suggest you immediately change your plan of attack on this case and start behaving like an ethical prosecutor. Otherwise, I will remove you from the case and report your misconduct."

Victoria nodded in understanding and silently seethed as Walker spun around, walked out of her office, and slammed the door shut behind him. She could feel the weight of the case and her questionable decisions bearing down hard on her. After a moment of tense silence, she backhanded her cup of coffee and watched as it sailed off her desk and onto the floor. She dropped her head into her hands and repeatedly whispered to herself, "Fuck!"

TWENTY

Elizabeth looked out a large second-floor window and watched as rain droplets splattered onto the red-brick walkway located adjacent to a large patch of grass that served as the Custom House Maritime Museum's public green. The Custom House Maritime Museum is one of the centerpieces of Newburyport's downtown shopping district. The gray granite structure was built in 1835 and served as a government station for the inspection of international cargo entering the northern Massachusetts port town until the beginning of the twentieth century. On the eve of the First World War, the building was closed by the federal government. Shortly thereafter, the structure served as a shoe factory, an accountant's office, and a junkyard. In the early 1970s, the building was granted a second life and became a maritime museum.

Over the past two years, the museum had become one of Elizabeth Pickering's primary clients for her consulting businesses. Every time the museum planned a new exhibition exploring a unique historical or cultural topic, it turned to her for help. Through her guidance and leadership, the staff of the Custom House put on a variety of award-winning shows, presentations, and static displays that challenged visitors to explore the lesser-known and often ugly aspects of maritime and coastal life.

After a moment of silently cursing her husband's name, she stepped back from the window and turned her attention back to the World War II display that she had been hired to design. She casually walked around a nearby female mannequin dressed in a reproduction United States Coast Guard SPARS uniform, studied the display, and occasionally tapped notes onto an iPad. She was so engrossed in her work that she did not notice Mary Beth Rose, an elderly museum volunteer and a fixture of Newburyport society, enter the room. After a moment of watching Elizabeth, the woman loudly cleared her throat. Elizabeth looked up from her iPad and smiled at the woman.

"Mrs. Rose," she cheerfully announced. "I did not hear you enter the room. My apologies."

Mary Beth looked around the room and nodded her head with satisfaction. "You have outdone yourself this time, Elizabeth. The trustees will be pleased with your work."

Elizabeth nodded with appreciation. "I certainly hope so. This exhibit has been a little more challenging than previous projects. Admittedly the Second World War is not my area of expertise."

"Your work does not reveal any deficiencies," the woman replied as she started to glide across the stone floor of the exhibit room toward Elizabeth. "If this exhibit is as successful as your last three projects, I am certain you will have clients lining up to hire you for years to come."

"One can only hope," Elizabeth quietly replied as she glanced away from her visitor. She was somewhat distracted by her idiot husband, and the last thing Elizabeth wanted was for Mrs. Rose to notice the distraction.

While Elizabeth was a highly sought-after museum consultant, some of her clientele was often challenging. Mere rumors of bad behavior, questionable affiliations, or scandalous conduct could be the death knell of a project. Shortly after it had been publicly revealed that Timothy had returned to the legal field and was representing an individual accused of a brutal murder, Elizabeth started to feel pressure from others in her own field of work. More than one Custom House Museum trustee openly questioned why her husband was representing the "Hispanic kid" from Salem who clearly had murdered his white girlfriend. Directors from other historical and cultural sites contacted Elizabeth directly and asked probing questions as to whether she approved of her husband's actions. Only yesterday, a client openly admitted that he was unsure if he wanted to hire her for a new project out of fear of being linked to her husband.

Elizabeth struggled to contain her fury at Timothy before resuming her conversation with Mrs. Rose. However, before the chat could continue, a teenage girl who earned school credits as a museum volunteer entered the room and shyly announced that her husband, Timothy Pickering, was waiting for her in the museum's lobby. Elizabeth's face turned a bright red with embarrassment. In response, Mrs. Rose's face soured, and she raised an eyebrow. She then shook her head in disappointment before reluctantly announcing that she would show the attorney upstairs to his wife. As the two volunteers left the room, Elizabeth tossed her iPad onto a nearby display case and cursed several times to herself.

She walked back over to the window and stared out beyond the museum green to the Merrimack River. She watched as the dark water rushed past the museum property and continued to the Atlantic Ocean. Elizabeth wondered to herself how far the river would carry her husband's body if she chose to dispose of him in the next few moments.

Her half-hearted plot came to an abrupt end as footsteps could be heard ascending the flight of granite stairs leading to the museum's second floor. Elizabeth spun around, folded her arms, and steeled herself for yet another confrontation with her husband.

Timothy entered the gallery, averted his eyes from his wife, and looked sheepishly around the room. Elizabeth noticed that he was wearing a rain-soaked coat and carrying a briefcase and umbrella. After a moment of awkward silence, she addressed her husband.

"You have some balls coming to my place of work," she softly hissed. "It's bad enough that you chose yourself over your family with this stupid stunt, but now you come to my place of work and put my job at risk?"

Pickering stammered and shifted uncomfortably for a moment and continued to avoid eye contact with his wife. Finally, he responded,

"I just want to come home, Elizabeth. I miss the girls. I want to see Catherine and Hannah and be with you."

Elizabeth eyed him suspiciously and shook her head in the negative. "No. It was bad enough that I had to find out from a fucking Massachusetts state trooper that you jumped back into criminal litigation. It was unforgivable when I had to read in the damn *Lawrence Star* that you ignored my explicit instructions to not continue handling this case."

"There were reasons to continue working on this case," Timothy quietly pleaded. "I just couldn't walk away from the matter."

"Yes, yes, you could have," she replied as her raised voice echoed in the gallery. Elizabeth quickly checked herself, clenched her jaw momentarily, and then narrowed her eyes as she glared at her husband. "You chose to continue representing this murderer without talking to me. You never considered the potential harm this case could cause to our relationship or family. Your actions are now having an impact on my ability to support our children!"

"What? How?" Pickering retorted with an almost incredulous tone.

Elizabeth took two steps forward toward Timothy, who instinctively shuffled slightly back to remain out of her reach. "How?" she seethed. "The people and organizations I work closely with are extremely sensitive about how they are viewed. That perception extends to those who perform work for them. No matter how progressive they try to present themselves, at the end of the day, they will undertake every measure to ensure they do not rock the boat with their financial backers."

"I see," Timothy replied matter-of-factly.

"No, Tim, you don't," Elizabeth replied. "Since you decided to represent that asshole, I have been receiving shit from several of my clients about whether or not they want to continue their business dealings with me. Until you get off this fucking case, you can't come home."

"Even if this kid may have been set up?" he demanded as he started to withdraw a file from his briefcase.

"Here we fucking go again," Elizabeth announced with exasperation. "Timothy Pickering, the ultimate true believer of the criminal defense bar. Let me guess. He's been framed by the police?"

"We think he might have been," Timothy replied as he dropped the file onto the display case and pushed it toward his wife. "Go ahead, read it."

Elizabeth looked at Timothy in stunned silence for a moment and then snorted in contempt. "We? Did you drag Adrian Watson into this mess as well?"

"Just look at the file, Elizabeth. Please. I know I screwed up with you and the kids, but you need to know why I am still in this case. Read what Adrian and I have found."

His wife stepped back from Timothy and slowly paced around the gallery in silence. Eventually, she walked back to her husband. She shook her head in disbelief, cursed underneath her breath, picked up the file, and walked away.

As Elizabeth poured over Timothy's notes, Adrian's reports, and the accompanying photographs, she felt her stomach churn. She brought her hand up to her mouth, and her eyes widened in shock as she realized that her husband and his investigator might have uncovered a river of lies that were part of a coordinated effort to frame an innocent man. With her hand still over her mouth, she looked over at her husband as a tear rolled down her cheek. His client may have been a consummate asshole, but he was an innocent asshole.

Elizabeth closed the case file, walked back over to her husband, and handed him the file. She sniffed loudly as she wiped the tear away from her cheek. "This changes nothing, Tim. You should have spoken to me first. "

"I agree," he conceded. "But now that you know why, will you at least let me come home?"

She stared at him for a moment before she started to exit the gallery. At the entrance, she stopped momentarily and turned back to Timothy. "You may come home but get used to the couch. That is the only place you're going to be laying your head down for an exceedingly long time."

"I understand," Timothy replied earnestly.

"However, I want to be perfectly clear, Mr. Pickering," Elizabeth announced, her tone ominous and cold. "If you are handling this case, then you had better be all-in. If you need to go for the fucking throat to save an innocent kid, I expect you to do so."

"I will."

"You also need to understand," she continued, "I will not, under any circumstances, come to your rescue if I hear you have collapsed into an emotional ball of mush because of this case. If you do, you are on your own. Am I clear, Timothy?"

"Crystal," Timothy replied awkwardly.

Elizabeth studied her husband to determine if he understood just how serious she was. Once satisfied, she turned around and started to walk toward the stairwell. Once at the landing, she turned again to address her husband one last time.

"Timothy, get out of my work site. Now please."

TWENTY-ONE

WEDNESDAY, APRIL 24

Pickering quickly pulled into a parking space behind the Everett Mills, grabbed his briefcase, and exited his car. As he walked through the parking lot, he eyed the nearby Stone Mill. The building was one of the oldest surviving mill buildings in Lawrence and one of the few remaining American mills from the early years of the Industrial Revolution that was made completely out of stone. The structure originally housed a forge and a foundry that was utilized to manufacture and repair machinery for neighboring mill buildings. By 1860, the Stone Mill was sold to the owners of the Everett Mills and was converted into a cotton mill. By the end of the nineteenth century, the building had been repurposed to manufacture steam locomotives and fire engines.

Pickering circled past the Stone Mill and approached a flight of wooden stairs located at the back of the Everett Mill complex. He quickly ascended them and walked toward a glass doorway. Waiting by the door was Adrian Watson. Adrian smiled and gestured for the professor to follow him inside. The pair entered the main building, turned right, and passed through the back entrance of the committee of public counsel services. After a second sharp right, the two entered Watson's office. Pickering dropped his briefcase onto one of the two wooden guest chairs and collapsed into the other. His counterpart remained standing as he looked out his office window to the mill parking lot.

"It seems we've had a pretty successful week; wouldn't you agree, counselor?" Watson inquired as he continued to stare out the window.

"Absolutely," Pickering replied as he struggled to pull the ever-growing Vaughn file out of his briefcase.

"I'm not sure which I should be more excited about," the investigator announced as he continued to look out the window with increasing interest. "The suppression of the fingerprints or the planting of evidence. Honestly, both have me pretty wound up, Tim."

"I'd say together these two revelations can put us on the road to . . ." Pickering stated before trailing off. He turned in his chair toward Watson and shook his head in confusion. "Adrian, what are you looking at that has your undivided attention?"

Watson looked over at Pickering and burst out laughing. "Tim, come here. You have to see this. There's a Pitbull that is eating a rat the size of a large cat."

"You have to be shitting me," Pickering retorted before hopping out of his seat and rushing over to the window.

Near the southwest corner of the Stone Mill, a brown, muscular Pitbull struggled to subdue a mangy, gray rat that was, as Adrian noted, the size of a cat. The two animals wrestled with one another until the rat finally broke free, nipped the dog in the rump, and then dashed off toward an overflowing dumpster. The Pitbull quickly gave chase.

Once the distraction was out of sight, Adrian struggled to catch his breath from laughing so hard, looked over at Timothy, and slapped him on the shoulder. "I love my office. I have some of the best views."

"I'm sure you do, but we've got to get back to work. We have a court hearing in Haverhill tomorrow," Pickering protested.

"All right, Professor Pickering, let's review what we've got," Watson stated as he walked over and sat down behind a large mahogany desk. He picked up a copy of his investigative report, cleared his throat, and started to review out loud some of the key points of what the pair had uncovered over the past few weeks.

"We know the Essex District Attorney's office is sitting on an unidentified fingerprint that is not our client's. Correct?" Adrian surmised.

"Correct," Pickering quickly answered and nodded in the affirmative twice.

"We also know that someone removed the necklace from Jillian's body after it washed ashore and planted it in Carmen's vehicle." Watson paused and reflected for a moment. "The question is who? Was it someone from crime scene services, a state police detective, or a Merrimac police officer?"

"I'd rule out a Merrimac cop right out of the gate," Pickering confidently declared. "No Merrimac police officer has ever had access to Carmen's vehicle or was even present when it was searched."

"So, that leaves crime scene services or the state police detectives," Watson announced. "We know both were present when Carmen's car was searched at Brighton College."

"All right, so let's flesh this out," the attorney replied as he shuffled through Carmen's case file, retrieved a crime scene services evidence log, and passed it across the desk to Adrian. "All of the forensic evidence obtained from the crime scene were recorded in that log. The document includes the start and end times that the crime scene was processed. We know that from 3:15 to 3:45 p.m., the forensic team was collecting evidence from Jillian's body and the tarp she was wrapped up in."

Watson studied the log for a moment. Afterward, he looked up at Pickering and gestured for him to continue.

"Massachusetts State Police investigative guidelines require that a photographer take images of a crime scene before and after processing," Pickering reported before withdrawing a series of photographs and passing them across Watson's desk. "We know that was done in this case because we've received overall, mid-range, and close-up images of Jillian's body before and after it was examined."

"Let me guess, the photographer has a log as well?" the investigator quipped somewhat sarcastically.

"Yes, but we don't need that log because all of the images were time-stamped," Timothy replied as he tapped the corner of each image with his index finger. "The last set of pictures was taken at

3:55 p.m., ten minutes after crime scene services finished processing the body."

Watson methodically studied the images of Jillian's bloated body
for several moments in silence. He had seen enough images of murder victims to become immune to the shock and queasiness that
often accompanied the sight of a dead body. Once finished reviewing the images, he looked back up at Pickering. "The necklace is in
those pictures."

"The necklace is in those pictures," Pickering repeated softly.

Adrian leaned back in his chair and thought back to the afternoon
Jillian's body was discovered near his home. "If I recall correctly, I
arrived to play spectator around 4:00 p.m. Crime scene services
had moved away from the body and was processing the crime scene
closer to the waterline."

"Exactly!" Pickering exclaimed as he bounced slightly in his
seat. His eyes were wide with excitement. "Based upon these
pictures as well as your observations of the crime scene services
team at the crime scene, there is no way a member of that team
could have removed the necklace and subsequently planted it in
Carmen's car."

"Overall, I agree," Watson replied with some hesitation. "But let us
play devil's advocate for a moment. Is it possible that a member of
that team could have returned to the body and removed the necklace before Jillian was transported to the coroner's office?"

Pickering paused for a moment to contemplate Watson's question. "It's possible, Adrian. But assume for a moment you might be
right; what is the motive of a member of an evidence collection team
to set up Carmen?"

Watson nodded in understanding as he again leaned back into his
chair. "You think the stronger candidate is one of the state police
detectives."

"I do," Timothy announced loudly before regaining his composure.
"Didn't you tell me that at least one of the detectives was hovering
over the body when you arrived?"

"I remember both Troopers Pullo and Eriksen being around the body when I got there," Watson quickly answered.

Timothy slid forward in his chair and eyed Watson with anticipation. "Did you see either one of them get really close to Jillian's body?"

The investigator contemplated for a moment and then looked up at Pickering in surprise. "Eriksen! Jesus Tim, I remember that he was crouched down by the body just before Donovan arrived."

"Victoria Donovan was at the crime scene?" the professor asked with a tone of curiosity.

Adrian sat up straight in his chair. After regaining his composure, he slapped his desk once and leaned toward his counterpart. "Jesus H. Christ! I just remembered, Tim. Fucking Victoria Donovan took pictures of the body with her cell phone shortly after she arrived."

"Holy shit," Pickering replied with a tone of surprise.

"If we can get our hands on the pictures on Donovan's phone, and they show the necklace is missing, then we pretty much know who took the necklace," Watson announced.

"Holy shit," Timothy repeated, but this time the tone of his voice was low and ominous.

"Yes," Watson responded as he tried desperately to remain calm, "holy shit. This is potentially a big game-changer."

"We're going to need to file a motion with the court tomorrow to get access to her phone," Pickering noted.

"I agree," Watson asked as he stood up from his chair and walked back toward his office window. "But tell me, Tim; if we're going to go down this road, we need to ask ourselves why a Massachusetts state trooper would try to set Carmen up."

"I've been thinking the same thing myself ever since I last visited Carmen at the jail," Pickering answered as he watched Adrian look out the window. "I think the person responsible for Jillian's death is this other boyfriend we've heard about."

"So do I," Watson replied as he turned and looked intently at the attorney. "But why would the police cover for him?"

"The only scenario I can think of right now is that the real killer is either related to a police officer or works for the police," Timothy speculated.

The investigator furrowed his brow and rubbed his chin with his right hand as he contemplated his partner's last statement. "Do you mean like a dispatcher?"

"No. No," the professor responded as he waved his hands in disagreement. "I mean an informant. The person who killed Jillian likely disposed of the body and then went to the police for help. He was probably an extremely valuable rat who has helped law enforcement investigations in the past."

Adrian stared at Timothy for a moment before responding. He sounded very reluctant. "I don't know, Tim. I agree someone inside law enforcement is setting Carmen up, but I am not convinced the person is an informant. I'm leaning toward the theory that the suspect is related to a police officer."

Pickering nodded in understanding. "Honestly, I think we'll get a better sense of who this person is after we speak to Jillian's best friend."

"You think she'll be helpful?" Watson asked as he walked back to his desk.

"I sure as hell hope so," Pickering conceded. "What time are we meeting with her?"

"Tomorrow afternoon at two o'clock at her mother's home in Salem," Watson replied as he checked his notes to confirm the meeting.

"Good. Once we're out of court, we can drive down," Timothy announced.

"Tell me, professor, what's the plan of attack when Carmen appears before the judge tomorrow morning?" Watson inquired. He was curious how the attorney planned to handle Carmen's hearing.

The attorney smiled and then leaned forward in his chair. "We pick our fights carefully."

"How?" Watson asked, somewhat surprised at Pickering's response.

"We're not going to reveal what we know about the necklace or the fact that it was planted in Carmen's car. I do not want to tip the government off about what we're up to. We're only going to focus on the fingerprint report taken and Donovan's cell phone pictures."

"No motion to dismiss for prosecutorial misconduct?" Adrian asked with a hint of disappointment. Secretly, he was hoping Pickering would toss a grenade into the room and pursue misconduct charges against Victoria Donovan.

Timothy detected the investigator's disappointment. "It's too soon, Adrian. I want to know more about this second boyfriend before we march down the road to a motion to dismiss."

Adrian nodded in understanding and smiled slightly. Pickering continued. "Adrian, I'm going to need you to write up a report regarding your interview with Emily and a separate report that you saw Donovan taking pictures of the body at the crime scene. I'll want to present both to the judge tomorrow morning."

The investigator spun in his chair toward his computer and began to type. A moment later, a nearby printer whirred and spit out a two-page report of Emily's interview. He handed it to Pickering before assuring him that the second report would be emailed to the attorney by the end of the day.

Timothy nodded in appreciation and placed the document in his briefcase.

"So, we have a plan of attack?" Watson asked as he watched the attorney thumb through the Vaughn file.

"We do. Are you ready?"

"I am, but are you?" Adrian replied with a tone of seriousness.

Pickering stopped perusing through his file and looked up at the investigator. He appeared confused by Watson's question. "Of course, I'm ready. Why wouldn't I?"

"I'm not just talking about tomorrow, Tim," Adrian replied softly as he studied his friend. "I need to know if you're in this for the long haul. This fight is about to get real."

"Of course, I am," Timothy hesitantly replied. The attorney knew where the conversation was possibly going.

"Are you sure?" Adrian quickly replied as he stood up, walked behind his chair, and leaned forward onto it. "We both know the circumstances behind how you became a college professor. Representing a student as a favor at an arraignment and during the early stages of pre-trial is one thing. We are about to go into unchartered waters and will be playing with a person's life. You think you can handle that?"

"I'm pretty sure I can, Adrian," Pickering replied as he felt the blood rush to his cheeks.

"Really, Tim?" Adrian asked again. "We are about to accuse the Essex County District Attorney's office and the Massachusetts State Police of misconduct and framing your client. I don't want to find out two weeks from now that you're had a complete relapse and are a babbling hot mess."

Pickering boiled with silent anger and struggled to keep his temper in check. He contemplated with himself whether he would be up for the task. After a moment of reflection, he gazed directly at Watson. "You don't have to worry, Adrian; my head's in the game."

"And what about your home life?" Adrian quickly countered. "Are you still occupying the Essex Street Inn, or have your squared things with your bride? I need to know because I don't need Elizabeth shutting us down."

Timothy paused a second time and clenched his jaw before quickly relaxing it. "I'm back home."

"Where are you sleeping?" Adrian pressed.

"On the couch," Pickering admitted awkwardly.

"You've graduated to the couch. Congratulations," Watson replied sarcastically as he eyed the attorney carefully. "I mean it, Tim. I need your head in the game before we go down this road."

"I'm in the game," Pickering replied with exasperation.

Watson snorted and then smiled. "Fine, Professor Pickering. I will take your word for it. But if we are going to go after these bastards, we need to go after them hard."

"I'm prepared to do that," Pickering quickly replied to assure Watson.

The investigator studied the attorney in silence before nodding in the affirmative. "Fine, professor. You and I are going to take these motherfuckers down."

TWENTY-TWO

THURSDAY, APRIL 25

Victoria quickly ascended the stairs outside the Haverhill District Court and brushed past several defendants who were waiting on the landing to enter the building. Unlike her last appearance, the media was noticeably absent on this occasion. In fact, the only reporter that was present was the *Star*'s Harriet Jenson. The journalist eagerly waited for the prosecutor near the front entrance. She was armed with a notepad and, upon seeing Donovan, walked quickly over to greet her.

"Good morning, Vicky. Would you care to comment on today's hearing? What do you expect will happen? Anything you could give me? The *Star* wants to make sure the Commonwealth's position is accurately represented," Jenson gushed with a slight hint of desperation in her voice.

Victoria chose not to acknowledge the reporter. Instead, she quickly waved the reporter away and silently entered the courthouse. Harriet watched as the prosecutor glided past the security checkpoint and walked farther into the interior of the building.

The reporter sulked as she watched Victoria advance farther into the courthouse. However, when she looked over her shoulder, she noted Timothy Pickering had arrived and was starting to climb the same courthouse stairs. Harriet studied the attorney and internally debated whether it was worth her time to even speak with him. From her perspective, defense attorneys served no purpose in the criminal justice system other than to get criminals off on technicalities or police error.

Nevertheless, Jenson was desperate for a lead as her editor was pressuring her hard to file an updated story on the Vaughn case. Unfortunately, as the matter worked its way through the courts and the grand jury, very little information trickled her way. She had hoped Victoria would give her an exclusive commentary when the prosecutor arrived this morning, but that attempt had failed.

The reporter swallowed her pride, waited until Pickering reached the landing, and then stepped forward to greet him.

"Good morning, Attorney Pickering. Any comment on today's hearing?" she cheerfully stated, hoping to disarm him. She knew Pickering was generally a very friendly and likable man, and she hoped to capitalize on that characteristic to secure valuable information from him.

"No, Harriet, I don't," Pickering replied somewhat coldly as he walked past her.

Surprisingly, Jenson blocked Timothy's path, looked him straight in the eyes, and spoke in a softened voice. "Tim, if your guy has a story to tell, I can help present it."

Pickering could sense the nervousness in her voice. It was clear the government had leaked all it had intended to, and Harriet could only keep regurgitating police reports as news stories for so long. She needed new information and perhaps a new angle on the case. For a brief, fleeting moment, he felt sorry for Jenson. However, the sympathy quickly disappeared as Pickering recounted the dozen or more articles published by the *Star* over the past three weeks that focused on Carmen's ethnicity and his overwhelming guilt. He looked over at the reporter carefully and answered her question in an equally low tone.

"Harriet, anything I have to say about my client's case will be said in court."

"Tim, there must be something you can tell me," she begged.

Pickering smiled and turned away from her. As he started to enter the courthouse, he suddenly stopped and looked back at the reporter. "After everything you and the *Star* have said about my client, you want me to help you out? Screw you."

He heard the reporter mutter loudly and curse under her breath as he entered the building, passed through the security checkpoint, and walked directly to courtroom two. He glided down the aisle between the gallery seats and entered the enclosed bar area where only attorneys and law enforcement were permitted to enter. He looked around the courtroom as he took off his raincoat coat, folded it, and placed it onto an old metal chair that was probably twice his age. He noticed Victoria Donovan was already carefully reviewing her case file while seated at the prosecutor's table.

Pickering withdrew his own file from his briefcase and started to walk over to her. Located just inside the file jacket were two motions he had prepared for today's hearing. The first was a motion asking the court to compel the Essex District Attorney's office to disclose all test results generated from the examination of the outlining how he and his investigator had discovered the government had suppressed the information. The second motion was a request to order Victoria Donovan to turn over all images that were taken at the crime scene currently stored on her phone. In support of that motion, he had attached an affidavit from Adrian Watson describing what he observed when the police were processing the crime scene the day Jillian's body was recovered.

As he walked toward the prosecutor, Victoria spun in in her chair, smiled warmly, and stood up to greet Pickering. After the exchange of a few small pleasantries, she retrieved a large manila envelope and handed it to him.

"What's this?" he asked.

"Fingerprint test results from the Massachusetts crime lab," Victoria announced confidently. "I was just made aware of their existence two days ago, and I wanted to get the information to you immediately. A sole fingerprint was recovered from the duct tape wrapped around Jillian's body. It was tested, and it came back inconclusive. Unfortunately, nobody from the state police bothered to tell my office. I apologize this was not sent to you earlier."

You are a lying bitch. If you only knew what I know, Pickering thought to himself as he took the envelope from her and thanked her.

"Is there anything else you need in the way of preliminary discovery?" Donovan asked coyly.

He opened his file and stared at the two discovery motions. He desperately wanted to hand over to her the first motion alleging the suppression of fingerprint evidence, but he recognized that now it would be fruitless. Instead, he withdrew the second motion seeking the crime scene photographs and handed it to her.

"My investigator tells me that he was present at the crime scene when you arrived," Pickering stated matter-of-factly. "Surprisingly, Adrian Watson lives about a block away and was playing spectator. As his affidavit states, Mr. Watson saw you taking pictures of Jillian's body with your cell phone. I want those pictures, Victoria."

Victoria froze in shock as her mind raced and she attempted to formulate a response to Pickering's announcement. She had forgotten about the images and chastised herself for not erasing them when she had the chance. "I'm sorry," she stammered. "Why do you need those images?"

Timothy smiled thinly. "These were images taken by you while at the crime scene. You were acting in your official capacity as a government official. I don't care if the images were taken on your personal phone or not; they are discoverable, and I'm entitled to them."

Victoria thumbed through his motion and tried to deduce what Pickering was up to. "Fine, but why, Tim? You have the images from crime scene services. Why do you need my pictures?"

"Vicky, I am entitled to the pictures under the rules of discovery, plain and simple. But if you must know, I want to make sure the crime scene was properly processed," Pickering quickly snapped as he stared at her knowingly.

The hairs on the back of Victoria's neck stood up. Had someone from her office talked to Pickering? Was he aware that there was a concern that Trooper Eriksen had possibly tainted the crime scene?

She signaled for him to wait, retrieved her phone, stepped away from the prosecution table, and started to thumb through images that included selfies, food, and sunsets. After a moment, she located the six images she took at the crime scene in Merrimac over a month ago. She looked up at Pickering, gestured she was still going through her phone, and then went back to examining each of the photos.

Donovan carefully examined each image, her thumb hovering over the delete button, as she tried to deduce if any of the images contained possible hints or suggestions of impropriety. From her initial cursory review, there appeared to be nothing of concern. Several feet away, Pickering started to grow impatient.

"Vicky, I'm not asking for a forensic analysis of your phone," he snapped. "I am only asking for the images you took at the crime scene. I do not know what you're thinking right now, but I want you to know that I can see you're examining the images that I want. Are you going to turn the pictures over to me, or are we going to argue about this when Judge Williams comes out onto the bench?"

The prosecutor seethed, realizing there was no way she could selectively choose which images she could turn over to Pickering. However, she decided she was going to buy more time so she could carefully review the images one last time. She smiled slightly and nodded in deference to Pickering. "Of course, I am more than happy to turn these images over to you. I can have my office download them off my phone, burn them onto a CD, and have it sent to you no later than tomorrow afternoon."

"No," Pickering replied as he waived his right hand in protest. "Your phone can send emails, can't it? I would prefer it if you sent the images directly from your phone. I would like to review these images with my client and investigator later today if possible."

"I'd prefer to send it via CD," Donovan quickly replied, her voice rising with anger.

Pickering eyed the prosecutor suspiciously for a moment before continuing. "The district attorney's office here has the ability to transfer the images from your phone onto a CD or a thumb drive. Let us go downstairs and do it right now."

"I would love to, Attorney Pickering, but unfortunately, you'll have to provide the CD or thumb drive, and I'm not sure if you have either right now," Donovan quipped.

Timothy could sense she was stalling. He knew it was a common tactic amongst Essex County prosecutors, particularly those assigned to the Lawrence and Haverhill District Courts, to refuse to copy discovery unless the defense attorney provided a CD or thumb drive ahead of time. Fortunately, he was prepared. Pickering withdrew from his suit coat jacket a brand-new thumb drive and handed it to Victoria. She sighed in frustration as she realized he had completely outmaneuvered her and gestured to Pickering to follow her down to the district attorney's office in the basement.

Fifteen minutes later, he was in possession of the six images from her phone.

The hearing before Judge Williams that followed was rather uneventful and brief. To preserve the record, the professor filed with the court a copy of his discovery motion seeking the cell phone images. However, he also reported to the court that Assistant District Attorney Donovan had already complied with his request and had turned the images over to him.

In turn, Victoria reported to the judge that she had started to present the matter to a grand jury and expected an indictment to be handed down within the next two weeks. As a result, both attorneys agree to continue the case for thirty days in anticipation of the coming indictment.

At the conclusion of the hearing, Attorney Donovan watched as Pickering whispered into his client's ear and then held up the thumb drive in triumph. She fumed over the fact that Pickering had completely outmaneuvered her and was able to get his hands on the pictures before she could have appropriately discarded them. Once again, her mind repeatedly reviewed the possible scenarios as to why he genuinely wanted the images so quickly. Each possible outcome pointed to the same conclusion: he believed the crime scene was tainted and was going to use the pictures to significantly damage her case.

After Pickering conferred with Carmen in the holding dock, he packed up his belongings, put on his coat, and exited the courtroom. He immediately walked out of the building, down the front stairs, and crossed the street to where his vehicle was parked. He climbed into the driver's seat, withdrew his laptop from his briefcase, and inserted the thumb drive into the device. He anxiously awaited as it loaded and then launched the images onto the laptop screen. Timothy studied the images one by one, zooming in on each image and then zooming out. The first five pictures were somewhat unremarkable and of mixed quality. The first displayed Jillian's body as viewed from the left side. The next two pictures were taken from the right. Two more were taken from the victim's feet, looking toward the victim's head. When Pickering reached the last picture, he gasped and then swore out loud. The final image was a close-up image of Jillian's shoulders, neck, and head.

The necklace was missing.

Victoria Donovan watched Pickering from the portico of the Haverhill District Court. After he put his laptop back into his briefcase and drove away, she retrieved her cell phone, dialed a number, and listened as the phone rang. Moments later, Trooper Eriksen's voice could be heard on the other end.

"Hey there!" Eriksen cheerfully exclaimed. "How did it go in court today?"

"Don't worry about that. I have a job for you," she angrily announced.

TWENTY-THREE

THURSDAY, APRIL 25

The Point Neighborhood District, also known as Stage Point, is a residential area located just south of downtown Salem, Massachusetts. A massive fire swept through the neighborhood in 1914, and shortly thereafter, the area was the target of a major redevelopment effort. With many of the multiunit residential buildings constructed in just under three years, the key architectural feature of the area is tightly packed yet cohesive multifamily dwellings.

Since the eighties, the neighborhood has witnessed a substantial rise in criminal activity, including gang enterprises, drug distribution, crimes of violence, and sexual assaults. Recently, with the arrival of the opioid epidemic in Salem, the Point has also witnessed a significant increase in property-related crimes as well as deaths because of narcotic overdoses.

Nevertheless, the residents of the Point, especially the Dominican and Puerto Rican residents, rallied together to fight back and reclaim their neighborhood. Block by block the residents struggled to drive out criminal elements. Neighborhood watches roamed the streets, police officers saturated the neighborhood, and local nonprofit organizations collaborated with residents to provide educational and economic opportunities to at-risk youths and adults.

In short, the Point had the potential of becoming a symbol of revitalization for Salem, but it also had an exceptionally long way to go.

Timothy Pickering parked his car in a lot adjacent to the Palmer's Cove playground and exited the vehicle. Adrian was already outside of his vehicle and leaning up against the back bumper. The investigator looked up Congress Street toward several rundown public housing buildings, took a long gulp of coffee from a stainless-steel mug, and then looked back over toward the attorney.

"How did court go this morning?"

"Better than expected. Donovan gave me the pictures off her phone," Pickering replied with a wide grin.

"Do you think she gave you all of the photos, or do you think she hid a few from you?" Adrian inquired.

"Doesn't matter. I got the picture I needed," Timothy proudly announced as he held up the thumb drive.

"Oh?" Watson replied with a tone of surprise. "How the hell did you pull that off?"

"Never mind," Pickering replied with a dismissal of Watson's question. "We now know who tampered with Jillian's body at the crime scene and removed the necklace."

"Who?" the investigator demanded, his curiosity piqued.

"It's either Trooper Pullo or Trooper Eriksen," the attorney announced as he placed the thumb drive back in his pocket. "My money is on Eriksen."

"Because he allegedly found the necklace in Carmen's trunk?" Arian instinctively replied.

"Because he found it in Carmen's trunk," Pickering repeated.

Watson contemplated in silence for a moment before looking over at Pickering. "You have any ideas or thoughts as to *why* one of these guys is setting up Carmen? I mean, Carmen doesn't know either of these troopers."

"I haven't forgotten. I keep going back and forth in my mind and the only plausible explanation I can come up with is they're either covering for a valuable informant or a family member," the professor retorted. "I can't fathom any other plausible explanation."

"Well," Adrian replied, "hopefully, Sandy Minerva can fill in the blanks for us."

"Where does she live?" Pickering asked as he looked around, trying to find the young woman's address.

Watson tapped the attorney on the shoulder and then pointed toward a white two-family structure diagonally across from where they were standing. The building was dirty, rundown, and in desperate need of a fresh coat of paint. A pair of porches were stacked one above the other on the right side of the building. The first-floor porch was cluttered with several patio chairs, two umbrellas, and a broken glass table. The second-floor deck was not much better. Adjacent to the building was a small grassy field that was littered with used condoms, needles, and cigarette butts. Several rundown cars were parked along the street in front of the structure. A fat Dominican man wearing a white tank top sat on the gray cement stairway that led up to the front entrance. He occasionally puffed on his e-cigarette as he studied Pickering and Watson.

"You bring your gun, Adrian?" the attorney asked cautiously as he watched the man on the porch.

"Of course not. I thought you brought yours," the investigator replied with a tone of disappointment.

"Wonderful., Timothy announced. "If this guy gives us a hard time, I'll be waiting in the car."

"I appreciate the support, Professor Pickering," Adrian softly retorted.

The pair started to walk across the street toward the two-family building. As they closed in on the building, the fat Dominican stood up and quickly waddled inside. Pickering watched as the man re-emerged on the second-floor porch, leaned against the railing, and looked down at the two men.

As they ascended the stairs to the main entrance, Watson noticed a clutter of mailboxes and concluded that the building was not a two-family but rather a multi-unit building that housed eight separate apartments. Adrian was not surprised. Having grown up in Lawrence, it was not uncommon for landlords to try and cram as many apartments as possible into small, post–Civil War structures to maximize profit.

"Which apartment?" Timothy asked.

"First-floor apartment on the left," Adrian responded as he studied the various names on the mailboxes.

The pair walked through the front door, past a stairwell that led to the second floor, and continued to walk down a common hallway toward an apartment door located on the left-hand side. Timothy knocked firmly on the door three times and then stepped back. Adrian looked farther down the hallway and waved to a thin, middle-aged Hispanic woman who had opened her apartment door and peered out at the two men.

"What do you want?" the woman demanded in broken English.

"Nothing, ma'am," Watson replied. "We're here to see Sandy Minerva. She's expecting us."

"I know," the woman answered curtly as she stepped into the hallway. "She lives with me. I'm her aunt."

Pickering and Watson looked at each other and shrugged at their mistake of knocking on the wrong door. Afterward, the pair walked toward the woman, who had stepped back into her apartment. The two men followed her inside and found themselves in a cluttered living room. Most of the furniture appeared to be beaten and torn, while images of Jesus Christ and smoke stains decorated the walls. An older Hispanic man snored loudly as he slept in a chair adjacent to a bay window. To their right was the kitchen that was in desperate need of renovation.

Seated at a table in the center of the kitchen was a young woman who was no more than nineteen years old. She was fair-skinned with black curly hair and big brown eyes. She studied Pickering and Watson carefully. Standing behind her with her arms folded and a scowl on her face was the aunt.

"Sandy Minerva?" Adrian asked with a slightly authoritative tone.

"Yes," she replied somewhat nervously.

"I'm sorry, I didn't catch your name," Pickering said to Sandy's aunt.

"I'm Michely Melendez," the woman coldly replied before sitting down next to her niece. "What's this about? Sandy tells me you want to talk to her about a murder. She had nothing to do with no murder."

"We never said she did," Adrian responded with a calm, soft tone. "Carmen Vaughn told us that Sandy was Jillian's best friend. We were hoping she could answer some questions we have about Jillian and her other boyfriend."

"Carmen's a fucking idiot," Michely hissed as she jabbed a finger toward Watson. "Why should my niece stick out her neck to help that *cabron*?"

Pickering smirked. "Because that *cabron* might be innocent."

She eyed Pickering in silence for a moment before muttering a string of curses toward him in Spanish. Afterward, she turned her attention toward Sandy and spoke.

"*No quiero que hables con estos dos imbéciles. Recuerda lo que te dijo el oficial de policía, tenemos que mantener la boca cerrada sobre Jillian!*" Michely shouted in Spanish.

Watson quickly stepped farther into the kitchen and interjected himself into the conversation. "*¿Qué quieres decir con que el oficial de policía te dijo que mantuvieras la boca cerrada?*"

Both women looked over at the black investigator with shock. Pickering walked toward his investigator and stood next to him. "Since when did you start speaking Spanish?" the attorney asked incredulously.

"When you grow up in Lawrence, you learn a few things."

"Apparently," Pickering replied as he shook his head with a sense of mock surprise. He looked over at the two women and continued his conversation with his investigator. "Tell me, Mr. Watson. What was the gist of the conversation you so politely interrupted?"

"Aunt Michely doesn't want Sandy to speak with us," Watson

announced. "It seems that a police officer visited these two women and ordered both to keep their mouths shut regarding Jillian. Oh, and she also thinks we're fucking morons."

"Well, she's right on that point," Timothy quipped as he walked toward the kitchen table, pulled back a chair, and sat down. Adrian followed. "Tell me, ladies; what department was this police officer from? Salem?"

"I don't know," Michely replied with exasperation. "I guess, sure, it was Salem."

"No, no. It wasn't," Sandy corrected her before looking over the two men. "He was a state trooper."

"Sandy! Do you want that cop coming back to visit us?" Michely warned with an ominous tone in her voice.

"Fuck that guy!" Sandy retorted. "I've been quiet long enough, and I'm not going to let that pig threaten me or tell me what I can and can't do."

Pickering found Sandy's answer somewhat troubling. He coughed nervously and then leaned forward in his chair. "Very well then, Sandy. Let us start with the basics so we can figure out what trooper paid you a visit. Do you remember what the trooper looked like?"

"Of course, I do; he was Jillian's boyfriend," Sandy replied with a tone of exasperation in her voice. "I met him at least three or four times."

"What?" Adrian exclaimed. "Are you telling us Jillian was dating a trooper? A Massachusetts state trooper?"

"Yes, he told me when I first met him that he was a Massachusetts trooper," Sandy calmly announced as she glanced over toward her aunt, who was shaking her head in disgust and gesturing for her niece to stop talking.

"What's his name?" the investigator demanded with a tone of disbelief.

"Brian Eriksen," she replied with disgust.

Pickering felt a chill run down his spine. He stumbled backward out of his chair, stood up straight, and stared blankly at Sandy.

Meanwhile, Adrian sat in stunned silence, attempting to wrap his head around this unexpected development. After a few moments, Watson looked over toward his counterpart, nodded, and opened his notepad to start scribbling a series of notes. Once he finished, he looked up at Sandy.

"Do you know how they met?" Adrian asked.

"I do. Jillian met Brian in a bar in Lawrence last September," Sandy calmly replied. "I think it was called the Claddagh. She told me that she and her roommates would often go to this place because they rarely checked IDs. She also said it was a place that cops hung out at after hours to drink and pick up younger women from Merrimack College."

"The irony," Watson quipped out loud. After some delay, Pickering nodded in agreement.

"When did you first meet this trooper?" the investigator inquired.

"Sometime last fall, Jillian brought him to Salem for Haunted Happenings. If I had to guess, I would say I met him toward the end of October."

"What was your impression of him?" Adrian asked with curiosity.

"He was an asshole," she simply stated.

"How so?" Pickering inquired, still stunned by Sandy's revelation.

"From the first time I met him, he was always acting like a macho jerk," she replied. "Worse, he always treated Jillian like crap. He was mean to her, he'd yell at her, he'd threaten her, he would—"

"Wait," Adrian interrupted, "how exactly did he threaten her?"

"Jillian told me he would often threaten to kick her ass. On a few occasions, she told me Brian threatened to kill her."

"Did you ever hear Brian threaten Jillian?" Pickering asked quietly.

"Once," Sandy replied nervously. "They had a fight in front of me. He told her he was going to slap the bitch out of her, and he could get away with it because he was a Massachusetts state trooper."

"Jesus Christ," Watson muttered.

"You ever see him hit her?" Pickering asked.

"Yes," Sandy replied with a shaky voice. Her hand trembled as she raised it to her face and wiped a tear away from her right eye. "The same argument where he threatened her, I also saw him hit her. He slapped her so hard across the face that she spun around and fell to the ground."

Adrian looked at her for a moment and then spoke. "What did you do when you saw this?"

"He was just standing over her as she was lying on the ground crying. He then started to crouch down and looked as if he was going to start beating her. So, I shoved him off her and told him I was going to call 911."

"What was his reaction?" the lawyer asked.

"He just laughed," she replied with a sniffle.

"Did you ever see him hit Jillian again?" Watson inquired.

"No. No," Sandy stated. "But I often saw bruises on Jillian's throat, shoulders, arms, and face. The son of a bitch was definitely beating her," Sandy replied as tears streamed down her cheek.

"Why didn't she dump his ass?" the investigator asked in a follow-up.

"She often tried," she announced. "But she also felt trapped. Jillian told me that Eriksen threatened to burn her family's house down if they ever broke up."

"What was the attraction to this guy?" Pickering asked with a sense of morbid curiosity.

"Jillian liked the attention of dating a cop," Sandy answered softly as she avoided eye contact with Watson and Pickering.

"She ever hit him?" Timothy asked.

"Oh yeah," the young woman replied. "She found out the asshole had another girlfriend on the side. A lawyer."

"Interesting," Watson noted. "Did she ever tell you who this lawyer was or where she worked?"

"No," Sandy conceded.

"How did she attack him?" Adrian asked.

"She told me that she was spending the night at his place in Haverhill when she came across some of the other woman's belongings. She punched him, threw a beer bottle at him, and slashed his tires when she left."

Watson cursed under his breath and then looked up from his notes. "Sounds like Jillian had a bit of a temper."

"She did. It was always drama with this girl," Sandy announced.

"Did she ever try and get a restraining order against Trooper Eriksen?" Pickering inquired.

"Really?" Sandy replied, annoyed with the foolish question. "What court would issue a restraining order against a Massachusetts cop? Besides, she said she didn't want to ruin his career."

"Did her parents even know about Trooper Eriksen?" Adrian asked.

"I'm not sure," she replied. "They may have met him, but I can't be certain."

"So, how did Carmen fit into this picture?" the professor queried.

The girl loudly sighed, wiped tears from her eyes, and sighed again. She looked at her aunt and then at Pickering and Watson. "Michely is right. He is a fucking idiot."

"What do you mean?" Watson asked.

"Don't get me wrong. Carmen isn't the nicest person. Although I never saw him hit Jillian, he often lost his temper around her."

"How did Jillian act toward him?" the investigator pressed.

"Jillian would always belittle him and intentionally push his buttons. She told me how she loved to tell Carmen how she was dating someone else just to make him angry."

"I've been told by one of her college roommates that the two were always fighting," the investigator interjected. "Is that what you observed?"

"Yes. A lot," Sandy conceded.

"Did Carmen ever come to you about Jillian's other boyfriend?" Pickering inquired.

"Yes. Twice. On both occasions, I told him what I knew," Sandy explained.

"How did Carmen respond?" the lawyer asked as he studied Sandy carefully, trying to gauge her credibility.

"He was upset," she replied. "He said that he was going to find this other guy so he could kick his ass."

The two men paused for a moment to collect their thoughts and review Watson's notes. Occasionally, they would ask Sandy for clarification or to confirm if a statement had been recorded accurately. Afterward, Pickering resumed questioning.

"Tell me, Sandy," he asked. "When did Trooper Eriksen last pay you a visit?"

"A couple of days after Carmen was arraigned in the Haverhill District Court."

"All right. Has he ever been to your house before?" the lawyer asked.

"No. Honestly, I was surprised to see him."

"You weren't expecting to see him?" Watson asked as he continued to take notes.

"Absolutely not," she replied. "I had just come home from classes at North Shore Community College, and he was waiting for me outside of the building."

"What are you studying?" Pickering casually asked.

"Nursing," Sandy replied.

"Good for you," Pickering responded before asking another question. "So, did he speak?"

"In this very same kitchen," she replied as she tapped the table with her index finger. "He sat where you two are sitting now."

"What did he say?" Watson asked, fearful of what the response would be.

Sandy exhaled loudly and looked at Watson and Pickering with a wild look. "He told my aunt and me that we needed to keep our mouths shut and talk to no one, not even the police, about Jillian's death. Brian also told my aunt that he could make life exceedingly difficult for us. He warned us that if we even thought about talking to anyone about Jillian or his relationship with her, he'd have no problem returning us to the Dominican Republic."

Pickering looked over at Sandy's aunt. She silently nodded in confirmation.

"Holy shit," Watson loudly proclaimed with a hint of disgust. He leaned back in his chair, folded his arms, and looked across the table toward Sandy. He quickly cut to the chase. "Sandy, who do you think killed Jillian?"

She hesitated only for a moment as if to catch her breath. "Brian Eriksen. I had some suspicions that he did something to her when she first disappeared. But I was completely convinced it was him after that asshole paid me a visit and threatened us. That is why I agreed to talk to the two of you. I'm not about to let that bastard get away with this."

"That man is trouble and thinks he can get away with anything," Michely exclaimed as she waved her arms in excitement. "He came into my home and threatened us. That *cabron* said that ICE would pay us a visit if we said anything about his relationship to Jillian."

"Did he come alone or with anyone?" Watson asked.

"Alone. And the visit was at night," Michely replied.

Pickering expected that Sandy or her mother would have provided information on a boyfriend who had remote ties to a law enforcement officer. He never foresaw Sandy pointing the finger at Brian Eriksen. But it all made sense now.

"Did he only visit you once?" the attorney asked.

"Yes, but he called me two more times to remind me to keep my mouth shut or he'd be back to visit me," Sandy stated as her voice shook.

"When did he call you?" Watson inquired.

"The day after the visit and three days ago."

Her aunt slapped the table and began to swear in Spanish. Timothy raised his hand to signal her to stop yelling. "Do you still have the numbers in your cell phone?"

"Of course," Sandy stated calmly. She pulled out her phone from her back pocket, tapped the screen several times, and then handed it over to Adrian. She pointed out the two calls made by Brian. Each lasted a little over a minute. The investigator nodded before taking screenshots of the call logs and forwarding the images to his own phone. He then handed the phone back to the girl and instructed her not to erase the log or destroy the phone.

Pickering was overwhelmed and struggled to comprehend the bombshell that had been dropped into his lap. He rubbed his eyes, shook his head, and reviewed the conversation repeatedly in his mind. Afterward, he looked over at Sandy.

"I have one last question. Do you have any pictures of Jillian and this trooper together?"

"Yes. I have two," she calmly answered.

"Two?" Timothy repeated.

"Two. One from the time I first met him and one from New Year's Eve."

"May I see them?" he asked.

Sandy tapped her phone again, and after some delay, she finally produced the two images. The first was apparently taken at night in downtown Salem during Haunted Happenings. In the image, Trooper Brian Eriksen had his arm around Jillian. The other was a closeup of the couple. Jillian was kissing the trooper on the cheek.

Pickering looked over at Watson and mouthed silently, "What the fuck?" The investigator nodded in understanding.

TWENTY-FOUR

MONDAY, APRIL 29

An informant is any person that provides information about a suspect or a criminal organization to a police officer. The term is typically used within the law enforcement community, where these individuals are officially known as confidential informants or "CIs." Quite frequently, confidential informants provided information to the police in exchange for money, lenient treatment following their own arrest, or simply for the police to overlook their own criminal activities.

Trooper Brian Eriksen was never a fan of confidential informants. He saw them as useless rats who would tell law enforcement officials anything they wanted to hear in exchange for getting out of a jam. Worse, many informants either misled the police or acted as double agents for drug dealers and organized criminal enterprises.

Despite their inherent lack of reliability and questionable motives, Brian Eriksen had his own small network of informants. As he saw it, on the rare occasion, informants could be somewhat useful; especially those individuals who had no pending criminal cases and were willing to provide valuable information in exchange for short money.

Eriksen's most recent operative was recruited in the days before Pickering and Watson visited Sandy Minerva. The trooper knew that Sandy was close with Jillian and that she was the only person who could tie him to the girl's death. He had spoken to Sandy and her aunt once before and had hoped that he had sufficiently conveyed the danger they would be in if they spoke to anyone about his relationship with Jillian. However, Eriksen also knew the reputation of Adrian Watson and knew there was a distinct likelihood that the investigator would eventually locate Sandy and speak with her.

After Trooper Eriksen had visited Sandy and her aunt, he walked upstairs to the second floor and spoke with the fat Dominican tenant who apparently spent his days and nights watching everyone from his porch. After identifying himself as a Massachusetts state trooper, Eriksen told the man that he would give him $500—$250 now and $250 later—for any information regarding individuals who were not from the neighborhood and who visited Sandy or her aunt. From Eriksen's point of view, it was a sound precaution to counter any efforts by Adrian Watson.

More importantly, it was an investment that paid off.

The Monday after Carmen Vaughn's second court appearance, Eriksen received a call from his newly recruited contact. The Dominican described in broken English how two men that matched the descriptions of Timothy Pickering and Adrian Watson arrived at the tenement in separate vehicles. They entered the building together and went directly to Sandy's apartment. According to the informant, the pair remained inside for almost three hours before leaving the building and then conferring briefly in the parking lot across the street. Afterward, the pair left the area.

Eriksen immediately recognized how the dire situation had become. It was more likely than not that Sandy had told the pair everything about his relationship with Jillian Russo. Worse, it was almost certain that the men had come to the correct conclusion that he was Jillian Russo's killer.

Since they first met, Brian Eriksen had known that Jillian Russo had a violent temper and would rarely hesitate to goad him into fights with her. Worse, she was a drunk who could not handle her liquor. Together, the two traits proved to be a dangerous combination.

On the night of her death, Jillian wanted to spend the night with Brian. She left a nightclub in Lawrence and traveled by Uber to Washington Square in Haverhill. However, because she was highly intoxicated, she stumbled around the neighborhood lost until she ended up on Essex Street. Unsure of her exact location, Jillian became frustrated and called Eriksen to come and pick her up, which he reluctantly did. He picked her up in his unmarked cruiser and brought her back to his condominium on Locke Street.

Once at his residence, she went directly to his kitchen and began to drink even more. She consumed several shots of rum and tequila and then started to complain about her high school boyfriend, Carmen Vaughn. At first, Brian feigned interest in her diatribe as he was more interested in getting into her pants than her feelings. He occasionally nodded and pretended to agree with what she said.

Eventually, Jillian became enraged when she realized Eriksen was simply not listening to her. She raised her voice and pointed out to the trooper that she was wasting her life with him. Brian simply shrugged his shoulders and told her to go back to her dorm room in North Andover.

The comment only made her angrier. She looked around the kitchen, picked up a metal ice bucket located on a nearby counter, and hurled it, striking Eriksen on the head.

The trooper touched his head and felt warm blood as it trickled down past his temple. Instinctively, he became enraged. He rushed forward, hauled Jillian off her chair, and slapped her twice across the face. She retaliated by kicking him in the groin and shoving him away from her. Eriksen closed in again and punched her square on the cheek with a closed fist, causing her head to snap back. She wobbled for a moment and then crumpled to the kitchen floor.

As her face began to swell and blood oozed from her lip and nose, she seethed at him and told him the relationship was over. She announced she was going to tell his other girlfriend, Victoria Donovan, about their relationship. Eriksen snorted and told Jillian that the prosecutor already knew about their relationship. Jillian stared coldly at the trooper for several seconds before telling him that she was going to his superiors.

Eriksen at first dismissed her open threat. However, Jillian quickly announced that she would tell Sergeant McCam not only had he repeatedly assaulted her but there was an occasion when he plied her with alcohol and drugs and then proceeded to rape her. She quickly recounted how her best friend Sandy, as well as her college roommates, had seen the injuries and would support her claim. As Eriksen stood there dumbfounded, Jillian sneered and announced that he would lose his job and become nothing more than a glorified mall cop.

Impulsively, Eriksen lunged down toward Jillian and seized her neck with both hands. He lifted her off the ground, slammed her against a kitchen counter, and began to squeeze her throat until the fingers of his right and left hands met. Jillian tried to break free of the grip by pulling at his wrists, but his hands remained firmly locked around her neck. Slowly, her eyes bulged, and she gasped for air.

Eriksen, his face wild with anger, repeatedly cursed at the girl as he choked and physically shook her. Eventually, Jillian released her hold of Eriksen's wrists and began to flail her arms and legs about as she tried to break free of the death grip. When that failed, she desperately punched the trooper in the face, arms, and shoulders. After what seemed like an eternity, her punches became weaker and weaker and then ceased. Jillian tried one last time to call out for help, but her voice was only a mere rasp.

The trooper continued to squeeze until he heard the girl's death rattle and then slowly let go. Jillian Russo was dead.

Eriksen disposed of the body early the next morning. He retrieved a tarp and some duct tape from a nearby room he had been painting. He wrapped her body up, carried her down to his cruiser, tossed her in the backseat, and then transported her to the Comeau Bridge located near the downtown section of Haverhill. In the predawn darkness, he tossed Jillian's body over the iron railing and watched as she sank into the depths of the Merrimack River.

Almost immediately, he began to formulate a plan to frame Carmen Vaughn. The trooper recognized that a jealous boyfriend who had had previous legal issues with Jillian would be the perfect suspect. Even Victoria Donovan agreed with the plan when he confessed to her later that day about what he had done.

But Eriksen never expected Pickering and Watson—especially

Watson—to get involved with this case. He expected that Vaughn would have received a court-appointed attorney who would provide a less-than-adequate defense and a hack investigator who would simply go through the motions. Instead, Pickering and Watson began to resemble a pack of wolves slowly circling their prey as they came closer and closer to uncovering the truth that he was the one responsible for Jillian's death.

When the trooper became aware that they had visited Sandy, he decided that it was time to cut the pair off at the knees. After speaking with his informant, Eriksen discovered that the girl would be home alone first thing in the morning because her aunt worked an overnight shift at Salem Hospital. He was also told that Sandy typically left for school around seven in the morning so she could go to the North Shore Community College library and study.

Thus, the same morning that his informant called him, Eriksen found himself standing in the common hallway outside of Sandy's apartment. He greeted her with a smile as the front apartment door swung open, and Sandy tried to exit to go to school. She looked up and recoiled in horror when she saw the trooper. She started to walk back into her apartment and slam the door so he could not enter. Eriksen easily pushed past the door and punched Sandy squarely on the nose. Her head bobbled back and then forward. He punched her again and watched as she tripped backward and spilled onto the couch behind her.

"You want to tell me what you said last week to Attorney Pickering and his investigator, Sandy?" Eriksen hissed.

"Fuck you!" she screamed as loud as she could. Blood poured from her nose down onto her chin, neck, and shirt.

"Yell all you want," Eriksen replied calmly as he unholstered his Smith & Wesson M&P .9 mm pistol. Sandy's eyes grew wide with fear. "Most of the people in this building or asleep, high, or working for me. No one is going to save your ass, Sandy."

"Fuck you!" she repeated as she tried to conceal her fear with a tone of bravado. "I told them everything. I even showed them the pictures I have of you and Jillian together. You are fucking done,

Eriksen. You killed her, and you're fucked!"

"Oh Sandy, if only you had kept your fuckin' spic mouth shut," the trooper replied with a tone of contempt as he brought up his pistol and squeezed the trigger. There was a loud pop followed by Sandy's brains splattering onto the wall behind her. The girl's body crumpled to the ground with a soft thud.

Trooper Eriksen quickly looked around, recovered the spent shell casing that had ejected from his firearm, re-holstered his weapon, and walked out the back door. He convinced himself that Sandy's demise should be enough to persuade the aunt to not only be silent but to get the hell out of town as quickly as possible.

As he walked around outside the building, he stopped to reflect for a moment. The trooper turned around, looked up at the second-floor porch, and went back inside. He quickly ascended a flight of stairs to the second floor. As he stood outside of his informant's apartment, Eriksen thought to himself that with additional investment, his Dominican friend could help lay the groundwork to charge the two men responsible for Sandy's murder: Timothy Pickering and Adrian Watson.

TWENTY-FIVE

The Claddagh Pub was the sole remaining traditional Irish bar in Lawrence and was located directly across from the Merrimack River at the intersection of Route 114 and Canal Street. The establishment occupied the former location of RJ McCartney's, a clothing store that once catered to the white residents of Lawrence and the surrounding communities of Andover, North Andover, and Methuen. For the few Irish residents that still lived in the city, the Claddagh served as a reminder of a time when their ancestors controlled the cultural, political, and criminal landscapes of the city.

The outside facade of the pub was easily recognizable from its Guinness beer advertisements and large swaths of overgrown vines. Adjacent to the main entrance was a rundown patio that was enclosed by a black rod iron fence and metal awning. The area provided a haven for those customers who did not mind being penned up like hogs while they sucked on vape pens and cigarettes.

Surrounding the Claddagh were several rundown mills, deteriorating parking lots, vacant buildings, and the Lawrence District Court. Ironically, the pub catered to all those that either visited or worked inside the courthouse. In fact, it was quite common on Friday evenings to see criminal defendants, police and probation officers, prosecutors, judges, and defense attorneys all sharing drinks and exchanging pleasantries within the confines of the dark and dirty establishment.

On this evening, Sergeant Dennis McCam sat by himself at a tabletop near the pub's fireplace and was drinking away his troubles. The Claddagh was sparsely attended because it was a weeknight. A bartender quietly conversed with a drunk district court judge in a corner while a tough-minded female waitress navigated from table to table, refilling drinks and taking orders from her few customers.

McCam drained the remaining beer in his glass, waved to the waitress, and signaled that he wanted another refill. After she retrieved his empty mug, he turned his attention back to the Red Sox game that was being broadcast on a television set closest to him. McCam was oblivious to his surroundings, and he never noticed Timothy Pickering until the attorney sat down next to him.

Dennis was not a fan of Pickering. Admittedly, he knew the attorney was a highly effective prosecutor who repeatedly secured convictions and favorable results for the Essex County District Attorney's office. However, the sergeant felt that Timothy was always jockeying for a better position in life. When he left to open his own law practice and represent criminal defendants, the trooper felt he was simply selling his soul for cash. Worse, when Pickering won several cases in quick succession, McCam's resentment and jealousy of the attorney expanded tenfold. When Pickering secured a very favorable result on a very high-profile trial that called into question the sergeant's own investigative techniques and raised the possibility of tainted evidence, any remaining fondness for the attorney quickly disappeared. From that point forward, he held nothing but disgust and contempt for the lawyer.

Now, the son of a bitch had pulled up a seat next to him. McCam intuitively knew that Pickering wanted something on the Vaughn case. He glared at the attorney for a moment, scanned the room to find his waitress, and then looked back to acknowledge him.

"What do you want?" the trooper asked, his voice dripping with contempt.

"Can't I pull up a seat next to a former coworker and say hi?" Pickering quipped as he signaled the same waitress to bring him a beer.

"Fuck you," McCam hissed. "Either you tell me what the fuck you want, or you go sit somewhere else."

Pickering glared at the sergeant for a moment. He could easily tell he was stressed and tense. "The Vaughn case getting to you, Dennis? Or are you simply drinking because the Red Sox suck this season?"

The sergeant ignored the sarcastic comment and thanked the waitress as she returned with two beers: one for himself and one for Pickering. He took a sip of his beer and watched as Timothy paid the waitress in cash.

"Don't think I owe you anything simply because you bought me a drink," McCam loudly announced as he jabbed his right index finger at Pickering. "Attorneys buy me drinks all the time, and it gets them shit."

"Of course," Timothy replied as he held up his hands to suggest he did not want an argument.

"What do you want, Tim?" McCam quietly but firmly demanded again. "It's clearly about the Vaughn matter. Make it quick because you're interrupting my personal time."

"It is about the Vaughn case," Pickering conceded as he looked around the room. "And this needs to be off the record for now."

McCam's interest piqued slightly. "Oh?"

Pickering looked around the room again and then leaned toward the trooper. "Listen, I wouldn't bring a bullshit story about the Vaughn case to you to waste your time. My investigator and I have uncovered evidence that you need to see."

"You are wasting my time," McCam quickly retorted as he became annoyed with the direction the conversation had taken. "Shouldn't you be talking to Victoria about this?"

Pickering sighed. "You and I both know Victoria's hands aren't clean in this case. Do you really think I didn't know about the fingerprint results she hid from me?"

McCam softly cursed and then nodded in agreement. "You knew?"

"I did, Dennis. But I also know that one of your investigators on this case, Brian Eriksen, removed evidence from the crime scene and planted it in my client's vehicle."

"Oh, bullshit, Tim. Now you're grasping at straws," McCam argued as he banged his fist against the countertop. He folded his arms across his chest, tightened his jaw, and stared coldly at the attorney.

"Am I?" Pickering replied as he withdrew several pictures from an envelope and dropped them in front of the trooper. "Tell me what you see, sergeant, in these pictures. The first picture shows Jillian Russo's body at the crime scene with her necklace still on her body. The next image was taken a short time after Trooper Eriksen was seen by my investigator hovering over the body."

McCam cursed again. He should have known that somehow Watson would have had a hand in these recent developments. Pickering continued.

"The second picture shows Ms. Russo without the necklace on her body. A little over two weeks later, the same investigator finds her necklace in the trunk of my client's vehicle."

The sergeant seethed as he sat uncomfortably on his stool. He always believed that Eriksen was sloppy and had often questioned why the trooper was assigned to the Massachusetts State Police Detective Unit. But he had strong reservations over whether Eriksen would truly plant evidence on a suspect.

"Come on, Tim. Do you really think Eriksen is going to set up a kid he does not even know? And those images mean nothing to me. For all I know, you photoshopped the necklace out of the picture."

The attorney looked at the trooper incredulously and burst out laughing. "Really, Dennis? You want to play this game? Then allow me to take it up a notch. Did Trooper Eriksen tell you how he was dating the victim?"

This time it was McCam who broke out in laughter. He took a large gulp of his beer and returned his attention to the attorney. "I've got to hand it to you, Pickering. You've got some balls coming to me with a fucking bullshit story like that."

Timothy remained perfectly calm, withdrew the two images provided by Sandy Minerva, and dropped them in front of the sergeant. McCam stopped laughing and became noticeably quiet as he studied the pictures of Trooper Eriksen with the victim.

"Where did you get these?" McCam asked as his face became flushed with embarrassment.

"From Jillian's Russo's best friend, Sandy Minerva."

"Who?" McCam asked in confusion.

"A witness you and your team clearly missed. She recently told my investigator and me that Brian Eriksen was in a relationship with the victim since last October. She also described how your trooper would often get violent with Ms. Russo. I also have a college roommate who will corroborate Sandy's account and describe how she saw Jillian with bruises and red marks on multiple occasions after she was with Eriksen."

McCam leaned forward in his chair and rested his elbows on the countertop. He swore several times, lifted his glass, and took two large gulps of beer. He then slammed the glass back down onto the table and looked away from Pickering.

"What was the best friend's name again?" the sergeant asked with dread.

"Sandy Minerva."

"Fuck," McCam exclaimed as he downed the rest of his drink. Any doubt that Eriksen was neck-deep in this quickly developing mess had all but disappeared. He took a deep breath and looked over at the attorney. "Sandy Minerva is dead."

"What?" Pickering exclaimed, unsure whether McCam was half-joking. "What do you mean, she's dead?"

"She was found late last night by her aunt after she returned from working a double shift. She had a gunshot wound to the head. No shell casings were recovered, but a slug consistent with a .9mm caliber was found."

"What?" the attorney stammered as he attempted to digest what was just revealed to him. "Adrian Watson and I just were with her yesterday!"

"She's dead."

"Holy shit," Timothy muttered as he rested his hands on the top of his head, looked around the room, and then loudly exhaled before he addressed the sergeant once again. "Dennis, listen to me. Sandy told Adrian and me that Eriksen had visited her shortly after Jillian's body washed ashore. She told us that he threatened her and her aunt and said there would be consequences if she told anyone about his relationship with Jillian."

McCam nodded in silence as he reflected upon the revelation. He cursed at himself for missing all the obvious signs. How could he be so stupid to miss this? How did he overlook interviewing Sandy, and worse, how did he miss the tampered evidence? Now he understood why Victoria Donovan was blatantly running interference for her boyfriend. Was it possible she knew what Eriksen did and was covering for him, or was she merely acting on his orders?

As the sergeant opened his mouth to speak, his phone started to ring. He gestured to Pickering to wait and stepped away from the tabletop and into a hallway. From his vantage point, Pickering could see that McCam was in a heated conversation. After five minutes, the trooper walked back over to the table and started to gather his belongings to leave. The attorney quickly objected.

"Dennis, this conversation is not over."

"I know," McCam responded. The sergeant sat back down and looked directly at Timothy. "Why did you come to me with this information?"

"Although we may no longer see eye to eye, at the end of the day, you always do the right thing, Dennis," Pickering conceded.

McCam slowly smiled in understanding. Maybe he had misjudged the lawyer. It was time to roll the dice and find out. "Tim, that was Lieutenant Alexander Desmond who just called me."

"The Essex County Drug Task Force officer?"

"The same one," McCam responded.

"How is he? Is he still busting dealers in Lynn?"

"Lynn and Salem, Tim," the trooper stated cryptically.

"Go on," Pickering responded as he eyed McCam suspiciously.

"He received a call from one of his informants who lives on the floor above Sandy Minerva," the sergeant responded. Pickering noted that the sergeant's face had suddenly lost all its color.

"Son of a bitch," Pickering snapped. "I bet it was that fat fucking Dominican!"

"I don't know," the sergeant replied. "But what I do know is that he told Lieutenant Desmond that another trooper matching Eriksen's description approached him recently and paid him $500 to keep tabs on Sandy Minerva. He was to report back to this trooper if anyone not from the neighborhood paid her a visit."

Pickering's mouth dropped open in shock. McCam continued. "After you and your investigator paid a visit to Sandy yesterday, the informant called the trooper. Of course, the informant told Lieutenant Desmond that he thought he was providing information for an ongoing investigation."

"Clearly, it wasn't Dennis," Pickering loudly interrupted.

"I agree. Please let me finish," McCam snapped.

"Sorry," Pickering replied.

"According to Desmond, the informant was startled from his sleep yesterday morning by a gunshot. Next thing he knows is this trooper—"

"Eriksen," Pickering interrupted.

"Possibly Eriksen," the sergeant rebutted.

"It is Eriksen."

"Fine," McCam declared with a huff. "Eriksen paid the informant a visit. He offered him an additional $2,500 to say that he saw two men break into Sandy Minerva's apartment and then heard a gunshot. He was also to report that he saw the two men flee from the apartment and drive away from the area."

Pickering felt a chill run up his spine. "Let me guess," he stated with a slight quiver in his voice. "The description of the two men matched Adrian Watson and me."

"Possibly. Lieutenant Desmond is trying to get that information now."

"Holy fuck," Pickering replied with a low whistle.

"Yes, holy fuck," McCam repeated. "The only reasons this informant didn't follow through with the request are Eriksen didn't pay him upfront and—"

"Wait," Pickering interrupted again. "You mean to tell me this dumb son of a bitch didn't pay this informant?"

"Nope. He was going to give him the $2,500 after the description of the suspects had been forwarded to law enforcement."

Tim started laughing and continued to do so until the sergeant was able to get the conversation back on track.

"We never said Trooper Eriksen was a bright man," McCam regretfully stated.

"What was the other reason?" Pickering pressed.

"The other reason why the informant got spooked was that he liked Sandy Minerva. He said at the end of the day, she was a good kid. He did not mind keeping tabs on the girl because he believed she would not be harmed. He changed his tune when the trooper appeared at his doorstep. There was no way he was going to lie for a murderer."

Pickering contemplated on the irony of the statement: a confidential informant doing the honorable thing. "Tell me, what happens next?"

Sergeant McCam once again gathered his belongings and stood up from the table. "What happens next is I have to meet with the first assistant and tell him everything you just told me. I also must plan to meet with Desmond's informant tonight to have him view a photo array. Let's just hope he'll identify Eriksen."

The pictures Pickering had shared with McCam were still on the table. The attorney pushed them across to the trooper and then handed him a manila envelope. "Those are your copies. I made them for you to keep."

McCam quickly picked up the images and placed them into the envelope. He thanked the attorney and started to walk away.

"Dennis, what about my client?" Pickering asked as the trooper crossed the room. "I assume you're going to recommend to Walker that he be released."

"One step at a time," the sergeant shouted over his shoulder as he continued toward the front entrance of the pub.

"Dennis, my client!" Pickering snapped as he followed the trooper across the room.

McCam stopped and quickly turned around to face the attorney. "Tim, once I get my ducks in a row, of course, I am going to tell Walker your client needs to be released."

"Thank you," Pickering softly replied with a slight, conciliatory bow.

"And Tim?" McCam continued.

"Yes?"

"Get your family to safety, now," McCam ordered.

Tim was taken slightly aback by the suggestion but quickly realized that not only were he and Adrian in danger, but his family might be as well. He felt his chest tighten and his legs grow weak. He started to breathe shallowly.

McCam instantly recognized what was transpiring and stepped toward the attorney. He saw that Tim was visibly sweating. The sergeant could have taken steps to calm the attorney down. Instead, he chose to emphasize just how serious the situation had become.

"Tim, are you licensed to carry a firearm?" McCam solemnly asked. "Because if you are, I would get your family to a safe place far away from here and then start carrying your gun until this shitshow is under control and over."

TWENTY-SIX

Timothy's vehicle roared and then let out a high-pitched screech as it quickly pulled into the driveway of his Lime Street home. As the car came to an abrupt halt, the attorney forcefully slipped the gear shift into park, swung open the driver's side door, and quickly sprung up from his seat. Pickering raced across the driveway, ascended the stairs of the back entrance, and fumbled with his house keys as he struggled to unlock the door. Once successful, he burst into the mudroom and made a direct line for the kitchen. He tossed his car keys and cell phone onto a nearby gray granite countertop and continued into the dining room. Seeing that no one was there, he retreated into the kitchen and made his way into the living room. The room was dark, and empty and there was nothing but silence throughout the house.

Trooper Brian Eriksen was still at large, and as Sergeant McCam had intimated, it was not outside the realm of possibility for the trooper to retaliate for exposing his criminal deeds. Pickering felt his heart race, and a wave of dread overcame him. A nightmare scenario of Eriksen torturing before executing his two daughters and his wife repeatedly played over and over in his mind. He cursed himself for taking on this case and potentially exposing his family to the wrath of Trooper Eriksen.

Timothy loudly exhaled through his nose and started to walk through the dining room to a flight of stairs that led up to the second floor of the residence. As he reached the foot of the stairs, he heard movement above him. Pickering instinctively bounded two stairs at a time and repeatedly shouted Elizabeth's name. As he approached the landing, his wife stepped out of their bedroom and confronted him.

"Jesus Christ, Tim, are you drunk?" she snapped as she pointed to their daughters' bedrooms located to the left of the stairway. "The girls are studying. There's no need to be that loud."

Pickering seized his wife by the left arm and forcefully guided her to their bedroom. He released her as they entered the room.

"Pack some belongings as well as for the girls. We're leaving now." He announced as he looked about the room momentarily before stepping toward their bed.

Elizabeth studied Timothy and then shook her head in disbelief. "Tim, this is a school night. There's no way we're going to go on a road trip."

Pickering ignored her as she continued to demand an explanation of what was going on. Instead, he knelt beside the bed, reached underneath it, retrieved a flat, black safe, and entered a numeric code into the electronic lock. There was a loud click. Pickering retrieved his black Sig Sauer P229 Legion pistol, slid the fifteen-round ammunition magazine into the base of the grip, and chambered a round. He then stood back up and turned to his wife.

Elizabeth's face had drained of all color, and she was slightly trembling. She struggled to speak and, for a moment, turned away from Timothy. After regaining her composure, she looked back and addressed her husband.

"Tim, what the fuck is going on? Are we in danger?" she whispered so their daughters could not hear the conversation.

He nodded silently in the affirmative before speaking. "Adrian and I were able to establish a Massachusetts state trooper was in a dating relationship with Jillian Russo. He killed her and a key witness."

"Oh shit," Elizabeth blurted out. "Not the girl from Salem."

"Yes. The police now know, and they're looking for the trooper now."

Elizabeth stepped back, and her mouth dropped open in horror. She started pacing around the bedroom as she spoke. "They haven't arrested the trooper? Holy fuck, Tim. Is he coming for us?"

"Sergeant McCam thinks it's either me or Adrian he's going to visit next," he matter-of-factly stated as he loaded two additional magazines with .9 mm rounds.

His wife looked out of the bedroom toward Catherine and Hannah's bedrooms before wiping tears from her eyes. "Then we need to get the girls out of here, Tim, while we can."

"We do. We will tell the girls when we get into the car. In the meantime, tell them to start packing for a few days," Timothy replied.

Elizabeth eyed him momentarily. "Where are we going to hide, Tim?"

"I'm thinking either a hotel in Portsmouth, New Hampshire, or down to Boston."

Elizabeth shook her head in disbelief. She stepped toward her husband and struck him hard across the side of the head. Afterward, she slapped his chest repeatedly with closed fists. "Damn you, Timothy Pickering!" she hissed. "Damn you! I wish you never took this fucking case. You put your wife and children in danger, you fucking prick!"

All her husband could do was nod in agreement. "I know, Elizabeth. I know."

His wife stepped back, sighed loudly, and then walked to the closet. She retrieved a set of luggage and tossed it onto the bed. Afterward, she jabbed at Timothy with her left index finger. "You're going to tell the girls why we're leaving. You're going to explain to them that some psycho cop might be trying to kill their father or even them."

Timothy quickly agreed to Elizabeth's instructions. "Very well. I'll tell the girls to start packing."

"And Tim?" Elizabeth called out as he started down the hallway. "Is this kid really innocent?"

"Yes," Pickering replied nervously as he returned to the bedroom. "He was framed by the cop as well as a prosecutor."

Elizabeth stared at Timothy in silence for a moment in disbelief. Eventually, she took a deep breath and then spoke softly. "Then you also need to tell Catherine and Hannah how their father and Adrian

Watson risked their lives to save an innocent man."

Timothy cocked his head in surprise as he was not expecting the verbal compliment from his irate wife. As Elizabeth started to quickly pack their belongings into a single suitcase, she continued to speak to her husband. "I love you, but I am still furious at you, Timothy Pickering."

"I understand," he replied.

Elizabeth stopped packing and looked over at her husband. "I also know that you and Adrian would not idly stand by if you both had the chance to stop an injustice. The two of you did that with this young man."

"Thank you," Timothy softly answered.

"That said," she continued without acknowledging his reply, "if you ever take on another case without consulting me first, I want you to know I will take that gun, shove it up your ass, and then squeeze the trigger. Am I clear?"

"Yes, Mrs. Pickering."

"Good. I will pack the girls," Elizabeth ordered. "You watch outside to make sure we don't have an unwanted guest waiting for us."

"How much time do you need?" Timothy asked as he started toward the stairwell. He held his pistol down by his side.

"No more than ten minutes," she answered.

Fifteen minutes later, the family raced out the front entrance of their home and ran directly to Elizabeth's SUV. Timothy was in the lead, Catherine guided Hannah, and Elizabeth brought up the rear. Timothy positioned himself at the end of the driveway as his wife and the girls quickly tossed their luggage into the back well of the vehicle and piled inside.

He nervously looked up and down Lime Street for any sign of someone watching him or hiding in the shadows. Convinced there was no one there, Pickering retreated to the vehicle and jumped into the front passenger's seat. He and Elizabeth had agreed as they left the residence that Elizabeth would drive while Tim, if necessary, would defend the family.

As the SUV backed out of the driveway, Tim again looked all around to check his surroundings. His adrenaline was pumping, and his heart was beating hard. He was almost certain that Eriksen was going to step out from behind a nearby building and open fire. As Elizabeth pulled onto Lime Street, Timothy looked behind him and made eye contact with both of his daughters. Hannah's blond hair was disheveled and hid her face. Nevertheless, he could see her blue eyes were wild with fear. Catherine was softly whimpering and playing with her long red curls as she looked nervously out the window.

The vehicle sped down Lime Street and turned left onto Water Street. After passing through the downtown area of Newburyport, Elizabeth navigated a series of back roads before pulling onto the city's main street that led to a nearby interstate highway. Shortly thereafter, the Pickering family was fleeing north to Portsmouth.

TWENTY-SEVEN

WEDNESDAY, MAY 1

Victoria Donovan stood in her office staring out the window toward the North River. In less than a month, her hopes and dreams of using the case of *Commonwealth v. Vaughn* as a springboard to a judicial appointment, as well as more money and power, had come to a crashing halt. The best she could hope, for now, she noted to herself, was to survive in her current dreary job that she solely obtained through her family connections.

However, that was the best-case scenario. She was keenly aware that there was a very real possibility that her role in the entire fiasco surrounding the murder of Jillian Russo could be exposed. Her mind raced as she replayed repeatedly in her mind the potential scenarios she could face, including criminal prosecution, disbarment, and public humiliation. She physically shuddered as she contemplated the potential charges and jail sentences she could face for witness tampering, evidence tampering, and accessory after the fact.

At first, Victoria believed the circumstances surrounding Jillian's death could be controlled and, at the same time, used to help advance her career. She always knew her romantic interest, Trooper Brian Eriksen, had an occasional side dish. It was typical within police culture to cheat on wives or girlfriends with young groupies who were more likely infatuated with the uniform than the person. Jillian Russo appeared to meet that profile. Nevertheless, for some stupid reason, Victoria chose to remain with Brian Eriksen. Maybe it was because she was in love with him, or perhaps it was because her relationship with him gave her some air of credibility amongst the law enforcement community.

When Eriksen came to her Salem waterfront condo the morning after Jillian's murder, she knew she had a choice: report the incident to her superiors or keep her mouth shut and cover for her boyfriend. She foolishly chose the latter. Victoria then used her influence as a high-ranking member of the Essex County District Attorney's office to get the Russo case assigned to herself as soon as her disappearance was reported. It allowed her to keep close tabs on the case and ensure that any exposure to Brian Eriksen was minimized.

When Eriksen informed her that Jillian had a boyfriend who had prior accusations of domestic violence, she found the perfect scapegoat for the crime. It did not help that Carmen Vaughn had gotten into a verbal and very public argument with Jillian in the hours before the girl's death. It was worse that he had followed her after she stormed out of the Lawrence nightclub. Trooper Eriksen quickly agreed to a plan to frame the young man and, together, the two quietly steered the focus of the case toward Carmen Vaughn.

Of course, as the case quickly developed, Victoria reached the conclusion that since she was risking so much for her boyfriend, she was entitled to some form of reward. As a result, she started to lay out the groundwork for a judicial appointment. From her perspective, a high-profile conviction of a violent Hispanic boy by a white Essex County jury would be a slam-dunk and an easy path to the bench. She started reaching out to her father's political connections and even went as far as to complete an application with the Massachusetts Judicial Nominating Committee for a political appointment.

However, Brian Eriksen was an idiot. Despite her repeated instructions, he decided to take an active role in the case and joined the investigative team. Eriksen tried to justify his presence as nothing more than self-preservation. However, slowly but surely, he started to make mistakes. At first, they were minor, like showing up in Merrimac when the body washed ashore and threatening Vaughn's family with deportation. Then they became more problematic when he started engaging in witness intimidation by threatening Sandy

Minerva and her family. However, he crossed into dangerous territory when he removed Jillian's necklace from the crime scene and planted it in the trunk of Carmen's car.

She never expected Timothy Pickering and Adrian Watson to enter the equation. As the case slowly worked its way through the court system, the pair started to sniff down the right paths. In turn, Victoria found herself having to run interference and play hide-the-ball to throw the pair off track. However, when Eriksen called her to tell her that Vaughn's attorney and investigator had visited Ms. Minerva, she knew it was only a matter of time before her role in this entire fiasco would be discovered. When Victoria was alerted of the girl's death the next day, she immediately knew that their fate had been sealed.

As much as she cursed her errors of judgment and her boyfriend's stupidity, she equally cursed the efforts of Pickering and Watson. Because of those two, her career and possibly her freedom were now in jeopardy. She vowed that if she ever got through this mess, she would find a way to make the two men suffer for their actions.

After a few more moments of reflection, Victoria stepped away from the window, composed herself, and exited her office. She turned left and started to walk down the hallway to a conference room where she knew the first assistant and Sergeant McCam were meeting. She stopped at the door, straightened herself out, took a deep breath, and entered the room without knocking.

Walker and McCam were standing across from each other and were engaged in a heated conversation. Both stopped shouting and glanced over at her. Almost immediately, the sergeant snorted in contempt. Walker pointed to Donovan to sit down in a chair.

"I'd ask you why you're barging into this private conversation, but I strongly suspect you already know what we're talking about," the first assistant stated coldly, his eyes carefully studying her.

Victoria was unsure if Walker was making a statement or asking a question, but she did not hesitate to respond. "I do. You're discussing Brian's possible role in the death of Jillian Russo."

Walker looked over at McCam and then back at her. "Interesting. Just so you know, Victoria, Sergeant McCam came to me a few weeks ago and expressed concern that you were playing games on the Vaughn case, including hiding potentially exculpatory evidence. Recently, I was informed that you are in a romantic relationship with Trooper Brian Eriksen, a fact neither you nor anyone in the state police detectives unit bothered to disclose to me when I honored your request and assigned you to this matter."

Victoria shifted in her seat but said nothing to Walker. The first assistant continued, his voice growing angrier.

"Last night, I was informed by the sergeant there is more than enough credible evidence to not only establish that Brian Eriksen was in a dating relationship with Jillian Russo, but that he killed her and tried to frame an innocent Hispanic boy. Even more horrifying, I now have been informed he most likely murdered another teenage girl who possessed incriminating information that could have tied him to Ms. Russo's death. Sergeant McCam believes you were aware of all this and had an active role by either encouraging or concealing Eriksen's crimes. Am I even remotely incorrect about anything I just said, Victoria?"

The first assistant gestured to McCam. The sergeant withdrew a sheet of paper, cleared his throat, and began to recite the Miranda rights to Victoria. Almost immediately, tears began to well up in her eyes, and she started to sniffle. She brought a shaky hand up to her face and wiped her eyes and cheeks. She tried to take deep breaths but struggled for air. Walker reached behind him and retrieved a box of tissues from an end table. He unceremoniously tossed the box at her. Afterward, McCam passed the Miranda rights sheet over to her and asked her to sign it. Surprisingly, she did.

The sergeant eyed her suspiciously and then glanced over to Walker. Victoria cleared her throat, looked down to her lap, and then back up at both men. She then spoke in a shaky voice.

"You are correct about some of what you said, Geoff," she softly stated as tears continued to roll down her cheeks.

"What am I incorrect about?" the first assistant asked.

"Since our dating relationship began, Brian has been physically abusive toward me," she lied as tears continued to stream down her cheeks. "At first, he was verbally abusive, but then he began to hit me."

"Are you fucking kidding me?" McCam demanded. "Geoff, are you going to listen to this bullshit?"

"Sergeant, please. Let us hear what Ms. Donovan has to say," Walker replied as he gestured for the sergeant to keep taking notes. "Go on."

"I always knew Eriksen had a temper. Hell, I know of three women he dated that he routinely smacked around. However, I thought he would be different with me."

"You have to be kidding me," McCam muttered under his breath as he continued to take notes. Walker glared at him for a moment before signaling Victoria to continue.

"He would often beat me, but never on the face. He almost always struck me in the chest, stomach, and groin. He struck me so hard one time he cracked a rib," Victoria announced, knowing the very public injury was the result of her slipping on motor oil in her driveway after a morning jog. "When I asked to be assigned to the case, I was unaware of Brian's role in her death and planned to disclose my relationship with the office, court, and defense. However, around the time her body washed ashore, I discovered he was in a dating relationship with Jillian Russo."

"How?" the first assistant asked.

"He slept over at my condo one evening. The next morning, while he was in the shower, I was on his phone looking at his images. I came across two pictures of Brian with Jillian. One was of the couple together at a bar, the other was at a cookout at her parents' house," she lied. "I confronted him about it."

"And what happened next?"

Victoria started to sob uncontrollably. "He retrieved his service weapon, chambered a round, and forced the barrel into my mouth. He swore he would blow my head off if I ever said anything to anyone."

"He put his service weapon in your mouth?" McCam asked incredulously.

Victoria sniffed loudly and then shook her head in the affirmative. Afterward, she then opened her mouth, pulled her cheek back with a finger, and pointed to a pair of teeth she had chipped when she played soccer in college. "When he forced the gun into my mouth, he chipped two of the teeth."

Walker's tone unexpectedly changed from one of anger and disgust to concern. He leaned forward in his chair and addressed his prosecutor. "Victoria, why didn't you come to us earlier?"

Victoria shuddered and silently sobbed for a moment before answering the question. "He was always around me. At work, at home, everywhere. He was constantly reminding me that if I said anything about Jillian, he would bury my body in a place where no one would find it. He also bragged to me that he was a respected Massachusetts trooper, and no one would believe he was responsible for her death. I felt I had no one I could go to because he was always watching me."

McCam rolled his eyes in disgust. He found Victoria's story completely unbelievable. However, he kept his mouth shut as it was the first assistant who was driving the bus. Unfortunately, Geoff Walker seemed far more sympathetic.

"All right, Vicky. What about the exculpatory evidence? Why did you sit on the fingerprints?" Walker asked.

"He ordered me to," she lied as she looked directly into Geoff's eyes. "When he learned there was a fingerprint recovered off of the duct tape, he instructed me to hide it from Attorney Pickering."

"Did he say what would happen if you revealed the prints?"

"He threatened he would beat the shit out of me and nail my cat to the front door of my parents' house."

"But you eventually disclosed the prints to Attorney Pickering?" McCam asked, interrupting Walker.

"I did. When Geoff ordered me to, I complied."

"And what was Trooper Eriksen's reaction when you told him I ordered you to disclose the fingerprint tests to Attorney Pickering?"

Walker demanded.

"He was pissed and lost his temper. He thought I should have somehow convinced you that the prints should not be disclosed. He told me there would be consequences if I followed your instructions."

"But you disclosed the information anyway," the sergeant pressed.

"I did. I somehow convinced Brian that I would make sure the prints would not be traced back to him."

"And he believed you?" McCam demanded as he studied Victoria's body language and eye movements.

"It took some convincing, but eventually, he did." She sobbed.

The room fell silent for a moment. McCam continued to scribble down notes as Victoria shifted slightly in her chair. Walker was staring out a window but eventually broke the silence. "Why Carmen Vaughn?"

Donovan was prepared for that question. "It was Brian's idea. He knew Jillian was in an on-again-off-again relationship with him and that Carmen had a couple of domestic violence charges involving her. His behavior the night of her disappearance simply sealed his fate."

McCam cursed silently to himself. He was not sure what was going to be worse: the press ripping apart the Massachusetts State Police for framing an innocent minority or the depositions that would be part of Carmen Vaughn's civil rights lawsuit against the Commonwealth of Massachusetts.

"Why are you coming to us now?" Walker calmly asked.

Victoria started to whimper and choke on her tears. "Brian told me a couple of days ago that there was a witness who could link him to Jillian's death, a girl named Sandy. He became aware that Pickering and his investigator had found this girl and met with her. Now she is dead. I don't want to be next."

"Maybe Attorney Pickering or Investigator Watson is next," the sergeant noted with a hint of suspicion in his voice.

Victoria paused for a moment. Was it possible that she was playing the victim card a bit too much? Should she had expressed concern for the defense attorney and his investigator sooner? She brushed the thought aside and addressed McCam's comment. "Yes. I believe they are in danger. Brian thinks he can make this go away by harming them, or he plans to go out in a suicide by cop scenario. Either way, someone is going to get hurt."

"Where is he now?" Walker asked softly but firmly.

"I—I don't know," she stammered.

Geoff Walker leaned back and stared at Donovan. After several moments, he stood up and stepped away from the table. He walked over to McCam, picked up the notes the sergeant had taken, reviewed them, and then dropped them back onto the table. He looked over at his prosecutor.

"You are off the Vaughn case immediately. I will be filing a nol pros and dismissing that matter before the end of the day. You better hope and pray prosecutorial immunity applies to your situation when Carmen Vaughn decides to sue everyone for this shitshow."

Victoria nodded, feigning understanding. "What is going to happen to me?"

"That's up to the district attorney now," Walker replied tersely. "But, effective immediately, you're suspended. Get your belongings out of your office and go to reception. We are going to arrange for a trooper to be assigned to you for protection until Eriksen is caught. He or she will meet you in reception."

"Thank you."

"And Victoria?"

"Yes?"

"Sergeant McCam will escort you to your office to collect your belongings. Don't you even fucking think of taking anything that doesn't belong to you or is related to the Vaughn case."

"Of course, Geoff."

"Thank you," Walker replied as he ushered her to the door. McCam followed behind her.

As she stepped out into the hallway, she smiled slightly. She knew McCam did not buy the story, but she couldn't give a fuck about what the sergeant thought. Victoria knew it was Walker who called the shots. If he had any suspicion of her true involvement, he would have had McCam slap cuffs on her and perp-walked her out of the office right then and there. Instead, he fell for her sob story. Granted, he would send detectives out to confirm her story, but it was a case of she said versus he said. In the age of the #metoo movement, she held all the cards and the advantage of credibility.

Victoria Donovan mentally congratulated herself as she concluded that she was going to survive this ordeal relatively intact and with her freedom.

TWENTY-EIGHT

WEDNESDAY, MAY 1

Adrian shifted the gears of his 2017 Jeep Cherokee downward as he exited off Route 495 and drove up the ramp to Broad Street in Merrimac. Once at the end of the exit ramp, he took a left and traveled toward River Road. Upon arriving at a stop sign, he took another left turn and drove directly past the park where Jillian Russo's body had washed ashore several weeks ago.

The investigator slowed down so he could look over toward the field. Unfortunately, it was enveloped in darkness, and Adrian could see little next to nothing. As his car rolled to a stop, he thought for a moment about Jillian and her tragic demise. His thoughts then wandered to her parents. He could not even remotely pretend to understand what they must have been feeling or experiencing since their daughter's disappearance weeks ago. Of course, with the developments throughout the day, he was sure that Jillian's mother and father were once again in hell.

Shortly after lunch, the charges against Carmen Vaughn were quietly dropped. Shortly afterward, Carmen was allowed to gather what little possessions he had inside the Middleton House of Corrections and was quickly escorted out of the facility by a deputy sheriff and Attorney Timothy Pickering.

Waiting in the parking lot for him with tears rolling down her face was his mother. As the two had a tearful reunion, Pickering quietly excused himself and returned to his family in Portsmouth.

Three hours later, just as the *Lawrence Star* was getting wind of the boy's release, the district attorney for Essex County appeared on a local television network and announced that a warrant had been issued for the arrest of Trooper Brian Eriksen for the murder of Jillian Russo and Sandy Minerva. By the end of the day, the story of a Massachusetts state trooper who had framed a teenage minority had been picked up by several national outlets.

Unfortunately, Brian Eriksen was still at large and considered heavily armed and extremely dangerous.

Adrian softly sighed, turned his attention back to the road, and continued to drive down River Road. A block later, he saw his house on the left-hand side of the road. He pulled into the horseshoe-shaped driveway, parked, and exited the vehicle. He grabbed his backpack from the backseat of his SUV, shut the door, and started walking toward his house. He withdrew his phone and scanned through several emails from national media sources requesting interviews as he approached a set of stairs that led up to the side entrance of his residence. When he reached the landing, he put his phone in his pocket, pulled out his keys, and fumbled in the dark for the correct one that unlocked the storm door. As he started to insert the key into the lock, he froze.

The door was unlocked.

Over the years, Watson had grown tired of solar panel salesmen, contractors, and religious figures who would repeatedly leave fliers and promotional materials in between his screen and entrance doorways. As a result, he adopted the daily routine to lock both his front and side doors when he left his house.

He pulled open the storm door and pushed on the entrance door. It was locked. The investigator questioned himself for a moment as to whether he locked the exterior door or had merely forgotten. He brushed off the concern and moved to unlock the second door. However, before he inserted the key into the lock, he stopped short. Whether it was instinct or an abundance of caution, Adrian decided to inspect the doorway.

He turned on the flashlight to his phone and started to examine the two doors, locks, and jams. As he neared completion of his inspection, he felt a chill run up his spine. There were several thin

pry marks on the inner door near the deadbolt. Watson stepped back from the doorway, turned off his phone's light, and quietly backed down the stairs. He stood in the driveway, studying his house and listening for any unusual sounds from within. There was nothing but silence. As he scanned the second-floor windows, he noted that no lights were on inside, which was unusual because his smart-home program was set to turn the lights on fifteen minutes earlier. Watson opened the Nest application on his phone and discovered that the entire security system, as well as the lights, were offline. Arian slowed his breathing and listened for any unusual sounds. He looked up again at the house and then quickly retreated to his car.

Once at his vehicle, Adrian opened the driver's side door and tossed his backpack into the vehicle. He turned and started to walk back to the side entrance. However, at the last minute, he turned quickly to the right and hugged the exterior side of his home as he maneuvered toward a white, wooden bulkhead located at the back of his home. Once again, Watson withdrew his keys, slowly unlocked a padlock on the doors, and quietly opened the bulkhead. He placed his keys onto the ground, withdrew his H&K VP9 9mm pistol that had been holstered on his waist belt, and cautiously descended a flight of stairs into his basement. He stopped at the bottom and allowed his eyes to adjust to the darkness. Afterward, he silently crossed the room until he positioned himself near a flight of stairs leading up to his kitchen.

A loud wooden creak followed by two heavy footsteps echoed throughout the basement. Adrian's heart started to race as an adrenaline rush kicked in. He tried to control his breathing and ignore the sweat that was starting to bead on his forehead. Suddenly, the door at the top of the basement stairs slowly creaked open. Watson cursed to himself as he realized that he was now in a tactically disadvantageous position. The intruder held the high ground and was in a better position for cover if a firefight broke out.

Adrian retreated across the basement to the washing machine located on the left-hand side of the stairway. He took up a defensive position, disengaged the safety latch on his weapon, and waited to see if the intruder would descend the stairs into the basement. If he did, the tactical advantage would shift to Adrian, who would enjoy the dual benefits of cover behind the appliance as well as attacking the intruder from a flanking position.

There was a moment of tense silence before the kitchen floorboards started to crack and moan as the intruder at the top of the stairway shifted his weight from one foot to another. Several more seconds of silence passed before there was a loud metallic click of a pistol round being chambered, followed by the heavy thud of footsteps descending the first three stairs into the basement. Watson crouched slightly backward and aimed his pistol toward the stairwell. He debated whether to issue a warning before shooting.

The person descended four more stairs into the basement. Although there was little light, Watson could make out the intruder from the chest down. He was wearing a bulletproof vest and carrying a Smith & Wesson M&P pistol in his right hand. Watson came to the realization that it had to be Brian Eriksen that was standing on his basement stairs.

The investigator recognized that he had entered dangerous territory and questioned the sanity of entering the basement in the first place. He quietly withdrew his cell phone with his left hand, dialed 911, and placed the phone face down on top of the washing machine. A hang-up or a dead call would automatically trigger the Merrimac Police Department to respond to his location.

Of course, Watson knew only one of two scenarios that were going to play out. On the one hand, Eriksen could descend farther into the basement and force the investigator to open fire in self-defense. On the other hand, the disgraced trooper could return upstairs, thereby allowing Adrian to retreat from the house. After careful reflection, Adrian decided he was going to try and influence the outcome and force the intruder back upstairs.

"Eriksen!" Watson shouted. "I have a bead on you, and I can take the fucking shot. Drop your gun and go back upstairs into the kitchen. I called the police, and they are on their fucking way. Do not make this any harder than it must be, trooper. I do not want to shoot you. It's over."

Even with the limited visibility in the dark basement, the investigator was able to see Eriksen's body stiffen. He watched as the trooper stood on the stairs and shifted his weight from one side to the other. Finally, the man responded.

"Fuck you, Watson."

"Brian, you don't want this to end this way. Please," Adrian pleaded.

"Why? My fucking life is over, thanks to you. You had to be just too fucking good and figure out what I did."

"Brian, you did that to yourself," the investigator responded calmly. "Do you really think you could have gotten away with what you did? If it weren't Attorney Pickering or me, someone would have eventually figured out what you did."

"No, no, no," Eriksen repeatedly shouted. "If you and that nut-sack attorney you work with had just done your jobs and convinced your piece-of-shit client to plead guilty, none of this would have been necessary."

"Really, Brian?" Watson asked incredulously. "You're willing to let an innocent man go to jail so that you could get away with murdering Jillian Russo?"

"Fuck yes. What do you think happens to a cop in Walpole?"

The Massachusetts Correctional Institution at Cedar Junction, more commonly known as "MCI Walpole," was the state's maximum-security prison. It housed violent felons, sexual predators, and murderers. If a disgraced police officer was sentenced to that facility, it was akin to a death sentence.

"Trooper, two people are dead because of you. You're going to Walpole," Watson retorted.

"The fuck I am," Eriksen coldly replied. "There's no way I am going down for this shit. I am checking out, and you and Pickering are going with me. You two stirred this crap up. Now I have to finish it."

"All because we did our jobs? You're going to kill us because we did our jobs?"

"Fuck your jobs. You two put my neck on the chopping block. Fuck you and fuck Pickering. There is no way I am walking out of here in cuffs."

"Brian, last I checked, you killed Jillian. Don't you feel any remorse for what you did?"

Eriksen paused for a moment to collect his thoughts. "I did. But those feelings are long gone by now."

"Attorney Pickering has a family," Adrian quietly noted. "Are you going to take a father away from his children?"

"What does that have to do with anything? He should have thought about his family before he took this case on."

This time, Watson fell silent. The situation was not improving, and he knew it could escalate even further when the police finally arrived. He decided to make one last-ditch effort to diffuse the situation.

"Brian. This is not going to end well. Put the fucking gun down and call it a day. Enough people have been hurt. Please, there's no need for any more suffering."

"I can't do that, Watson."

"Brian, please put the gun down and just walk away. Walk out of this house and disappear, for all I fucking care. But you cannot go out in a shootout with the police. All that is going to happen is more people will get hurt, including people you work with and the people you care about. Please just walk away."

As Watson tried to reason with the trooper, off in the distance, the wailing of police cruiser sirens could be heard. It was soft at first but gradually grew louder. Eriksen began to shuffle his feet nervously on the stairs and then turned his attention back to the investigator.

"You called the police?" he asked softly, his voice almost monotone.

"I told you I did," Adrian replied. "What did you expect me to do?"

"I'm not going down for this, Watson. I won't."

The investigator remained silent. He could hear the trooper mumbling and grunting to himself. Adrian knew the conversation was over. Eriksen was determined to check out through "suicide by cop," and it was almost certain that he was going to try to take Adrian with him.

Eriksen started to descend the stairs. As he did, he brought up his pistol and started to turn toward Adrian. From Watson's perspective, everything appeared as if it was happening in slow motion. He aimed his own weapon at the trooper and squeezed the trigger twice. There were two deafening pops and flashes of light. The first round missed the trooper and slammed into the wooden frame of the basement stairs with a loud crack. However, the second bullet struck Eriksen's leg just above the right knee. The trooper let out a painful howl and spilled down the cellar stairs. As he sprawled out onto the cellar floor, Eriksen's pistol slipped from his hands and bounced across the floor with a loud metallic clank.

Watson rushed forward from his defensive position and closed in on the trooper. As he neared the man, he planted his left foot on the cement floor and swung his right foot forward, kicking Eriksen's wounded leg. The trooper yelped in pain and rolled over onto his back. Adrian back-peddled a couple of steps, turned, and kicked the trooper's firearm out of reach. The weapon skated along the cement floor and came to a final stop when it collided with a stone wall. Adrian then raised his own pistol and aimed it at Eriksen's head. Surprisingly, the trooper pulled himself up, rested on his elbows, and begged for Watson to shoot him.

"Shoot me, you mother fucker. Just fucking shoot me."

Adrian started to squeeze the trigger but caught himself. After a moment of reflection, he lowered his weapon until the barrel pointed at the ground. He straightened himself up and looked out through the bulkhead. Blue and white lights flickered outside of the basement. He turned his attention back to the trooper.

"No, Eriksen; you don't get off that easy."

EPILOGUE

Four months after Trooper Brian Eriksen's apprehension for the murders of Jillian Russo and Sandy Minerva, he appeared before a judge in the Newburyport Superior Court to plead guilty. It was surprising to many as most believed he would fight the charges to the bitter end. The hearing was emotional as the parents, siblings, and relatives of each of the victims took the stand and testified about the impact the crimes had on their lives and well-being. Even Carmen Vaughn was permitted to testify as to how he was affected by Eriksen's actions.

At the end of the hearing, the defendant was sentenced to two consecutive life sentences without the possibility of parole. Pickering, who was seated in the gallery with Watson, Vaughn, and his mother, watched as Eriksen was led away in shackles by court officers. The disgraced trooper sobbed, whimpered, and pleaded for the judge to grant him leniency and mercy. The irony was not lost on anyone in the courtroom.

As he stood up to leave, Pickering noticed Victoria Donovan, who was standing at the back of the courtroom, eyeing the professor with a cold, icy stare. He met her gaze for a moment and then smiled knowingly at her. It clearly rattled the prosecutor as she gave him a look of disgust, turned around, and stormed out of the courtroom.

"The sad thing is the district attorney only whacked her with a four-month suspension. She is already back to work in our office, and it absolutely sickens me that she got away with this," Sergeant McCam stated calmly as he walked up and stood next to the attorney.

"You think she had a hand in this?" Watson asked, keenly aware of the police report that detailed her statement to Walker and McCam after Eriksen had been exposed.

"I don't think; I know," the sergeant responded matter-of-factly to the investigator. "She gave us a bullshit story about how she was abused and forced to be complicit in this case. Geoff Walker and the district attorney may have believed her. I do not. I know she played a much bigger role in this matter, and if I have to spend the rest of my career building a case against her, I will."

Pickering, Watson, and Vaughn remained silent. McCam eyed the pair for a moment and then continued to speak. "Just promise me that when I take her fucking down, you two are not there to represent her."

"Can't promise you that," the professor replied sarcastically. McCam again eyed the two and started to walk away. He stopped and turned around to face the pair.

"You two did well. I may not have liked that you kicked my ass in the process, but I respect what you both did for that young man. Nice job, gentlemen."

"See you around, sergeant," Watson announced as the trooper casually waved goodbye and resumed exiting the courtroom.

Timothy watched McCam leave and then turned to his client. The young man had been through hell and back. After spending over a month incarcerated as well as being crucified in the press, the attorney hoped Vaughn would be able to move forward. Fortunately, through the efforts of Pickering and Carmen's mother, they were able to get the young man reinstated as a full-time student at Brighton College.

With Watson's assistance, Carmen and his mother were also able to secure the assistance of a civil rights attorney from the Boston area who intended to file a civil rights lawsuit against the Massachusetts State Police and Brian Eriksen. Timothy knew Carmen and his mother would likely receive a very hefty settlement to make this matter go away. What the young man would do with that money was up to him. Pickering could only hope that he would spend it wisely.

"Mr. Vaughn," Timothy stated as he extended his hand to his student. "It has been an honor to work with you."

"Professor, I can't even begin to express my thanks," Carmen replied humbly. "I am so grateful that you decided to take my case. I was looking at life in prison, and the two of you saved my life."

"Well, thank your mother," Watson interjected with a chuckle. "She was the one who ensured you had the two of us on your case."

"How can we even begin to repay you?" Carmen's mother asked, her voice shaking with emotion.

Pickering held up his hands in protest. "No, ma'am. We will not take your money. We had a rare opportunity to ensure justice was served. But with your permission, I'd like to speak with Carmen in private."

"Of course," she replied.

Pickering led Carmen away from Watson and his mother and, together, they walked to the back of the courtroom. The professor looked around and then leaned toward Carmen.

"Final piece of advice?" he asked.

"Of course. Anything, professor."

"Don't date for a while."

"I don't understand," Carmen stated.

"If I were you, I'd stay away from women other than your mom for a while. Your entire relationship with Jillian was toxic and helped contribute to this mess. In speaking with your mother and friends, it is pretty clear you tend to be drawn to women that come with their own set of problems. Give romance a bit of a break until you can get your shit in order. Do you understand me?"

Carmen smiled nervously and appeared somewhat embarrassed. "Yeah, I understand you, Mr. Pickering. I'm going to look out for just me and my mom."

"Good. I assume I'll see you in class next week, Mr. Vaughn?"

"Absolutely, professor."

Pickering and Watson exchanged final greetings with Carmen and his mother. Afterward, the pair walked out of the superior courthouse and stepped onto the Bartlett Mall, one of the oldest public grounds in the Newburyport area. As the two started to walk across the park, Watson looked inquisitively over toward his partner.

"You do realize you were the only idiot in this entire case who didn't get paid?"

"I know," Pickering responded.

"No, seriously, I got paid. The prosecutors all got paid. The judges got paid. Hell, even that shit reporter from the *Lawrence Star* go paid. But you? You got nothing."

Pickering smiled broadly. "Well, maybe on the next case, I'll charge extra to make up for any money lost on this one."

The investigator stopped in his tracks, turned, and rested his hand on the attorney's shoulder. "Tim, are you saying you want to do this again?"

"I think under the right circumstances, yes, I would."

Watson stared at his friend in silence for a moment and then burst out laughing. "You can't afford me."

"No, I probably can't," Tim replied sarcastically.

"Besides, I don't have time to hold your hand, Attorney Pickering. As a result of this case, I've got requests from lawyers all over the Commonwealth asking me to help them out on their cases."

"Let me ask you something, Adrian. Will any of those other law-yers let you shoot intruders in your basement?"

"Now that is cold, Tim."

The two men resumed walking across the Bartlett Mall. As they neared a World War I artillery piece, Timothy resumed the conversation.

"I'm serious. If it is the right case, I may consider coming back."

"I know you'll be back," Watson replied with a tone of sincerity. "And when you return, I'll be right next to you fighting the good fight with you."

ABOUT THE AUTHOR

John Crossan is your classic New England Yankee. Growing up, he divided his time between Massachusetts, New Hampshire, and Coastal Maine. After graduating with honors from both college and law school, he spent several years working as a litigator in New Hampshire, Massachusetts, and Rhode Island. Ultimately, he decided to put the practice of law behind him and pursue a career as a writer. A *River of Lies* is his first foray into the world of fiction. John currently resides along the New England coast with his family.

Be sure to visit John's author page for the latest news, scheduled appearances, and upcoming releases: JohnCrossanAuthor.com.

What does an author stand to gain by asking for reader feedback? A lot. In fact, it's so important in the publishing world that they've coined a catchy name for it: "social proof." And without social proof, an author may as well be invisible in this age of digital media sharing.

So if you've enjoyed A *River of Lies*, please consider giving it some visibility by reviewing it on the sales platform of your choice. Your honest opinion could help potential readers decide whether or not they would enjoy this book, too.

Made in the USA
Middletown, DE
08 February 2022

60188708R00166